Books by Lillie Todd

Single Titles

The Possibility of You and Me

The Possibility of You and Me

ISBN # 978-1-78686-030-9

Cover Art by Posh Gosh ©Copyright 2016

Interior text design by Claire Siemaszkiewicz

Finch Books

Published in 2016 by Finch Books, Newland House, The Point, Weaver Road, Lincoln, LN6 3QN, United Kingdom.

Finch Books is a subsidiary of Totally Entwined Group Limited.

THE POSSIBILITY OF YOU AND ME

LILLIE TODD

Dedication

For T & A
Keep reading my darlings, and keep dreaming.

Prologue

The car honked and the whoops from my girlfriends pierced the previously quiet air. With a laugh, I waved goodbye and opened my front door. I could still hear them when it closed behind me, the engine revving and music blasting from the radio.

"Anyone home?" I called out. "Mom?"

When no answer came, I let out a sigh of relief and headed into the kitchen for a soda. Mom and Dad had been on me about getting my friends to tone it down when they dropped me off. They were enthusiastic...so what? It beat the hell out of boring.

I headed to my bedroom to get changed and figure out what to wear later when the girls would come back to pick me up. Something cute...or something hot that my boyfriend would appreciate.

Out of habit, I sniffed the air. An empty house would usually have been too great a temptation for my brother, and the telltale smell of his weed would creep out from under his door.

But today I could smell nothing but the lemon bathroom cleaner Mom used. I let out a sigh of relief and pushed open my bedroom door. I kicked off the sandals that had been rubbing my little toes all day then flopped down on my bed. The pillow beneath my head crinkled, as if there were something on it. I lifted my head and rooted around, coming up a moment later with an envelope from the stationery set Grandma had given me at Christmas. Snore.

I ripped the envelope open and pulled out a handwritten note.

My heart began to thump as I read the words.

What is this? This can't... No...

My heart was in my throat as I vaulted off my bed and raced out of the room. I skidded on the rug in the hall and threw open his bedroom door — and stopped.

The world around me went silent.

After an age, I took one clumsy step forward and another until I reached the side of the bed.

I reached out to touch him.

He was cold.

Chapter One

Laughter filled the warm day. Shrieks of excitement echoed all around, adding to the cacophony coming from the parking lot and the front steps. Students flitted past me, paying no attention to the new kid who had a world of torment swirling inside.

First days suck.

Especially when you're the new kid.

Especially when you're only sort of the new kid.

Poised on the brink of my first day as a senior, I had returned to the school I'd thought I would never see again. It had been a year since I'd left and, while everything looked the same, I had changed irrevocably.

I guessed that was what came when your parents shipped you off because your face reminded them too much of your brother's, who had decided to party a smidge too hard and OD.

After Derek's funeral, none of us had been able to cope. My parents most of all, who had ignored his drug problem the entire time and therefore hadn't seen the disaster from a mile off. Their solution had been to send me to live with my grandma six hours away.

Being away from home and everything that reminded me of my brother was...different. Somehow both easier and harder all at the same time.

It had been refreshing to be in a place where no one had known my history, no one had known what I'd run away from. The kids at my new school had seen me only as a real new girl... With them, I'd had a clean slate. There, I had been able to breathe again. I hadn't been tied down with the superficial crap that came with who I'd been before with my old friends.

But... I missed my brother. I missed him in a way that I would never be whole again. He was one half of me and I wasn't sure who I was without him. We had walked different paths in life, were completely different people. In fact, as twins, we couldn't have been more different.

I had to wonder if Derek would even recognize me now. Once upon a time, we had been best friends — had camped together, had eaten s'mores together and had broken bones together. Who knew umbrellas didn't have the same effect as parachutes? But then along with growing up, we'd grown apart. I'd found my friends and clothes and accessories... and Derek had found prescription medication.

So now here I was...again. Molded into a new shape by grief...again. Three months ago, I had come home from school to find Grandma slumped on the kitchen floor having suffered a massive stroke. It had left her paralyzed and unable to talk, and my parents with no other option but to bring me home.

I had no way to predict what I would walk into. Before I'd left, I'd known where I fitted in. But what if, now, I didn't fit anywhere? Or what if there was no longer space for me?

One thing was for sure — I wouldn't find out by hiding outside.

I squared my shoulders to take the first step. My stomach knotted and my heart pounded. I had never been more aware of every single part of my body, from my sweaty hands to my awkward feet.

Heels had been my staple before I'd left, but after a year of ballet flats and sneakers, the cute, summery wedges strapped to my feet felt more like vise grips that threatened to send me tumbling the moment I stopped concentrating.

I released a long breath and climbed the steps leading into the school. There were a few minutes left before the first bell, and I knew exactly where I had to go. I wouldn't slip quietly into school, waiting for the rumors to announce my return, though that sounded like a much better option. If I didn't feel like the girl I used to be, I could at least act like it until I did. And that meant showing no fear as I faced the friends I hadn't heard a word from since Derek's funeral.

Once upon a time, I belonged to the most powerful clique of my school. Which meant, as seniors, they could only be in one place.

The quad was a beautiful suntrap, part of the reason it made such a popular hangout. People from all groups of social standing could be seen scattered across the space, but as the reigning monarchs of Westbrook High, my friends' undisputed territory had to be the most central table.

All around, kids shot them glances, some not exactly warm ones. The elaborate fountain behind them framed their table and with the picture-perfect blue sky above, they could have been plucked from an airbrushed magazine spread. They sported the latest hairstyles, hottest lip gloss, killer nail polish and matching tiny bags.

None of them saw me coming. They actively ignored everything around them — something I myself had once been a master at.

It was Sarah Kaye, bubbly and permanently happy Sarah, who saw me first. She broke into a wide grin and pushed her enormous designer sunglasses on top of her head. "No way!"

I smiled at her, and my nerves disappeared a smidge. But Sarah was the easy one — the one I didn't have to worry about. I slid my gaze to the next girl, now second in line to our leader. I'd bet the ink on my transfer papers hadn't even dried before she'd stepped into my empty spot.

Rachel Rosenberg arched a slender eyebrow at Sarah's eager outburst and flicked her dark gaze to me. Her eyes widened for a beat before she regained composure and pulled one corner of her lips into a half-smile. Rachel bumped her takeout coffee cup against the top of the one beside her, which belonged to the remaining girl who point blank refused to acknowledge me.

She would make me work for it.

With a deep breath, I stepped forward, hoping I had my game face on. "Hi, guys." I shifted to confront the girl who had once been my best friend. "Jill."

Jill Myers cast her eyes up to me. She coolly observed me for half a second before flashing a dazzling, yet ice-cold smile. Slowly, so everyone would have a chance to check out her bod, Jill stood, one hand on her popped hip. Every move Jill made had a motive behind it... Even one as simple as standing up. "Lori Black," she purred. "So. You're back then. For good?"

She didn't sound pleased to see me, despite the smile on her face. For a flicker of a second, I wondered if they were mad at me...but that was absolutely ridiculous. No way they could be pissed because I hadn't called or texted in my absence. For chrissakes, they didn't even send my family a condolence card. Most of all, I'd never forget that after texting Jill the time I would be leaving, not one of them had showed to say goodbye.

Part of me had to wonder just why I wanted to put myself through this ordeal. If they wanted to be my friends, I would have heard from them this past year. I wouldn't have been hurt by their silence. Maybe I was crazy for wanting them back in my life. But senior year would go a hell of a lot more smoothly if I was in their circle rather than out of it. "Seems that way."

"It's been a while." Jill's face softened. "We've missed you around here, Lo." And with that she pulled me into a gentle hug, her overpowering perfume assaulting my nose. Jill let me go and flicked her hand to the empty seat beside her. "Sit down and tell us all about what you've been up to."

"Oh." I looked down at my hands and saw they trembled. From Jill's use of my old nickname, or because being with these girls made me feel as if I'd traveled back in time? Only I had gone back in time and there was a world of difference between us. And still no Derek, either. "There's not much to tell. What about you guys? I bet you have a lot to fill me in on."

Sarah giggled. "Rachel got a nose job."

Rachel gasped and swatted Sarah's arm. The pair squabbled until everyone forgot about questioning me and remembered how much they loved talking about themselves.

As the girls talked, and talked, and talked, about things and people I had no idea about, I let my eyes roam over the quad, seeing who had changed, who looked the same and who I figured would never, ever change. One face stuck out from the crowd for the simple reason that I'd never seen it before.

And I would remember a face like that.

He sat on the ledge of the fountain, slouched over with one elbow on his knee and fist supporting his cheek. In the other hand he held open a paperback book—the cover both too new and too interesting for it to be required reading from a teacher. Even though he appeared lost in his novel, he looked as though he had intentionally closed himself off to everything around him. He definitely looked as if he didn't give a crap. He wore dark jeans and a rumpled dark gray T-shirt. His inky black hair shone in the sun, casting rainbows like a raven's feather, and the shadow of a few days' worth of stubble on his jaw.

"Hey," I said, interrupting Rachel's monologue about the guy she traded makeout sessions for tutoring with. "Who's the new kid?"

Jill tittered a little laugh. "You?"

I frowned. "I meant the guy at the fountain."

The girls peered around to look at him before collectively rolling their eyes and turning away.

My eyebrows shot up. I'd never seen my friends dismiss such a hot guy, regardless of who he was or what he was like. So for them to react the way they did, it had to mean he was different from their usual worshipers. "What? Who is he?"

"Don't waste your time," Jill muttered. "The guy's an

asshole — a major one. Doesn't talk to anyone, doesn't party, doesn't do anything. Except read. And glare. A lot."

My cheeks flushed. "I wasn't planning on wasting my time. I'm just curious." I sneaked another glance at him, wishing I hadn't brought it to the gossipmongers' attention that I'd noticed him. "Why is he all alone? Doesn't he have any friends?"

Rachel laughed. "Archer? Seriously, what part of 'doesn't talk to anyone' aren't you getting?"

I shrugged. "Everyone's got to have someone, right?"

"Not him. He started here junior year and I haven't seen him hang out with anyone." Rachel's eyes widened, further trying to drive home her point.

The bell rang for homeroom, and I watched him rise to his feet, slowly, and with a huge dose of resignation. I couldn't help but notice how tall he was. And buff. While hunched over his book it had been hard to see the true extent of his physique, easy to pass him off as lean, bordering on skinny. Now that he stood, I saw the powerful curves of his shoulders, the corded muscles of his arms as he swung a messenger bag over his neck. He wasn't skinny, far from it. *Just really, really...um...wow.* Lean and sculpted. From solid rock. The way he moved made my stomach all weird and jittery.

I glanced around, sure I would see a gaggle of girls reacting exactly like me — one notch away from panting like a freaking dog in heat. Nope. Not one person even looked at him, let alone lusted after him.

Rachel and Jill marched in front of me, apparently done with my homecoming. Every school has a student hierarchy. Our clique came with one of its own. Jill was the undisputed queen. Undisputed because no one had the courage to challenge her, lest social suicide occur.

Sarah was — I hate saying it, despite it being completely true — the dumb one, happy enough with simply being in the group at all. She was the sweetest member, the only one not likely to stab you in the back for social leverage. Rachel strove to be next to the top girl, never actually wanting to usurp her, and therefore had the easy acceptance of our fearless leader, Jill.

I had met Jill my first day of freshman year — a force to be reckoned with, even then. Our lockers had been side by side. I'd struggled to figure out how to open mine as the lunchtime crush in the hallway jostled me every other second, but Jill had simply pouted and stuck a hand on her hip.

An upperclassman — a cute one, if I remembered right — had halted and shot her a dazzling smile and had asked if he could help her. She had giggled and touched his arm, saying that would be wonderful. He had opened the locker, but before he'd left, she'd flickered her gaze to me and ordered him — in that way of hers that made you think it was your idea — to open my locker too. He had, paying me about a hundredth of the attention he'd given Jill.

He'd hung around for another minute, no doubt hoping she would repay his kindness somehow, or at the very least act like a simpering female. When she had merely started transferring books to her locker, he had given a half-hearted wave and disappeared into the crowd. I had watched, in awe of her, wondering how one little person could wield that kind of power over another human being. She had closed the locker and flounced down the hall, leaving me in her wake.

In a way, Jill became my obsession. I wasn't stupid. I knew she would use me just as she used that upperclassman. But if I played by the rules and didn't rock the boat, Jill could be my ticket through high school and be my social bulletproof vest. If I befriended her then I wouldn't be alone. After that one encounter on my first day, it was obvious Jill would be powerful later in high-school life. Hell, she had been even back then.

The next day I had come to school prepared. I'd begged and pleaded with my mom to take me shopping the afternoon before, swearing it could be my birthday and Christmas presents for the next fifty years if that's what it took. I had gotten a whole new wardrobe. Before I was a jeans and a T-shirt girl. Now the only jeans that graced my body were Seven jeans, and the only T-shirts I wore were slashed in the right places to allow for ample cleavage opportunities. Short skirts had become the new staple from that day on, with tiny purses and funky hair slides and makeup worn at all times. And heels. That took some getting used to.

I had also gotten my hair cut into a more stylish look, ensuring for the rest of my high-school career I got up a full two hours earlier than necessary. On the second day of school, when I had opened my locker at lunch and Jill had sidled up next to me, she'd paid attention. I'd watched her size me up in my peripheral vision, probably deciding whether it would be worth being allies or enemies, when she had gasped and grabbed my locker door.

"What?" I had asked, stepping back.

"Where did you get this?" she exclaimed, her eyes wide.

I had looked at where her manicured fingernail poked at The Howlers band poster taped to my locker door. "At a gig I went to in the summer. Why?"

"I love that band! No one else around here has even heard of them!" And that was it. A local indie band had put me on Jill Myers' radar.

Rachel had joined us later in the year, earning Jill's undying respect by hooking up with a senior. Sarah had come last, almost stumbling into our group by accident. Jill, Rachel and I had been having coffee at a place downtown when Sarah had dropped down beside me in the booth. She'd laughed and said she was avoiding her ex who she hadn't gotten around to telling was an ex yet. After that she had been a permanent feature.

And there we were. The A-Listers. The In Crowd. The Popular People.

Oh, how things had changed.

Once upon a time, I had spoken to all these girls at least twice a day after we'd parted ways, usually texting during class and late into the night. Now I resembled a dog begging for scraps from the dinner table. Rachel had gotten her wish, claiming my spot next to Jill. And the way she laughed at whatever Jill said told me she was threatened by my reappearance, and wouldn't give up her position without a fight. And Rachel fought dirty.

Only Sarah matched her step with mine, making an effort to talk. "Are you in any of my classes this year?"

I doubted it. Sarah, while lovely and at times sincere, fell short in the brains category. It was the one difference that was always apparent between me and the other girls. While they coasted and focused more on the social side of school, I maintained decent grades. I would never be top of my class, but I also wasn't at the bottom either. The others weren't as orientated as me. But I knew exactly where I was going.

I fished my new class schedule from my bag and held it out to Sarah. "Here."

Sarah gave it a quick once-over. "Aw, that sucks. We don't have any together."

"What about Rachel and Jill? Are they in any of my classes?" Maybe things would be really different and suddenly both girls had turned into masterminds while I had been gone.

She shook her head. "None. Looks like you're on your own."

Another pang of fear shot through my stomach. Even though my reception had been frosty at best, facing all my classes alone terrified me. Sarah squeezed my arm and gave me a small wave before disappearing in the crowd of the hallway.

I really was alone then.

Chapter Two

By fourth period English, word had spread across the senior class that I was back. I had the same teacher that I'd had sophomore year and out of habit I took my old, usual seat—second row back, window seat.

Just as I pulled out my notebook and pen, a shadow fell across my desk. I peered up and looked into the cold, hard eyes of the bitchiest girl I'd ever met. For two years Kimmie Jones had plotted my demise. And judging by the expression on her face, she wasn't done yet. I had no idea what I had done to piss her off. I had once thought she wanted my spot in the group, but even in my absence, she hadn't secured it.

No wonder she still hated me.

"Yeah?" I asked, swallowing the knot of unease and finding my voice.

Kimmie folded her arms below her chest and pinned me with an even colder glare. "Get up."

I lifted my eyebrows. "Excuse me?" I had expected cruel barbs, curiosity and vindictive speculation.

"You're in my seat. Get up."

I glanced around and my stomach dropped when people avoided my eyes. No one wanted to shift the heat from me to them. Especially for a girl who had disappeared for a year. Once, my standing in Jill's group would have been enough to keep the likes of Kimmie off my back, or even for someone to discard her for me...but not now. "Are the seats assigned in this class now?" I asked, trying to keep my voice level.

Kimmie smiled, a cold and calculating smile. "No. Now

move."

If Kimmie stopped being such a bitch, she'd actually be really pretty. Kimmie was all curves and angles, wavy dark brown hair framing a small heart-shaped face with high cheekbones, a ski-jump nose and a pair of seriously intense dark eyes.

But the ugliness of her personality overshadowed all her pretty features.

I wanted to tell her where to jump, but I couldn't seem to bring myself to do it. Whatever fake confidence I had mustered that morning was depleted now. So with my cheeks burning, I scooped up my things and left the desk.

Most of the class had taken their seats already, leaving my options scarce. Only one choice, in fact. Back row, second seat in the opposite corner. Next to the only person with fewer friends than me.

He didn't look up at my approach. Didn't acknowledge me as I slid into the seat next to him. Didn't seem to notice me at all.

"Hey," I murmured, figuring it couldn't hurt to reach out to him. "How's it going?"

Nothing.

"So, you're the new kid?" I winced, remembering Rachel's words. *Man, how rude am I?* He had probably been called New Kid since his first day here. "Well, I guess I'm the new kid now. Which is weird."

The guy remained silent. He turned his head away, staring at a spot on the wall.

I forced a carefree laugh, which sounded anything but. "Because, you know, I'm from here. Originally, I mean. I left, but I came back. I guess I'm the old-new kid." *Why am I pushing this?*

Thankfully for me, and my dwindling pride and self-respect, Mr. Poole started his lecture. When the bell dismissed us, Archer pushed out of his seat and had disappeared through the door before any of us were even halfway ready.

* * * *

The cafeteria was packed and booming with noise, which did nothing to help my nerves. My run-in with Kimmie, then being snubbed by Archer, had left me raw and vulnerable. I craved solace and reassurance and I hoped to find it with my old friends.

So with my head held high, and purpose in my step, I wove around the tables until I got to the most central one. "Hey. So, classes still suck around here. Guess some things never change, huh?"

None of the girls said anything as I sat down in the one remaining chair at their table. Rachel smiled thinly, casting nervous glances at Jill. That girl needed to get a mind of her own.

Sarah, true to form, beamed at me. "I know, right? I have the suckiest teachers this year."

"Sarah, what's the name of that guy you met over the summer? The tall one?" Jill glanced at me as she asked the question. Sarah's smile spread across her pretty face and she started gushing about her summer romance.

No one spoke to me again.

I tried to tell myself that they weren't ignoring me on purpose, it was only because I'd been out of the loop for so long. Sarah, in her defense, didn't realize she ignored me. She was too caught up in describing in great detail how awesome her summer beau's pecs were, and whatever melodrama Jill and Rachel had cooked up since I last saw them.

Though relieved when I could escape the cafeteria, it was short-lived when the staring in my classes started again. But not even hell can last forever, and the school day finally ended.

I walked home alone. The house was empty when I got there, my parents still at work.

As much as I wanted to disappear into my private sanctuary and not reappear until graduation, I couldn't let myself shrink away. I had to keep myself together and make the effort. Force my way back into the social scene, if that was what it took. I guessed I just didn't want to be alone anymore. I'd spent the last year alone.

Most weeknights, kids from school hung out at Urban Grill, a trendy restaurant downtown. It was the only decent place to both eat and hang out, and aside from a few early-bird diners, students from school filled Urban Grill. Because of the pool tables and the dart board in the back, and because the staff didn't care if you stayed for four hours and only ordered one Coke, it was the perfect place to kick back.

The bar downstairs was officially off limits to us high-school kids... Unofficially, if you tipped the bartender, he never carded anyone.

As expected, Jill, Rachel and Sarah camped out at a table near a group of guys playing pool. I wore the same skirt and tank top I had to school, but the others had all changed and now sported Seven jeans and cute shirts. The way Jill's eyes flickered over my ensemble told me she noticed I hadn't changed.

Lori, you idiot, why didn't you change? "Hey, guys," I said when I reached their table. Sarah was the only one who smiled. I tried to ignore the glance Jill and Rachel exchanged. "How's it going?"

Rachel avoided my eyes, but Jill held steady. "We heard a rumor today," she said.

I laughed, hoping my nerves didn't show. "Oh yeah? Don't you hear rumors every day?"

Her expression didn't soften. "About you." Jill leaned forward and lifted her eyebrows in disbelief. "Did you really let Kimmie Jones push you around in class?"

My cheeks burned. Great. Now I couldn't lie even if I wanted to. "She was being a bitch. I didn't want trouble my first day back."

Jill's eyes tightened. "Are you serious? You used to be Lori freaking Black."

A hard lump formed in my throat. "I still am."

She snorted. "Right. You've been MIA for over a year. You're different."

Of course I'm different. *Is she for real?* My brother died for chrissakes. Why couldn't they see that I still was me, just a more broken version? "What does it matter if I'm different?"

"It matters when you associate yourself with us then let trash like Kimmie dominate you. The old Lo would never have let that happen. You'd have stood your ground and told that witch to buzz off and find her broomstick."

True. But I would have been terrified doing it.

"Fact of it is, Lo, things have changed around here. You're not the hotshot you used to be. That thing with Kimmie was a challenge. She, and everyone else, wanted to see if you could still handle yourself — see if you could still rule. You failed. Badly."

My throat constricted. I couldn't do this... Not now. I should have stayed home and given things at school a chance before throwing myself in at the deep end like this.

Jill leaned back in her chair. "I mean, have you even looked at yourself lately? You used to, I don't know, shine or something. And, FYI, the self-harming thing? Totally over the top."

"Excuse me?" I frowned.

Jill looked pointedly at my arms then back up at my face. Glancing down, I saw the long, angry-looking red scratch up my arm. I'd forgotten about that. Hazard of the job, I guessed.

"Are you serious? You think I'm a cutter? For chrissakes, Jill, I work with animals." When I got back home in May I had begged and pleaded the local veterinary surgery for a job — any kind of job, just so long as it filled my colossal chunks of free time and helped me on the path to my future. They thought I was crazy for wanting to work from four to close four days a week and all day on weekends if they needed me.

I had one afternoon off a week and so far I'd worked every weekend paid or otherwise. I loved the vet's—there was always something for me to do, something for me to help take care of. I answered phones and worked the reception desk, cleaned kennels, assisted the vet when he needed it, and fed whatever needed feeding.

She shrugged. "Are you going to tell everyone in school that cover story? Even if it's true, who's going to believe you? Everyone will assume you missed out on a year's worth of sympathy for your junkie brother OD'ing and are trying to get it now by hacking up your arm."

Assuming makes an ass out of 'u' and 'me'. Derek's voice tinkled in my ear. His favorite saying that drove me nuts.

"My *friends* are supposed to believe me." Despite my pounding heart, I managed to keep my voice level. I kept eye contact and my face void of fear as I rose from the table.

I could hear them whispering as soon as I was clear of the table. Returning home was the last thing I wanted to do, especially when it had been so lifeless earlier. The stairs down to the bar proved too tempting, and after a glance around to make sure no one was watching, I bounded down them.

The dim lighting in the basement cast long shadows across the space. The place was practically deserted. It was barely dusk—too early for the night crowd that frequented the bar. I ordered a Diet Coke and ignored the disapproving look from the bartender. I slid my eyes along the bar and they landed on a person sitting on a stool a few feet away, half hidden in the shadows.

Archer.

Once again my heart gave a frantic splutter at the sight of him. His entire body language screamed that he was as unapproachable as a bear—but there was something about him that drew me in like a moth to the flame.

Archer wore the same dark jeans and gray T-shirt he had at school. He rocked the bad boy image and while I'd never been the type to dig bad boys...I totally dug Archer. His long fingers curled around a beer bottle, so I figured they still didn't card down here too often. I took a deep breath and moved to stand next to him.

"Hey." I didn't bother trying to keep the false upbeat tone in my voice like I had every other time I had spoken this past year. "Are you having as crappy a night as I am?"

Shockingly, he ignored me.

"I don't blame you for being down here. Upstairs is just as bad as the cafeteria or the quad before school. Preppy assholes as far as the eye can see."

The bartender placed my Diet Coke in front of me and I handed him the money. I looked at the quiet, strange boy again for longer than was socially polite. With a sigh, I gave up and retreated to a booth in a dark corner.

An hour passed and neither the quiet boy nor I moved. My Diet Coke was almost drained and staying for another was way more depressing than just going home. But just as I had decided to leave, a guy slid into the booth opposite me.

He couldn't have been any older than twenty-five. His dirty blond hair was styled into a messy fin that no doubt took way longer to achieve than it looked and his deep tan told me he spent a lot of his time outdoors. He was probably a jock — in high school, at least — but I couldn't tell how good a body he had under his scuffed and faded leather jacket.

"Hi there. All alone tonight?" he asked, his pale blue eyes twinkling.

I narrowed my eyes. After the day I'd had where the rest of the world had made it painfully clear they wanted nothing to do with me, this random guy and his attention put me on edge. "Why?"

He laughed, a soft, musical laugh, revealing dazzling white teeth. "Easy. I'm trying to figure out why a beautiful girl like you would be alone. You've got to have a line around the block of guys waiting for you to give them the time of day?"

I snorted a laugh. "Hardly."

He leaned forward and folded his arms on top of the table. "I don't believe that for a second."

The dull lighting helped disguise the blush that stained my cheeks. I'd had guys flirt with me before, but this dude was way into the flattery. It helped to settle the blanket of suspicion, and if I cared to admit it to myself... I liked the attention. Especially after the day I'd had.

"Are you okay?" he asked, a crease forming between his brows. "You seem a little sad."

I chuckled, a witty retort on the tip of my tongue that refused to be spoken aloud.

Opposite me, the guy straightened himself and a warm smile appeared. "Tell you what, I'm at a loss for something to do right now. My so-called friends ditched me, so how about I get us a couple of drinks and we can talk?"

I arched an eyebrow. "That's awfully presumptuous of you. Who said I'd have a drink with you?"

His smile turned coy and a hint of boyish charm appeared. "I'm just keeping my fingers crossed you say yes."

Despite myself, a smile played on my lips.

The guy sensed my resolve crumbling and jumped on it. "We don't even have to have a serious talk. I mean, we can if you want to. I can tell something is bothering you. I'm a good listener if you feel like unloading, and I'm always free as a shoulder to cry on."

A laugh bubbled in my throat when he waggled his eyebrows. "Sure. What the hell."

He smiled. "Huh. Thought it would take longer to break you. I'm almost disappointed."

Before I had time to react to his strange choice of words, he was out of his seat and striding toward the bar. When he returned to the booth with two beer bottles, instead of sitting opposite me like before, he slid in next to me. He kept a safe distance, but close enough that the action screamed intimate. Or intended intimacy.

"So, it's about time you told me your name," he said with a smile as he placed a beer in front of me.

"Lo," I said without even thinking about it. But was I Lo? Did I even want to be Lo anymore?

"No last name, Lo?"

Even I knew better than to tell a total stranger my full information. I forced a smile. "Nope. I'm like Madonna. Or Pink."

He smiled wider. "Don't you trust me enough to tell me your last name?"

Am I being stupid? I mean, what did I expect him to do if I told him my last name? I leaned my elbow on the table, rested my chin in my hand and lifted my eyebrows. "Why do you need to know? You haven't even told me your first."

"Touché. I'm Cam," he said with a nod.

I held out my hand for him to shake. "It's a pleasure to meet you, Cam."

He accepted my hand, holding on to me for a moment too long. "Likewise, Lo."

Two hours, three beers later and Cam had successfully taken my mind off the horrendous day. Despite being a little full-on at first, Cam backed off and gradually I found him easy to be around. He was interested in what I had to say without pushing and even though drop-dead gorgeous, he wasn't a vapid narcissist. Cam told me about his job as a mechanic and how he'd happily be a grease monkey for the rest of his life, he loved tinkering with engines and it was his dream to bring a vintage car back to life, fully restored.

Cars and engines weren't really things I knew an awful lot about and, rude as it was, my attention wandered... along with my eyes. The bar hadn't filled up much, only a handful more people than when I arrived.

Archer still sat at the bar, lonesome as ever. A sudden and unexpected pang for him burst in my chest and I wished he was sitting with me. Which was totally stupid and pointless — the guy had only ever ignored me. But he looked just as lonely as me, and I wanted to change that.

Cam brushed his fingers over the scratch on my arm and I jumped from the unexpected touch. "What happened here?" he asked.

"Oh, nothing," I said, removing my arm from the table and hiding it underneath.

His eyes bore into me. "Someone been rough with you, Lo?"

"No, it was an accident. Really," I stammered. Stupid Jill, putting doubts in my head. But maybe she had been right, and no one would believe it was simply a hazard of my job.

He nodded thoughtfully and didn't take his gaze from my face. Cam leaned an inch closer, invading my personal space so much that when he spoke next, his breath gently wafted on my face. "You really are beautiful," he murmured.

Another blush scorched my cheeks. I didn't consider myself classically beautiful. Out of all my friends — or were they ex friends? — I had always considered Sarah the prettiest, for the simple reason that she was the happiest and it showed — it lit her up somehow.

Jill and Rachel were pretty but they worked for it. A lot. Jill carefully maintained a year-long tan, had perfect long brown hair and a face that could smile and put someone at ease or harden and they'd know their days were numbered. Rachel had long, dark blonde hair from a bottle — a fiercely guarded secret — and cheekbones sharp enough to slice cheese.

And me? I guessed I'd never really thought about it. Sure, I kept in shape but I wasn't the tallest girl in my grade, and neither was I the shortest. I didn't wear a lot of makeup anymore out of habit. Mostly because once I stopped putting on the mask I wore to school and was away from Jill long enough to stop being so painfully insecure, I realized I had good skin already. Olive-toned skin gave me nice coloring without needing to bake myself under the sun in the summer. My black hair remained poker straight at all times, no matter what I did with it.

Derek's hair had been the exact opposite of mine. Similar in coloring only, where mine was orderly, his had been unruly. It didn't matter how many times Mom had dragged him to get it cut and styled, or how much product he'd used, his hair had done whatever the hell it wanted. Some days it had flopped forward, some days it had stuck up at every possible angle. Some days half had stayed flat, the other half hadn't.

I blinked.

Allowing myself to think about Derek was like someone throwing cold water in my face. Cam's eyes wandered over my face, focusing on my lips, and whatever was happening with Cam and me it wasn't happening now. "Um, I should really get going," I said quietly.

"What's the matter? We were getting along." Cam's eyes tightened, but his tone remained friendly with a hint of disappointment.

"We were — are," I corrected. "I just have somewhere to be, that's all."

Cam's smile slid clean off his face. "Are you lying to me, Lo?"

I frowned as unease prickled under my skin. "No, of course not. I had a lot of fun, Cam. You really took my mind off a truly heinous day." I glanced again at Archer and wondered if he would pick up on my apprehension and come to the rescue. As if.

Cam followed my eyes. "What are you looking at?"

"The clock above the bar," I lied quickly. All at once I was exhausted, and I wanted to go home... Lonely as it was. The day had been an all-out disaster, and Cam's sudden intensity made it all the worse. "My friend wants to meet me when she finishes her shift upstairs. She'll probably be waiting on me already." I tried to smile as I got to my feet but failed. "Thanks again for the drinks, and for the company. I'll see you again sometime?"

Cam stood to let me out of the booth. "I'm sure you will," he said as I walked past him.

My heart pounded in my ears and I forced myself not to run at breakneck speed up the stairs and out of the door. I could have just told him I needed to leave and left out of the door downstairs, but, for some unexplainable reason, I wanted Cam to think I would be with someone.

I couldn't put my finger on why panic crept into my gut, but there was something off about Cam that flared to life the second I went against what he wanted, or expected, from me. I'm a firm believer in listening to my instincts, and my instincts told me to hurry home.

At the top of the stairs, I didn't bother to check and see if any of the girls were still there. I just wanted to go home to my sanctuary. It was full dark when I made it out into the cool air. I paused for a breath and tried to slow my racing heart, and dug around in my purse to find my cell.

No missed calls.

So my parents really didn't care that I had been absent without warning for hours. I shoved the phone back in my purse and a wave of fury rolled through me. At my parents. At my old friends. At everyone in this goddamn town. In that tiny second I hated them all.

My uncharacteristic bout of anger shattered the second Cam stepped out of the dark mouth of the alley next to the Grill. A cold thrill of fear crept up my spine as he took a slow step toward me, a smile that didn't reach his eyes at play on his lips.

"Off so soon? Where's your friend?" Cam asked. He circled around me, forcing me to turn my back on the alley.

I swallowed. Had I badly misread Cam? It seemed he wasn't just intense. For the first time that night, I got a dangerous vibe from him. "She... She, uh, had to work late."

Cam took a step closer, forcing me to take one back. "Why didn't you come back and find me? Didn't you have a good time with me?"

"I did," I said in a rush. "But I'm a little tired now, and —"

"You're lying to me," Cam said. He took another step, and as I retreated back another, I realized he was herding me into the dark, isolated alley.

"No," I said quietly. My mind raced. I had to figure a way

out of this situation before it turned ugly.

"No?" Cam asked, lifting his eyebrows. He smiled wider, with teeth. "How about I walk you home, then?"

And have him find out where I lived? Absolutely not. I forced a smile and tried to walk around him, but he turned his body and didn't let me pass. "That's okay. You've already been so great with me tonight, I couldn't impose on you any more."

Cam chuckled quietly and reached out for me, his hand like lightning. He gripped my elbow and squeezed—not hard enough to cause me pain, but hard enough that I got the message that he wasn't letting go any time soon.

How I heard the footsteps over my racing heart I'll never know, but the second I heard them hope streaked through me. For a second nothing happened. The quiet boy from school merely watched us, slowly assessing the situation.

Cam peered over his shoulder. "Keep moving, buddy."

Archer dropped his head and carried on walking. My stomach dropped, making my legs tingle and jellify. *That's it,* I thought, *my only hope… And he isn't even going to try to help me…*

With my eyes wider than they'd ever been, I dragged my gaze back to Cam. He smiled, slow and sure.

A fist came flying out of nowhere and connected with Cam's face.

Cam stumbled back, releasing his iron grip on my arm. Archer pushed him away, making Cam stumble and fall into a pile of garbage bags.

I opened my mouth to speak, but Archer flashed me a look that silenced my voice in my throat.

"Go home," he said quietly, his voice rough and seriously pissed.

One last glance at Cam on the ground was all it took to spur me into motion and I ran home.

Fast.

Chapter Three

Every step home took a hundred times longer than usual. As though my feet weighed a ton and slowed my pace to a crawl. In my head, at least. In reality I'd probably never made the journey faster. I focused solely on getting inside. Get inside and lock the door. Get inside and lock the door and shut all the blinds. The thick darkness of the night made me achingly vulnerable, convinced that sinister things lurked in the shadows, just waiting to devour me in their jaws. Every noise I heard was Cam. Anything that moved was him coming to finish whatever it was he had been about to start.

Though I wanted to rip open my door with every ounce of strength I possessed, I forced myself to go slow — to ease it open just like always. I closed the door more rapidly than normal, but crouched and extended my hand. From the shadow, a low, slinking and trembling body emerged — no doubt from my slamming the door back into place.

I clicked my tongue. Ears flicked up at the familiar sound and he trotted closer, sniffing my hand. Checking my pockets, I found a few treats and pulled them out. His tongue lapped at my hand, teeth gently nipping to get the food. Once my hand was empty, I stood.

"Hey, Kit," I whispered, moving to turn on the lamp.

Kit sat in the center of the room, staring up at me expectantly. Once again, my unusual pet worked a calm through me. I dropped onto the couch, my fox jumping up to sit on my lap, licking at my face and ears. He let me burrow my face into his coarse coat and I let out a breath, shocked when it turned into a sob.

At the noise, Kit leaped away from me.

Once my breathing had returned to normal, I stood from the couch and headed to my bedroom. Once dressed in my comfiest PJs and wrapped up in bed, my fear of what could have happened slowly dissipated and I reassured myself that nothing did happen.

I had thought it would have been Cam's face that allowed me no peace that night, but mostly Archer occupied my waking thoughts. My heart slowed its frantic beating when his face fluttered past my mind's eye. I wondered if he realized how grateful I was... Wondered if he knew what I owed him.

* * * *

When the outfit I planned on wearing really wasn't wearable anymore thanks to Kit taking a hairy nap on it while I showered, and my makeup taking longer to apply because of the serious baggage happening beneath my eyes, I was late for school. My lateness left me no chance to seek Archer out to thank him for what he had done.

The day crawled by agonizingly slow, and I arrived to English before anyone else — not a shocker since I had raced from my last class. I headed straight for the desk I had sat at the day before. I chewed on my fingernail as I anxiously waited on him arriving. Kimmie entered the room before he did, smiling sardonically and sitting in my old seat.

Eventually he loped into the room with so much nonchalance I wondered why he even bothered showing up in the morning. If he really didn't want to be here, why didn't he drop out?

"Hi," I said a little too eagerly when he sat down beside me. Did he sit beside me on purpose? Was this his usual seat and I happened to be beside it? Or because it was the only free desk left? *Lori, you need help...*

He reached into his bag and pulled out his copy of William Blake poetry that we studied this unit, and his notebook and pen.

"Hi," I repeated, determined to engage with him. "I just wanted—"

"Problem, Miss Black?" Mr. Poole asked from the front of the class.

I scowled. Mr. Poole had always had a problem with me, and he made no secret of it. It probably stemmed from freshman year when Jill and I had had him and we'd done nothing but gossip the entire class. "No."

"Good. Then would you mind if I did the talking?"

I shook my head and folded my arms. I would just have to try later.

Just like the day before, Archer jumped out of his seat the second the bell rang. I tried to catch up with him, but between the droves of students on their way to the cafeteria and the length difference in our legs, I didn't have a chance in hell of catching up to him.

For a while I went with the masses, hoping to spot him. In the doorway to the cafeteria I stood watching, scanning the tables and the lunch line, turning a few times to see if he approached the door. After twenty minutes it was clear he wasn't showing up for lunch.

I circled the campus, figuring he might be sitting outside brown-bagging it or something, though I avoided the gym where the smokers—and therefore Kimmie—spent their lunch breaks. If he was friends, or even distant associates with the likes of her, he didn't deserve my thanks.

Even if he had saved me from a fate worse than death.

Archer remained invisible the rest of the day. I scoured the hallway between classes and waited until the parking lot emptied before walking home at the end of school.

I never saw him.

* * * *

The next day at school I tried to rearrange my priorities. Yes, I owed Archer a huge dose of gratitude. I'd bent over backward trying to find him to give him that gratitude, but his loner-boy rep seriously got in the way. While I wouldn't quit until he realized exactly how much him stepping in like that meant to me, it was in my better interests to pursue other social leads at school.

Only Sarah smiled her thanks when I placed the four takeout coffees in the center of their table in the quad.

The night before I'd taken some of the sleeping pills the doctor had prescribed me after Derek had died when my mind refused to let me have the solace of sleep. I rarely took them — I saw them more as an admission of weakness rather than something that could help me.

They did, however, bring me ten blissful, uninterrupted hours of sleep, ridding my eyes of the heavy bags and giving my complexion a bit of color again. I'd spent careful time getting ready that morning, painstakingly choosing the perfect skirt and top with adorable shoes. I reasoned I might not feel like the old Lo, but I sure as hell could look like her.

Remembering how Sarah made her introduction to the group, I decided to try her tactic by just sitting down and not leaving.

Open-heart surgery would be less intimidating. "I don't know about you girls, but I'm seriously lagging this morning." I snagged a coffee and gestured for the others to help themselves. "I was at the coffee place anyway."

Sarah made 'awwing' noises and picked one for herself. Rachel glanced at Jill, as though searching for a hint as to how she should react.

Jill smiled a smile that held as much warmth as a day in December in the Antarctic. "How sweet. You wouldn't be trying to butter us up, would you, Lo?"

I rolled my eyes. "Drink them or don't — makes no difference to me. Like I said, I was there anyway."

She smiled again as though she didn't expect my nonchalant response. Jill pulled the lid off one cup. "Mochas? Really, Lo?"

Rachel looked at the remaining coffee as though she wanted to devour it whole. Sarah glanced at her own coffee with a guilty expression. With a shrug she took another drink.

"Forget buttering us up, she's trying to fatten us up!" Rachel hissed.

I held a hand over my heart. "You think I'd do that to you girls? Cappuccinos. Swear to God."

Sarah looked at her drink. "I thought it tasted different."

"Cappuccinos are still ridiculously high in empty calories. What about the milk?"

I winked. "Non-fat." Perhaps. Well, I didn't *not* know it was regular milk—I didn't watch the barista make the drinks. In all honesty I had forgotten about Jill's obsession with calories and weight. As though one lousy coffee had the potential to turn her obese. Sometimes I wished she had real problems and could finally get her priorities right.

The bell rang and I drained the last of my own coffee. I grinned at the girls—Jill and Rachel still trying to decide if it was worth giving up the coffee just to spite me. "Wow, perfect pick-me-up. Bye, girls."

Tossing my empty coffee cup in the trashcan, I fought back the coffee that threatened to return.

Phase one—complete.

Phase two would be a hundred times worse than phase one. Show no fear.

Like the day before, I rushed to fourth period English, eager to beat someone there. Only this time it wasn't Archer. Before I could freak out and tell myself that this really was a heinous idea, I sat in my old seat. Second row, beside the window.

The kids in the room stopped talking when I sat down. Out of the corner of my eye I saw them exchange looks and whisper, jerking their heads in my direction. I caught one girl mouthing 'suicide' to her friend. I didn't need them to tell me this was a kamikaze mission.

What Jill had said to me the night at the Grill really

bothered me. Mainly because a lot of what she said was true. Before I'd left at the end of sophomore year, I would rather have died than let Kimmie push me around. Probably because my life wouldn't be worth living if I did. Had Jill not proved that at the Grill?

If I let Kimmie push me around now then my life within the group would be finished. If I fought back, showed her I wasn't the weakling she pegged me for, the girls would see I was still the shit and welcome me back with open arms. Then I would be untouchable again.

In theory, anyway.

Kimmie walked into the room a few minutes before the second bell rang, laughing with one of her sleazy buddies. She followed him to a desk three rows back in the second aisle from the door. He dropped his bag onto the desk and Kimmie took the desk beside him.

I wasn't surprised. It had never been about the desk. She wanted to prove she could take whatever she wanted of mine just because she could.

As she twisted around, she caught me staring. Kimmie made a show of turning back to her skeezy guy friend, kissing him on the cheek and flouncing across the room to me.

"Aw, thanks, Lo. How sweet of you to save my seat for me," Kimmie said, smiling so sickly sweet I wanted to hurl then and there.

"I'm not saving it for you," I said, dropping my eyes. First mistake. Note to self—maintain eye contact at all times, no matter how freaking scared you are.

"Keeping it warm for me then? It must be handy having an ass that big to keep the whole seat warm."

A few laughs tittered around us.

I looked back up at her. "Kimmie, I'm not moving, so give up already."

She rested her hands on the desk and loomed over me. "This is your last chance," she hissed in my ear. "Move, now, and I'll forget about this stupid attempt at growing a pair."

I pushed her hands off my desk. "I haven't grown anything, Kimmie. Unlike you. I can recommend a great waxer for that 'stache if you want." Below the belt. And not even true. Like that ass comment of hers wasn't. Why did I even care about hitting back at her? Oh right, I wasn't evil like her.

The laughter rose, more out of shock than anything.

Kimmie's face clouded over. Shit...

"Get up."

"No."

"Get up."

I forced myself to laugh. "Are you not hearing me right? I said no, Kimmie. Go pick on someone who cares."

"You think you're such hot shit?" Kimmie growled, leaning closer again. "No one missed you. No one even remembered you. *Or* your junkie brother."

I yawned, even though her words cut me deep — just like she wanted. "This all you got, Kimmie? Tell you what, I'll make it real easy for you — " With that, I held up the first three fingers of my right hand, palm facing me. "Read between the lines."

She frowned for a moment before flushing a violent shade of red. Laughter came from all around the room as people got it.

Mr. Poole came into the classroom, slamming the door behind him. "Find a seat, Ms. Jones."

Kimmie glared at me for another few seconds before turning on her heel. I didn't see where she sat. I didn't hear any of the lesson. The blood rushing past my ears blocked all noise.

After class, Mr. Poole kept Kimmie behind to talk about making an effort to learn or something. I took the opportunity to hightail it out of there before she exacted her revenge. Jill and the girls were already seated at their usual table in the cafeteria.

"Hey," I said, approaching them.

"Oh, Lo, we didn't expect you to sit with us today. We didn't keep a spot free for you," Jill said, no apologetic tone in her voice.

"No big deal." I smiled, swiping a chair from the next table. "I'm sure you can make a little room."

Sarah moved her chair closer to Rachel's, creating a spot for me between her and Jill.

"Thanks," I said smiling, shuffling in. Cramped. Awkward as hell. Least enjoyable lunch period of my life so far. But I was in. By the skin of my teeth, I was in.

"How was English, Lo?" Rachel asked, slurping from the straw in her can of Diet Coke — the only lunch meal I had ever seen her consume.

I rolled my eyes and ignored the jibe. "Sucky as always."

"No Kimmie threats?" she asked innocently.

So they hadn't heard yet. I laughed as if I didn't have a care in the world. "Plenty." I looked up and caught Jill's eye. "But when has Lo freaking Black let a witch like Kimmie Jones push her around?"

Jill arched a perfect slender eyebrow, but didn't comment. She turned to Rachel. "Mall on Saturday? I need some new shoes."

There was no invite for me.

Chapter Four

It didn't take a rocket scientist to find the girls. They said right in front of me they would be at the mall on Saturday afternoon, and as an In Crowd veteran, I knew how they operated. On first arrival they sat at one of the wrought iron tables that surrounded the coffee cart on the lower section in the east wing. A java jolt helped Jill prepare for flashing the black Amex card that Daddy gave her, apparently.

Next they went onto the second level to work their way along the high-end boutiques before switching sides and hitting the accessory stores. If the mood struck, they would browse the perfumes in the department store at the rear of the mall before getting smoothies and sitting on the lip of the giant fountain in another section of the mall. And the busiest section, might I add. What was the point of buying crap if people didn't see how much you'd acquired?

I checked my watch as I entered the mall. Two fifteen. Usually the girls got to the mall around one, coffee taking anywhere from twenty minutes to a half hour. Jill would have bought a few outfits in the first boutique by now, so they should, in theory, be at the second stop, and Rachel's personal favorite haven – the lingerie store.

Sure enough, as soon as I stepped inside, I spotted them. Sarah browsed the bras, Jill looked at some torturous-looking corset and Rachel tried to choose between a teddy and a few scraps of lace that in some cultures must pass as a nightgown.

Since I needed some new PJs anyway, I picked up a few tank top and shorts sets. I threw them over my arm as I wandered along the rails, picking up things but not really seeing them.

"Lo? Hey!"

At the sound of Sarah's voice, I looked up. I grinned as she enveloped me in a hug. "Hi, what are you doing here?"

Jill sauntered over and smiled tightly. "Didn't we mention we were coming to the mall today? I'm sure we did."

Not everyone would hear the thinly veiled threat in her words, but I heard them loud and clear. She wasn't happy that I had dared attend a public place without her explicit invitation first. "I don't remember. Any good buys so far?"

Jill nodded, seemingly thrown when I didn't roll over and show her my belly. "A few."

"Just a few?"

Her lips twitched into a true smile. "The day is still young."

My smile widened. It was almost as if we were having a real conversation.

"Lo, help me choose," Sarah said, holding up two bras. "The satin or the lace? I can't decide."

I looked back and forth, trying to remember what the 'old Lo' would say. "Both?"

Sarah giggled. "Both. Cool. No wonder you're the smart one."

We all paid at the same time, Sarah lingering beside me so the others couldn't rush off and abandon me just because they had finished paying. "What are you doing now?" Sarah asked as we stood near the store entrance.

I shrugged. "Just browsing. I might get a smoothie later."

Sarah linked her arm through mine. "Come with us, I need an outfit for next weekend. Tommy's taking me out on his dad's boat."

"Sure, that sounds great." I bit my tongue to keep from adding 'if that's cool with you guys'. The 'old Lo' wouldn't have asked permission.

Three hours and a serious dent in my savings later, Jill and Rachel had loosened up and no longer acted so standoffish with me. We all sat at the fountain, sipping our smoothies, admiring the cluster of pretty bags at our feet.

"What are you guys doing tonight?" I asked.

"Ugh," Sarah said as she rolled her eyes. "Rachel wants to go to some party in Muskego. Those parties are all the same. I am so over Muskego."

"What's wrong with Muskego?" Rachel demanded. "I don't remember you hating it when you met that guy."

"Which one? We've met all the Muskego guys."

I laughed at their banter.

Rachel's eyes flickered to mine. "I suppose you have better plans, Lo?"

"Not really. I'm going to Franklin, I've got tickets for The Howlers tonight."

Jill's eyes widened. "You got tickets for that show? They've been sold out for weeks — not even my dad could get any."

Thank God for eBay. "Yeah, I won a contest in the summer. I might not go. No else I know is." See, Jill? I can dangle a carrot too...

"How many tickets do you have?"

"Three spare ones."

"We could go with you," Jill said, smiling as if it was her doing me the favor.

"What about Muskego?" Rachel huffed.

"What about Muskego?" Jill asked, her tone turning cooler. "Sarah's right — it's old news."

"Well, I'm still going," Rachel said, shooting me a poisonous glare.

Jill's eyes narrowed with annoyance. "With who? What kind of loser goes to a party alone? Don't be a skank. Take the ticket." She turned back to me, her face warming. "Pick you up at seven, Lo?"

I wanted to laugh and grin and swoon with relief. If I pulled off the concert tonight then I would be on track to getting my old life back. Instead of acting like an embarrassing fangirl at a Bieber concert, I smiled and said, "Sounds great."

"Perfect. We can get some dinner afterward."

"Perfect." Perfect.

* * * *

I'd forgotten how much effort was required to make me look as if I'd made an effort. Even though my naturally straight hair didn't need to be straightened with the hot iron, I did it anyway, just to make it edgier and shiny. Smoky dark eye makeup followed. I wore my black skinny jeans with ballet flats and a cute fitted waistcoat that showed off my hipbones and accentuated what little cleavage I had.

I waited on the front steps of my house, the evening air losing a little more heat as night approached. A car turned into the driveway and for a second I thought it was Jill.

It wasn't.

My mom got out of her car, bringing with her a few bags of groceries. She paused when she noticed me, but mustered a semi-convincing smile. "Are you going out?"

"Yeah. Jill's picking me up in a few." I picked my jeans at the knee, worrying a worn patch.

"Good, good. You haven't really... I haven't seen the girls since you got home."

You've barely seen this *girl since I got home.* I nodded.

"Well, have fun." Mom passed me on the stairs. She opened the front door and stepped inside, turning back at the last second. "And don't stay out too late?"

"Sure thing, Mom," I said, turning back to face the road.

The door closed quietly behind me and I released a long breath.

Mom asking me to be home at a decent hour was pretty pointless. She wouldn't know when, or if, I made it home.

Eventually Jill's sleek black convertible pulled up. The drive to Franklin took about forty minutes, with me and Sarah in the back of the car laughing. Jill and Rachel barely cracked a smile in the front. But even Jill's unfazed exterior cracked when we waited in line to get into the club to see the band. The doormen didn't card us. Score for the hot girls.

At the abundance of cute, older guys inside, Rachel soon cheered up. And when her attitude finally disappeared, it was as if something clicked with all of us. We were back—the girls who ruled, who commanded attention wherever we went, who didn't take shit from anyone. It was intoxicating. We danced to the music, losing ourselves to the lyrics. After the band's first set, I motioned to the bar and Jill came with me.

I ordered four waters from the bartender, fanning my face with my hand when he left.

"I thought I'd never see her again," Jill shouted in my ear above the DJ music that filled the time before The Howlers returned to the stage.

"Who?" I asked with a frown as I glanced behind me.

She tapped my hand. "The old Lori. Our Lo." Jill grinned.

I looked down for a beat. Just how real could I be with Jill? Before Derek, I wouldn't have hesitated in calling her my best friend, said that she knew me better than anyone, the only exception being my brother. But now? I had to wonder if she had ever really been my friend, or if I had simply been someone she could use for a while. I pushed the concern from my head and said, "I never left, Jill. Just with Derek, I'm, you know…"

"Yeah, I do know. But I have to admit, when you came back I barely recognized you. I'm so happy you're back to your old self again." The bartender placed the bottles of water on the bar. "I got it," Jill said as she handed him the money. She took two bottles and motioned for me to follow her.

Something made me pause as I watched Jill push her way back through the crowd.

I should be doing cartwheels. Jill had basically just let me back in—what I had been aiming for since my return.

So why did I feel like I had the chance to win the million bucks, but came away with a microwave instead?

* * * *

A buzzing noise pulled me out of a dreamless sleep. A pillow over my head didn't do anything to block out the noise. Kit stuck his nose under the pillow, perhaps wondering if I'd hidden something interesting from him under there. With a groan I tossed the pillow away and admitted defeat. I was awake.

Jill had dropped me off the night before some time after two. Dinner after the concert had turned out to be a handful of pretzels at a party Rachel had insisted we hit before going home.

I groped around on my nightstand for the phone. It had to be my boss—no one else called me anymore. I flipped it open. "Hello?" I answered past a yawn.

Jill laughed. "Lo, are you still in bed?"

I bolted upright in bed and shoved a mass of hair out of my face. Despite last night going better than I could have expected, that was not a voice I expected to hear. "Jill? Uh... yeah, I am, why?"

"You're late."

"For what?" I asked, frowning. I didn't remember the others asking me to meet them anyplace the night before.

"Brunch, stupid," Jill said with derision. "The diner, eleven thirty... Any of this ringing any bells? We always have brunch together on Sundays."

That's right, we did. A long time ago I'd been part of the tradition. Apparently my invite had been reissued. "Um, I can be there in a half hour?"

"Okay, see you soon, babe."

I closed the phone and stared at the ceiling above me. My heart thumped. Had that just happened or was I still dreaming? Part of me couldn't believe that, despite the rocky start, my transition back into the group had been relatively painless. But, like the night before, that other part of me wondered what I even wanted anymore.

Chapter Five

The quad on Monday morning at school bustled as always. I walked toward the table with mild curiosity, wondering what reception I would get. At brunch the day before things had been normal. Normal for a year ago, at least. The girls talked as if I'd never been gone. But that hadn't been on school grounds. At school, everything could change.

An elbow in my side jolted me back to the present. "Are you dragging your heels for any particular reason, Lo?"

I turned and saw Jill smiling. Guess that answered my question. "No, just...tired I guess."

Jill handed me one of the takeout coffees she carried. "Got the perfect thing for you right here."

"Thanks, Jill," I said as I accepted the drink.

She leaned closer as we approached the table. "I got mochas. Little treat, you know? Rachel's is non-fat — don't tell her. She needs to lose a few pounds. Did you see how she looked in that top yesterday? I could barely eat my fruit cup."

Wow. I'd forgotten that side of Jill. The side that was convinced all her friends could stand to lose a pound or two, even if they absolutely couldn't. My own body insecurities had melted away since leaving last year. I had other things on my mind than my figure. "I won't say anything."

"There's my girl," Jill said with a wink.

That day in English, I claimed my old seat and watched with interest as Kimmie shot me a filthy look, but didn't attempt to remove me. She muttered something to her skanky friend, who also turned my way to glare.

Had word gotten out that I was once again an untouchable?

A few minutes later, I discovered that my new social standing had indeed made its way around the school. Joel, a cute guy in our class, took the seat beside mine.

"Hey, Lo. Glad to be home?" he asked as he dropped down into the seat.

I'd been back two weeks — at school anyway. The welcome wagon was late. Better late than never, I guessed. I could tell myself that Joel simply hadn't had the opportunity to seek me out yet, but his locker was four down from mine and I had seen him at least a dozen times since returning.

Joel belonged to the male equivalent of Jill's group, and was one of the beautiful elite whom she deemed worthy of our time. I'd lost count of the number of times she'd ragged on me for talking to a guy she didn't approve of, let alone converse with. And at six foot two, with tan muscles topped with a killer smile and dusty blond hair, there was no doubt that Joel was elite.

"Yeah," I said, forcing myself to smile. "It's like I never left."

He twisted farther in his chair to lean closer to me and lowered his voice when he next spoke. "I don't know if you remember, but you owe me a date."

A laugh bubbled in my throat. "I do?"

Joel smiled, one cheek dimpling. "Yeah, right before you left you said 'see you around'."

"I did?"

He nodded. "I'm taking you for your word. See, in my book, 'see you around' is a sure thing. So, what do you say you see me around eight tonight?"

I laughed again, so out of practice with flirting I found the whole thing ludicrous. "Um…"

He placed a hand over his heart. "Aw, come on, Lo, don't hurt a guy. You'll be at the Grill tonight, won't you?"

Would I? I didn't particularly want to go back after what had happened the last time I was there…but I also didn't plan on going downstairs or walking home alone. And to keep my place I had to play my role harder than anyone else. Yes, I decided, I'd be there. "Yeah, I'll be there."

He nodded. "So, if you're going to be there, and I'm going to be there, what do you say we're there together? You can still sit with your friends, laugh and whisper about me if that's what you really want to do." He grinned. "I'll be doing that with my friends. Just as long as you agree to one drink with me and a game of pool."

I leaned my elbow on my desk and rested my chin in my hand. "Oh, is that all?"

"Yeah. No — you let me drive you home after."

A ride home with a guy usually meant he wanted something. It was like some unwritten rule or something. I glanced over Joel's shoulder to the back of the room, where Archer had just slouched down low in his seat. He pulled out the book we were studying and folded back the cover.

If there was one person in this school that popularity meant absolutely nothing to, it was him. It didn't matter if I was a loser or a Queen Bee. He hadn't rushed to talk to me now that I was fair game again. He had no ulterior motive. There wasn't a single other person I could say that about.

A fierce pang of longing coursed through me. In that second, I wished Archer sat beside me, asking to meet me after school and drive me home after.

Archer's eyes flitted up and locked with mine.

My breath caught in my throat and I quickly looked down, embarrassed to have been caught staring.

"Lo?" Joel prompted.

A quick glance back at Archer confirmed that he had turned away and, embarrassed as I was, I couldn't help but be disappointed. I looked back at Joel and forced another smile. "I'll hang out with you for a while, but I'll get a ride home with the girls."

* * * *

By three that afternoon, word had spread across school

that Joel and I had a date for that night. Jill gushed when she met me in the parking lot, insisting on giving me a ride home. The entire drive she lectured me on how I should behave and what I should wear. Had it been this much work before? Taken this much energy?

I settled for a short denim skirt, black ballet flats and a white tank top. Clean and fresh-looking. I was a jittery mess of nerves by the time Jill arrived to pick me up, once again reminding me what I should say and how I should definitely not act.

Like a psycho freak, how I'd been shortly after Derek had died, apparently.

Sarah rushed toward us when Jill and I walked into the Grill. "Joel's here, he's been waiting forever!"

I placed my hands on her arms. "Sarah, breathe."

She laughed. "It's just so exciting! You're really back." Sarah threw her arms around me as if I'd been brought back from the dead.

Jill extracted Sarah from me. "Sarah, go sit down. You're embarrassing Lo."

I winked at Sarah so she knew I didn't agree. She smiled back, and followed orders. Jill and I followed her, but Jill stopped me before I could sit down. "I want a Diet Coke."

"Okay," I said, frowning.

She flashed a sickly sweet smile. "Go to the bar for me?"

I held back a sigh as I realized her game. "Sure."

We both knew she wouldn't get her drink. It was just to give Joel the opportunity to find me alone. Sure enough, the moment I reached the bar he appeared at my elbow, smiling beside me.

"Well, that wasn't as painful as I thought it would be. You girls usually travel in such tight packs no guy stands a chance. I figured I'd be waiting all night to find you on your own." He grinned. "So you're here, I'm here…"

"We're here together?" I guessed, a laugh bubbling in my throat at his easy, awkward charm.

He laughed. "Right. Can I get you a drink?"

"Water, thanks."

"You want to sit first, or have that game of pool?"

Crap. I'd forgotten the pool. This skirt would give any guy in the vicinity a happy every time I took a shot. "Sit, please."

He nodded, handed me the bottle of water and led the way to a quiet booth away from the rest of the students who loitered at the Grill. I glanced at Jill to find her watching us with her keen eyes. Tonight was as much a test as every other encounter had been so far. I waggled my fingers at her and turned back to Joel.

When we sat down, Joel looked at me and let out a quiet laugh.

"What?" I asked, hoping I didn't have something on my face.

He shook his head. "Nothing, it's like I've taken a step back a year. All sophomore year I tried to get the courage to ask you out."

Right. I had once been intimidating. I'd forgotten about that. "Seriously?"

Joel laughed, his eyes lighting up with mirth. "Yeah, seriously. Your friends used to scare the crap out of me. I was sure if I asked you out they'd make my life a living hell."

Well, he was right about that. If Joel had pursued me, he would have opened himself up to the same level of scrutiny that I lived with. Not to mention our relationship would never have been private. "But you always seem so confident."

"There's confident and there's suicidal — which I make it a point not to be." Joel chuckled. "Jill's the worst, but you... You came a close second."

It was as if he'd thrown a bucket of iced water in my face. "What?"

Joel lounged back in his chair, seemingly oblivious to my distress. "I don't mean it in a bad way, just that you were intimidating to a guy like me."

"Oh," I said, praying that I wasn't as much of a bitch as he was making me feel.

"I was never on your radar." He laughed and sipped his soda. "Then you started dating Drew, and I knew I didn't have a chance."

So I really was one of those horrible, bitchy popular girls. Jesus...

"But here we are now, so I must be doing something right."

"I'm sorry, Joel," I said quietly.

"Why? What's wrong?" he asked, a frown creasing his forehead.

I twisted my hands. "For being awful before."

Joel shrugged, his face losing the easy-going nature as he sobered and realized my shame. "Don't blame yourself. You were just falling in line." He nodded his head to Jill's table.

Sweet of him to say, but blaming Jill only went so far. What was worse — the one ordering, or the one following the orders? "Give it to me straight — how big a bitch was I?"

Joel shifted in his seat. "It wasn't that you were a bitch, I wouldn't have had a crush on you if you were... It was more like you just didn't see people. Your eyes only saw a certain level and anything under that fell by the wayside."

Is that better or worse? I couldn't decide.

"Want to play some PacMan?" Joel asked.

"What?" I said, the conversation change so abrupt it made my head spin.

"They put in a few arcade games last year. I'm hooked on PacMan. Want to see if you can beat my high score?" He lifted his eyebrows, his eyes once again light and playful.

That was the thing about Joel. He had the ability to flip a mood around and bring the vibe up. I smiled. "Deal."

I still wouldn't let Joel drive me home that night. I made my excuses to Sarah that I had a headache and she gave me a ride instead. Jill had already left an hour before, no doubt hoping if she left I'd have to get a ride with Joel. Rachel had gone with her—only Sarah lingered, as though she knew I'd need her.

Chapter Six

My date with Joel solidified my presence as an Untouchable, backed up by Jill vocalizing how awesome it was to have me back. The hallway crowds once again parted when I walked them. People talked to me in my classes, waved to me in the hall, invited me to parties and complimented my shoes.

It was weird. Disconcerting. And, underneath my apprehension, a relief. My popularity shielded me like a bulletproof vest, protecting me whenever I stepped outside.

But what Joel told me that night at the Grill seriously opened my eyes. I couldn't do anything to change the past, but I could do something about my present. I vowed to use my popularity for good instead of evil.

The next week, I sat in the warm sunshine in the quad one morning with the girls. Sarah flicked through a fashion magazine, Rachel texted and Jill kept a watchful eye over her public.

"Jesus, would you look at that girl?" Jill said, motioning to a junior girl sitting by the fountain.

"I know," Rachel agreed, taking her eyes off her phone. "She's so tragic."

Jill laughed. "Look at her clothes—I bet she borrowed them from the janitor!"

My mouth hung open at them. Had it always been like this? The only real conversations we had were about other people and their crappy fashion tastes?

None of them knew what I was afraid of. Or what I wanted to do after graduating college. Or what my favorite movie was. Or where the tiny scar on my kneecap came from.

My so-called best friends had no idea who I was.

That thought made me lonelier than ever.

"Drool much, Lo?" Jill asked with a giggle.

She snapped me back to reality and I couldn't come up with a plausible excuse that would explain my mental vacation.

"I know right?" Sarah said, touching my arm. "Super cute."

My eyebrows puckered together as I frowned in confusion. How long had I spaced out for?

Sarah nodded her head to the guy standing a little behind Jill and Rachel. His name was Paul, or Saul, or something. I didn't have any classes with him, but I was sure one of the girls used to date him. "I almost drooled, too." Sarah winked at me, and I realized that she had just saved my butt.

How had Sarah, sweet Sarah, who couldn't see past the end of her nose unless there was a guy in the vicinity, realized that I had actually gawped at our friends?

Jill and Rachel turned to see who Sarah meant. Rachel sighed. "Saul Valentine. So cute."

"Didn't you lose your virginity to him?" Jill asked.

Rachel smiled. "He thinks I did."

Jill settled her eyes on me, a daring expression on her face. "Go give him your number, Lo."

"What? No." I scoffed.

"I'm pretty sure he's gay now," Sarah said. "Tommy told me he saw Saul flirting with some guy at the Grill this one time."

Jill rolled her eyes. "Whatever. Seriously, Lo, go talk to him."

"No way," I said, shaking my head. "I'm not looking for anything. I was just, you, know, looking."

"Yeah, admiring the view," Sarah agreed.

Jill shrugged and asked Rachel what Saul had been like in bed. With her attention diverted, I hoped I could make a quick escape.

The bell wouldn't ring for another five minutes, but the table had become claustrophobic. "I'll see you guys at lunch," I said, rising from the table.

"You're going already?" Sarah asked, disappointment in her tone.

I smiled thinly. "I need to stop by my locker."

Sarah nodded. "Okay, see you later."

That part, at least, was true. But not until third period. Still, it never hurts to be prepared, I guess. Midway down the hallway I rummaged around in my messenger bag for some lip balm. I had just touched the cool tin with my fingertips when someone shoved into me.

Kimmie caught me hard with her shoulder and sent me careening into some poor unsuspecting student. "Ouch, Lo, what did I ever do to you?" Kimmie asked in a hurt voice, cradling her arm.

I flipped her the bird. Kimmie glared and stomped down the hallway.

With a sigh I crouched down to help the person I'd knocked into, collecting the stuff that had spilled to the floor from my bag and theirs. "Sorry about that," I said. When they didn't answer me, I lifted my head. My breath caught at the nearness of Archer, who frowned at me.

Archer straightened his long frame, bringing himself to his full height. He extended his hand to me, and for a second I thought he offered to help me up.

"What are doing down there, Lo?" a voice behind me asked.

I twisted away from Archer to see Joel make his way over with a warm and easy smile on his face.

With an irritated sigh, Archer pulled the book I held out of my grasp and stalked down the hall, leaving me sitting on the floor, like a complete idiot. So. Not a helping hand then—he just wanted his book.

Man, I'm a moron.

With a sigh, I slumped against the row of lockers.

Archer was long gone by the time Joel reached where I sat

on the floor. He crouched down in front of me, a concerned frown marring his forehead. "Are you okay?"

Aside from wishing I could do bodily harm to Kimmie, and also that I didn't turn into a complete idiot around Archer? I went with a simple "Yeah."

"Was he a jerk to you?" Joel asked. He looked in the direction Archer had disappeared, as if he wished he could do bodily harm to him. I had forgotten about Joel's protective instincts.

"No," I said quickly to pacify him. "I plowed into him by accident. He could have been an ass, but he wasn't."

Joel's frown didn't smooth out. "I don't like that kid. Are you sure he wasn't a jerk?"

I reached out to touch Joel's tan forearm and gave him my most reassuring smile. "I'm sure."

He glanced at my hand on his arm and nodded. A moment later a smile of his own stretched across his handsome face. "So what are you doing sitting on the floor?"

"Taking a break from the world—kind of like a mini vacation," I said with a laugh.

"Can I join you?"

I shrugged. "Why not?"

Joel sat down, leaning against the lockers and stretching his long legs out in front of him. "I love vacations."

"Me too. I wish this one would last longer."

"Take one with me later," Joel said, his smile turning dazzling. I had seen him use it before. Girls turned helpless in its presence. Part of me wished that I would too. "I'm sure I can think of a better destination than the school hall."

"Where did you have in mind?"

"The beach? We could leave right after school." He nudged me with his shoulder. "I could teach you to surf."

A laugh bubbled in my throat. "That sounds dangerous."

"You'll be in safe hands."

"I have to work this afternoon, or I'd love to, Joel." While I didn't have butterflies, and I didn't dissolve into a puddle of girlish mush when faced with his most charming smile, I did like Joel. He was a nice fun, guy. And, selfishly, another date with Joel would buy me a little more leverage with Jill.

And…he got that we were only friends…right?

"When do you finish?"

"Seven."

"Would you let me pick you up?"

"Depends."

"On?"

"How strong your sense of smell is."

Joel grinned. "It's terrible."

Guilt panged in my stomach. Something told me that Joel was way more excited about later today than me.

* * * *

All day I wished for the butterflies to flutter in my stomach, but they never did. Things would be so much simpler if I was into Joel. While I liked him, Joel's face didn't send my nerves jolting or my heart pounding. My boss, Doug, and I were close. I didn't tell him about my impending date. If I told him then I'd have to analyze the situation. That, and he would tell me to be honest with Joel.

At the end of the day, I dragged my heels, finishing up my jobs and taking my time saying goodnight to the animals.

Why the hell did I said yes? Stupid, Lori.

When he picked me up, wearing a pale blue T-shirt, crisp jeans and a wide smile, my heart sank. He looked everything I didn't — enthusiastic, happy, nervous. Joel drove us to the lookout, the town spread out below us. We sat on the hood of his car as dusk settled around us and the lights from the town flickering to life.

"I brought snacks." Joel reached into his satchel and handed me a sandwich.

I smiled. "I'm starving. This is great, thanks."

Joel grinned and dug into his own sandwich.

He kept the conversation light, nothing heavy, focusing mainly on school and football, and what I had missed last year. When he drove me home, the inevitable moment came.

"Are you doing anything this weekend?" Joel asked, his voice casual, but he scanned my face, as though uncertain of my answer.

The more time I spent with him, Joel made it clear how much more he wanted from me. I chewed my lip, my stomach twisting with nerves at what I was about to do. "Joel, I have to tell you something."

He let out a breath, his face falling. "Am I getting the brush-off? I came on too strong, didn't I?"

"No, Joel, this is all me." I cringed. "I'm sorry, that's a cliché. But here's the thing — I'm trying to get my life back on track. And this time I'm going to live it with other people in mind. What you said that night at the Grill... It really opened my eyes."

"Crap, I *did* upset you saying that."

"Yeah, but not because of you." I looked down. "I can't be that person again, Joel. And because of that I have to tell you that I'm not ready for this to go anywhere. I really like you, I do. Just not enough. I'm sorry."

Joel gave me a half smile. "Don't be. I appreciate your honesty. It's more than a lot of girls would give."

"No hard feelings?"

"None."

"Good. I'd like us to be friends, Joel."

Joel touched my arm as I opened the car door. "Just be careful, okay? All that honesty could get you in trouble with certain people."

I chuckled. "Believe me, I know. But I can't be who I used to be."

"Then I guess I should say good luck." I got out of the car, laughing as Joel saluted me. "And God speed."

* * * *

My biggest test of change came four weeks after my

official reintroduction to the group.

After we finished eating lunch, the four of us headed to the bathroom to check our makeup. Kristy, a girl I sort of knew from around school, stood in front of a mirror, rooting around in her purse for something. She flushed scarlet when we walked in, avoiding eye contact.

Jill and Rachel pretended she wasn't even in the room at all. Sarah was talking on the phone to some guy she met over the weekend.

"Are you okay?" I asked Kristy.

Silence rang in the room. I could have heard a pin drop.

Kristy looked up and studied my face as though trying to work out if this was some kind of trap. I smiled to show my sincerity.

"Um, I forgot to transfer all the stuff from my old purse to this one," she said, blushing harder.

"I do that all the time. What do you need?" I asked.

"Lip gloss and a tampon," Kristy whispered.

I produced both. "It's clear gloss, that okay?"

Kristy smiled and nodded. "Perfect, thank you."

"No problem."

Jill cleared her throat and motioned for us to leave the bathroom. The moment the door closed behind us, she turned on me. "What was that?" she asked, hissing between her teeth.

"What?" I asked, playing dumb.

Jill stabbed a finger toward the bathroom door. "The goodie act."

I laughed. "I gave the girl a tampon. Yeah, we're besties."

"One time I had to borrow one from this guy's mom. It was so embarrassing," Sarah said.

An eruption of noise nearby took the attention off me. Jill looked to the hall where the math club were laughing about their latest victory at…some math thing. "There should be a law that says they can't exist that close to us. I mean, look at us and look at *them*. Beauty should repel geeks, not attract them," Jill said with an ugly sneer.

Jill's unnecessary comment about a couple of harmless kids prickled my skin, and I clenched my fist. "Do you have to do that?" I asked quietly, anger bubbling in my veins.

Her eyebrows slowly lifted. "What did you say?" Jill asked, incredulous.

"What does it matter, Jill?" I asked, throwing my hand out toward the group in question. "Stop being an asshole. They don't affect you and, trust me, you don't affect them."

Jill laughed, surprising everyone — no one more than me. At Rachel's look of horror, she said, "Don't worry, Lo's kidding."

I am?

Jill slid her eyes over to me, a tight smile on her face. "I can tell because Lo would never say that to me, especially how I don't affect people. I affect everyone."

I took a breath and swallowed the anger welling in my throat. I'd wanted to be a better person than I had been... But I also didn't want to get on Jill's hit list. *Just get through this year... Just get through this year...* "Whatever you say, Jill," I agreed with a smile as fake as Jill's.

"Did you guys hear Ms. Walsh is pregnant?" Sarah asked, her face alive with excitement. "I told you guys she was screwing Coach Parks."

That night, Jill didn't pick me up for our nightly drop-in at the Grill.

Chapter Seven

After work, and after I'd got the smell of animal off me, I made my own way to the Grill. I refused to hide away, too scared to defy the omnipotent Jill Meyers.

"Hi," I said, sitting beside Sarah and snagging one of her fries. "What are we talking about?"

She slid the basket closer to me. "Jill's party on Saturday night," Sarah said.

"Awesome." I grinned. "No one throws a bash like Jill Myers. Who made the cut?"

"Everyone who deserves it," Jill said, smiling.

Was that her way of saying I didn't? Sarah saved me from answering. "Who's the guy, Lo?"

"What guy?"

She giggled and pointed in the direction of the pool table. "The one who hasn't taken his eyes off you since you came in."

I followed her finger, searching for who she meant. I locked eyes with Cam, and my blood went cold. He smiled and a shiver crept up my spine.

"So? Who is he?" Sarah probed.

My face burned and I dropped my gaze to the cooling fries. I prayed with all my might that he would stay away. "Uh, just a guy I met," I said quietly.

"Well, he's coming over."

Bile rose in my throat. *Oh, God...*

"That guy is hot, Lo." Jill said, showing the first real emotion since I arrived. Ah, how quickly she forgives when a cute guy is in the mix.

I twisted my fingers and in my periphery I saw Cam

saunter closer to the table, as if he knew I was trapped and took delight in drawing out my discomfort.

Nothing happened, Lori. Nothing actually happened, I repeated in my head, trying in vain to reassure myself. But then a traitorous voice whispered, *Only because Archer made sure it couldn't.*

Cam crouched in front of me, putting himself at eye level. "Hey, Lo. Long time," he said in a sexy, husky voice. Once it would have thrilled me. Now it terrified me.

My heartbeat pounded in my ears.

Jill rested her elbow on the table and flipped her hair over her shoulder. "Hi, I'm Jill," she purred.

Cam glanced at her before settling his eyes back on me. "Hey."

Sarah nudged me in the back, mistaking my flushed cheeks for his hotness, and not the real reason that the last time I'd seen Cam he was a heartbeat away from something horrifying.

"We should get together. Soon," Cam said, smiling. He reached for my hand, but I snatched it away and hid it beneath the table.

Jill, ever helpful when faced with a hot guy, offered, "I'm having a party on Saturday. Lo will be there."

"Will you, Lo?" Cam asked.

"Of course she will." Jill reached into her purse for a pen. She scribbled her address on a napkin. "Here, you should show. It's going to be epic."

Cam took the napkin from Jill and winked at me. "Be seeing you."

"You're welcome," Jill said, grinning when Cam went back to his pool game.

"You've gone really pale, are you okay?" Sarah asked, placing her hand on my shoulder.

I jumped about a mile in the air from the contact. I shook my head. "No, I feel kind of weird."

"Hotness on that scale will do that to you," Jill said.

Sarah ignored Jill's comment. Her eyebrows puckered

together in concern. "Do you want me to take you home?" she asked.

"Yes, please."

Sarah and I said little on the drive to my house. She hummed along to the radio, filling the silence with something better than idle chitchat. When she slowed to a stop outside my house, Sarah twisted in her seat to face me. "You know you can talk to me, right?" she said.

I nodded.

"No, Lo," she said quietly. "I mean you can *really* talk to me. Get some sleep, I'll see you tomorrow. I hope you feel better."

I smiled thinly and got out of her car, her words echoing in my head. Kit was in an affectionate mood that evening, staying curled against my side as I tried, and failed, to watch TV then sleeping on my pillow when I eventually went to bed. It's amazing that something that can't even speak can comfort you better than a human ever could.

* * * *

A few days after the reappearance of Cam, Kimmie made good on her threat. I crossed the parking lot to head home to change for work, when she slung an arm around my shoulders.

"Hi, Lo," Kimmie said, grinning. "I figured you could use a friend. Seems yours are forgetting about you. Again." She shoved my back against a tree, out of sight of the kids making their way to various cars in the lot. This could not end well.

"What do you want, Kimmie?" I asked, sounding bored though my heart pounded.

The fake grin slid from her face as her eyes turned cold. "I told you there would be consequences if you messed with me. You should have stayed clear of me, you pathetic slut."

"I'm the slut? Take a look in the mirror, Kimmie, I'm nothing like you."

Before I could blink, Kimmie shot her hand out and slapped me hard across the face. For a second I was so stunned her action didn't even register. Then the stinging came, then the red-hot throbbing. Girl could pack some power into her hands.

She smiled without a hint of warmth. "Remember what I said. Keep out of my way." Kimmie walked away before turning back to wave. "And, of course, if I say jump you say..."

I wouldn't say it. She could hit me again but I wouldn't say it.

And she did. When I didn't answer, Kimmie came straight back and hit me again. Same place, same pain.

"Take it easy, Lo," Kimmie said in a friendly voice as though she hadn't just smacked me. Twice.

When she was gone I reached into my bag for the soda I'd picked up from the vending machine for the walk home. The ice-cold tin provided blissful relief to my stinging cheek. So much so that I didn't think anything of walking out from behind the tree with a soda can pressed to my face.

And as luck would have it, when I would have happily seen no one and curled into a ball and hidden from the world, why did it have to be the one person who seemed to actively hate me, who saw me after Kimmie used me as her punching bag?

His eyes met mine before flickering to the soda can. Archer turned and looked at Kimmie, who stood laughing with a group of her friends—about me, no doubt—before looking back at me again.

I opened my mouth to speak, but nothing came out. What would I even have said? Weirdly, I wanted to apologize. But why would I apologize for getting smacked in the face? And why apologize to him?

He shifted his stance as though he meant to walk toward me.

"Lo!"

I turned at the sound of my name, seeing Sarah waving

and walking toward me. When I looked back at Archer, he was striding away from the scene.

"Hi," I said as Sarah reached me.

She laughed. "What are you doing with that soda?"

"What?" Crap! The can! "Oh, it's so hot out this afternoon, you know?"

Sarah nodded. "Tell me about it. I can't wait to get into my car with the AC on."

"Must be nice."

"You want a ride?"

I grinned. "Yeah, that would be—"

"Nice welt, Lo," Jill said as she sidled up beside us.

I dropped my eyes, ashamed as though I'd done the beating, not the one being beat on. This place...with these girls... It was suddenly the last place in the whole world I wanted to be. I looked back at Sarah. "Thanks, but I'd rather walk."

Before I could walk away and die of shame, Sarah threw her arms around me. "Don't let the bastards get you down," she whispered.

I nodded and turned away before she could see the emotion on my face. With my eyes stinging, I wrapped my arms around my middle to try to keep from breaking.

* * * *

If I hadn't had that run-in with Kimmie after school yesterday, I would have sought out the girls in the quad in the morning. I would have sat with them and forced conversation. I would have taken my usual seat in English. But, because of Kimmie, I didn't do any of those things.

I loitered off school grounds until the bell rang, so I could pretend I was running late and would have a plausible, if not flaky, reason for not seeking out the girls.

Kimmie beat me to English. She sat on top of a desk in the front row, a smile creeping onto her lips when I walked into the room.

Today I didn't have any fight in me.

I sat in the back row.

Archer ducked into the room a few minutes later. His stride faltered when he spotted me sitting in the desk next to his. He dropped into the seat beside mine and pulled his stuff out of his messenger bag, actively not looking in my direction. I didn't blame him. He must have the worst opinion of me, thanks to the drama with Cam and Kimmie.

Bad opinions or not, I still owed him a thank you.

"Hey," I whispered, hoping I wouldn't attract attention from anyone else. The last thing I needed was a rumor to break out that Lori Black was into the loner kid. "Hey, can I talk to you?"

Archer sighed and reached into his jeans pocket. I heard a dull, thudding noise, and I noticed the thin white cable peeking out from the collar of his gray T-shirt, running up to the ear bud in his ear. He actually wanted to drown out my voice.

Talk about rude. I only wanted to thank the kid for helping me out. Jeez.

Archer got my blood boiling and I refused to take his rudeness as an answer. When he rushed out of class, I leaped after him and trailed him down the hall, only catching up with him when he stopped at his locker.

"Okay, I'm getting the whole antisocial vibe, all right? I just—"

"Stop it," he hissed through his teeth. "Just leave me alone."

"No. I need to thank you for..." The glare he flashed took my breath away. The fury in those eyes was unmistakable. The stubborn side of my nature reared up and I refused to be silenced any longer. He might not want to hear it, but I had to say it. "Look—"

He slammed his locker shut. "No, you look." His raised voice rang out along the crowded hallway, earning us looks from passersby. "What the hell is your problem? You haven't figured out yet that I don't want to talk to you? Fine,

I get it—you're crushing on me. Deal with it. Stop following me around like the delusional psycho stalker you are. It's pathetic."

His words sliced through me, making my eyes sting with tears. It didn't help that a whole lot of the student body witnessed his outburst. Like I needed this embarrassment. Seriously. I backed away from him, refusing to flee. Or at least give him the satisfaction of seeing.

As I approached Jill's lunch table, their faces told me they had already heard about Archer's outburst. "So you said Archer was a loner, you guys forgot to mention the guy is a total asshole."

Jill and Rachel exchanged a glance.

"Why'd he blow up at you?" Sarah asked, reaching out to squeeze my hand.

I shrugged. "Hell if I know. I tried to thank him, he helped me out a few weeks ago. He's unstable, seriously."

"You need something to take your mind off him," Sarah said wisely.

"Definitely." I sighed and looked at Jill. She looked right back. Oh yeah, she would make me work for it. Though I had—thanks to Cam, at least—got myself invited to the party, Jill would rescind the invite in a heartbeat. "This weekend would be perfect to blow off some steam. What do you say, Jill? Want to show the school how we girls used to party?"

She smiled, happy with my begging. "See you Saturday."

Chapter Eight

I used to get ready with Rachel and Sarah at Jill's and help her set up. But this time I flew solo. Rachel and Sarah would already be there, having been there all day no doubt. I chickened out and came an hour and a half later than Jill told me to, hoping people would be drunk enough not to make a big deal out of my entrance.

Jill's place was enormous — a sprawling estate set on the outskirts of town with a long, curving driveway cutting a path through a dense woodland. Everyone loved her parties, which she threw often thanks to her folks always being out of town.

I wrapped my arms around myself, unable to help peering into the wooded darkness either side of me, imagining hands grabbing me. With a shiver, I picked up my speed.

The warmth from all the bodies hit me when I opened the door. Music boomed so loud I couldn't hear it so much as it pounded through my body. A few couples were intertwined on the staircase, lost in each other's mouths. People danced everywhere, in the hallway, in the den, in the TV room where the flat screen on the wall blared music videos. Someone thrust a red Solo cup into my hand. Stale beer.

Not my favorite.

A hand touched my shoulder. Adrenaline coursed through me as I spun around, expecting to come face to face with Kimmie, or, worse, Cam.

Nope. A boy in the shape of the ex-boyfriend.

"Hey," Drew said, smiling. "I didn't expect to see you here."

"Why?" I asked, realizing too late I had frowned instead of smiled.

Drew's confident smile fell. Drew and I had been hot and heavy before I left, together for five months, reaching third base and well on our way to a home run. I wondered if he could remember trying to score with me after Derek's funeral, claiming it 'would make me feel better'.

Ass.

He didn't score with me — didn't have a chance after that.

"Things seem weird with the girls since you got back," Drew said, shifting from foot to foot.

I shrugged. I bet he regretted talking to me. "It's been a long time. These things take time."

Drew nodded and folded his arms across his broad chest. "You didn't keep in touch with anyone when you left. They're probably still sore about it."

Didn't keep in touch with anyone... Christ! My brother died, my priority had been trying to figure out a way to live without him, not make sure I remembered to call Jill once a week.

"But whatever!" Drew exclaimed, smiling broadly. "You're back now, that's all that matters. How about a drink? Celebrate your homecoming?"

My homecoming? I had been back at school for two months. I bit my lip. I really should find Jill. But a drink first sounded...better than finding Jill without having had a drink. And if Cam made an appearance, I'd feel a hell of a lot better if Drew was around when he did. "Sure. What the hell."

Drew grinned and clasped my hand, leading me into the kitchen. A few guys from the football team guarded the keg, running a 'you're not hot enough to get a drink' carding system. One guy, Sam, slapped Drew on the back and gave him two beers.

"Aw, happy couple back together?" Kimmie asked as she stepped out of the shadows, her eyes trained on my face.

"I'm just getting Lo a drink," Drew said, discreetly putting some space between us.

"I'll bet," Kimmie purred, taking Drew's beer and disappearing as fast as she had appeared in the first place.

Okay. That wasn't so bad. She'd seen me. She hadn't tried to do anything… Like smack me in the face again.

My beer disappeared in record time.

"Another?" Drew asked.

"Drink? God, yes. Beer? No way," I said, laughing.

Drew's eyes crinkled when he smiled. "I'll find us something better."

Drew moved away from the keg and the kegger-heads guarding it. He pushed us through the crowd to get to the countertop beside the fridge. I fanned my face with my hand, blowing my bangs out of my eyes.

"Hot?" Drew asked.

I nodded.

Drew leaned over me and opened the window. He smiled and placed his hands on my hips, hoisting me up onto the counter as though I weighed no more than a bag of chips. He set out two glasses and poured vodka into each.

I laughed. "I am so not drinking straight vodka. Again."

Drew rolled his eyes. "And have you barf in my car again? No way, Lo." He rummaged around in the fridge and pulled out a few cartons of fresh fruit juice. He added some ice for good measure, and handed me my drink.

"What do you call it?" I asked.

He tapped his chin. "Reunited."

I laughed and took a sip. I could barely taste the vodka through the juice. It tasted good. Alcohol that tasted good meant I'd drink too much and get off-my-ass drunk. Not on the cards for tonight.

Drew leaned on to the counter, tracing circles on my knee as he told me about his junior year. He didn't ask much about my year away, and instead told me all the gossip I'd missed, who'd hooked up with who, who'd dated who.

I noticed he left one person out.

"What about you?"

"What about me?" Drew asked, smiling.

"You've told me all about the love lives of pretty much everyone in our class except yours. Don't tell me I ruined you for other girls," I teased.

Drew grinned as I nudged him. He placed a hand over his heart. "But you did, Lo. I spent your year away in a pit of depression. In fact, I only recovered when I found out you'd rejoined our ranks."

I swatted him. He caught my hand and played with my fingers. "Shut up. Come on, tell me."

For a second he looked uncomfortable. "Why do you want to know?"

I shrugged. "Just curious. Why? Is it really embarrassing?"

"It might be," he murmured.

"Just tell me already."

"Okay." He sighed. "When you left… Jill and I kind of fooled around for a while."

I snatched my hand out of his. "You and Jill? As in Jill Myers? As in my best friend?"

He shrugged. "We were lonely and we missed you."

Yeah, right.

"We'd been hanging out with a crowd at the beach one afternoon and we went for a walk, started talking about you. Next thing I know, we're behind this big sand dune and—"

I chuckled. "I really don't need to hear the end of that sentence."

"It didn't mean anything," Drew said quietly, taking my hand again and making me meet his eyes. "Not like we meant something."

Before I could even begin to tell him just how wrong that statement was, a bundle of energy shoved Drew out of the way.

"Lo! You made it!" Sarah squealed. She tugged on my hand, pulling me off the counter so she could hug me. "Come dance!"

I went willingly with Sarah into the den, happy to leave

my ex and his poetic waxing self in the kitchen.

"So, I heard Drew and Jill had a thing when I left," I shouted over the music as Sarah and I danced.

She made a face. "Totally nasty, right? So in bad taste."

Sarah and I danced for a half hour before Jill and Rachel found us. Rachel pulled Sarah away, telling her she'd seen the guy Sarah had met over the summer.

"So," Jill said once we were alone. "You came."

"Why wouldn't I?"

Jill shrugged. "I didn't think you'd have the balls to come to a party alone."

I sighed, suddenly exhausted with this dance Jill and I seemed to do around each other. "Why are you being like this?"

"Like what? You're the one being unreasonable. You left, Lo, and you thought, what? You'd come back and everyone would have kept their lives on hold for you? You're rejoining us, not the other way around."

Realization slapped me in the face. "When did you stop being my friend, Jill?" I asked in a small voice.

"When did I stop being yours?" she asked back, folding her arms across her chest. "You took off and didn't even tell anyone. You missed my Sweet Sixteen."

I snorted. Jill's birthday was three days after Derek's funeral. What a shocker I had missed it. "My brother died! How the hell are you making this out to be about you?"

Jill rolled her eyes. "He died a year ago! Let it go."

Oh, she did not just say that to me.

"You can't expect to come back after a year and expect nothing to have changed. It has. You need to deal."

A bitter laugh escaped my throat. "Yeah, I'm learning that, Jill. So, just out of interest, how long did you wait to make a play for my boyfriend?"

She smiled. "You left him behind too, Lo. We did what we had to."

"You wanted to get back at me."

"What does it matter now?"

"It matters because you're spouting all this shit about me letting you down as a friend, when you don't have the first clue how to be one! Why are you making me jump through all these hoops when all I want is my life back?" I cried, throwing my hands out to the sides.

Jill folded her arms beneath her chest and flashed me a cold, hard glare. "Because you haven't proved to me yet if you even deserve to have it back. All you've shown is attitude, acting like you're better than the rest of us and looking down your nose at us."

I laughed ruefully. That was it—I was done. I was so done. Getting through the rest of my senior year with no friends had to be better than trying to be someone I wasn't anymore just to impress a girl who wouldn't know how to be a real friend if there was an app for it. "I act like that because I can't believe you're still this shallow! You haven't changed one little bit! So you know what? I'm glad that you think I've changed, because I have. I don't treat people like crap anymore, and I'm not a vapid narcissist."

"You do realize I can make your life whatever I want it to be, don't you? I did you a favor when you came back. I gave you the chance to prove you were still worth having around. You can take all the AP classes you want, it won't make you any less stupid. You should have played the game right."

I took a step back. "What is the matter with you? Do you even hear yourself? I mean, do you hate me or something?"

Jill smiled. "Lo, to hate you I would have to care."

Her words punched into me. I looked around, fully expecting to see a crowd of onlookers. But no one paid us any attention. There wasn't a single person who cared enough to stand by me... To take my side. Jill gave me a smug smile and turned to rejoin her party.

I headed to the kitchen, hoping Drew would still be there and hopefully wouldn't be too drunk yet and I could talk him into giving me a ride home.

He was in the kitchen still all right, but I hoped he was

completely wasted given the person his mouth was attached to.

Someone way worse than when he hooked up with Jill.

He was making out with Kimmie.

She opened her eyes and caught me staring.

I rushed away from them, crashing into bodies around me.

"Hey!" a drunk guy shouted. He grabbed my arm and swayed on his feet. "Lo! What the fuck are you doing here?"

"Nothing. I was just leaving." I couldn't place the guy's face. But apparently he knew mine.

"Wait." He grinned. "You bring any with you?"

"What?"

"Your brother's stash." He laughed.

"Asshole," I mumbled, tugging my arm free.

It had been a mistake to come here. A huge mistake.

Chapter Nine

I walked down the driveway as fast as I could. Only when I had made it onto the main road did I realize that I'd left my jacket behind at the party. Crap. It wasn't worth going back for. No chance in hell was I going back there, not for a jacket. I'd rather freeze, especially when running into Cam was a distinct possibility. I wore a pair of faded skinny jeans and a black low-cut sleeveless top and ballet flats. Within minutes goosebumps dotted my arms.

The five miles home would be five long miles indeed. It seemed the longer I walked the slower I seemed to go. The cold seeped into my bones, making my legs stiff and awkward. I had walked about a mile when a car passed me, the first I'd seen since leaving the party. It slowed down, drifting for a few yards before stopping completely, as if the driver couldn't decide whether or not to stop.

I froze. I'd seen The Hitcher more times than I could count. And while yes, technically, the hitchhiker in this equation was me, but out of the two of us — assuming the driver was alone — I wasn't a psychotic serial killer.

The same couldn't be said for whoever drove that car.

I didn't have a whole lot of options. The road was deserted and there wasn't a house for at least another mile. I could set off running across a field, but the driver could easily get out and catch me.

I looked behind me to check if I could still see Jill's place. Nope. I turned back to the car that I didn't recognize. I doubted they had come from the party. It was too beat-up to forget. I didn't know anyone at the party who drove a car like that.

What if it's Cam?

Without warning, the car jumped into life. The tires screeched as the driver reversed the car back to where I stood.

I yelped and stumbled out of the way, landing in a heap on the side of the road.

The driver threw the passenger door open with a loud creak, and they leaned across the front seat to glare at me. "Are you getting in or not? I'm not waiting around all night."

My breath caught in my throat. "Uh..."

"Well?"

"Are you talking to me?" I asked, just for clarification.

He swore under his breath. "Do you see anyone else wandering along the side of a road at one in the morning?"

Wow—had I spent that long at Jill's? I glanced at my watch. Yup. Guess I had. I looked back at the driver and got up, brushing off the seat of my pants. With a deep breath, I got into Archer's car.

* * * *

"Where do you want to go?" he asked when I shut the car door.

"Anywhere but here," I whispered.

Archer didn't question my request of destination—or lack thereof—and started driving again, one hand on the steering wheel and the other elbow on the lip of the window with his hand supporting his head. Seemed he drove as moodily as he acted the rest of the time.

The urge to curl up into a ball still hadn't left me. I wrapped my arms around my middle and rested my head against the cool glass of the window. Of all the stupid-ass things I had done in my life, why the hell had I gone to that party? I'd only proved I was different and couldn't fit in where I'd once fit perfectly. My life before I'd left hadn't been just shallow, it had been bullshit. If Jill and I had been really true great friends, she would never have been able to fool around with Drew.

What a skank.

No, I had to be fair. They were both assholes.

"Asshole," I mumbled.

Archer turned his head to me with a single lifted eyebrow. I cringed. "Not you. Sorry."

He looked back at the road.

"You ever wonder why people are such jerks?"

"You're asking the wrong person," he eventually answered, his voice quiet and restrained.

The inside of Archer's car smelled like fast food and cigarettes. I'd never seen Archer smoke, and I couldn't smell it on him in class, so I guessed it was a pre-owned car whose previous owner smoked like a chimney.

With Archer back to glaring at the road, I drew my knees up to my chest. The seat covering was already wrecked and held together with duct tape, and I figured he wouldn't care about my ballet flats on it. I rested my chin on my knees, hugging my legs so tight my arms got real sore real fast. The lights in the dash lit Archer's face, the soft artificial blue glow causing hollows under his eye, accentuating his cheekbones and lips.

Butterflies rolled in my stomach as I observed him, probably not even half as subtly as I thought I was being. Drew had used his best lines, softest eyes and gentlest touch with me tonight and I'd felt nothing. Now just looking at Archer turned my insides into a puddle of girlish mush.

Archer, who aside from giving me a ride tonight had been nothing but a jerk to me. What did that say about me?

With a sigh I dropped the hold on my legs and put my feet back on the floor. I leaned my head back against the window before deciding the chill from the glass wouldn't help to warm me up.

"Christ, do you ever sit still?" Archer mumbled.

"Sorry, I tend to fidget when my body resembles a Popsicle."

Archer reached for the heater and cranked it up, the sound of air whooshing into the car. He leaned across me to adjust the heating vent so it blew in my direction. I leaned into the vent, smiling as the warm air tickled my face and defrosted my nose.

"Stupid of you not to have a jacket."

I pulled a face at him when he wasn't looking. "I left it at the party. So I'm not stupid enough not to bring one. Just stupid enough to leave it behind." Wow. Not my greatest comeback.

"Why didn't you go back and get it?"

"You found me wandering down a stretch of road, alone, at one in the morning. Did it seem like I would want to go back there?"

"Why'd you go in the first place?"

I chuckled sadly. "Hell if I know." I settled back against my seat, able to sit still finally. The air around me warmed, making me relax, but not as much as the smell. The previous owner must have had a dog, as a definite wet dog smell lingered in the fabric of the seats. It didn't gross me out as it would some people. I worked with animals. The smell was comforting, the way some people enjoyed baking bread or vanilla. Guess I was weird. But to me, it smelled like home. It was so comforting that I didn't fight the wave of drowsiness that came over me. I let it lull and caress me until I sank into the peaceful oblivion.

* * * *

When I woke the car had stopped, but the engine idled, still allowing heat to blast through the heating vent. Archer was slouched in his seat, knees up against the steering wheel. He had the overhead light on, a paperback resting against his legs. As I stretched, his body stiffened at my movements, as though he had forgotten I was even there.

"How long was I out?" I asked, clearing my throat when I sounded like an eighty year old with a three-pack-a-day habit.

"Few hours," Archer mumbled.

Few hours? "Why didn't you wake me?"

He shrugged. "Looked like you needed it. I've been on the receiving end of angry girls when they get woken up. Didn't feel like getting smacked in the face."

My stomach seemed to flutter with happiness and curdle all in a matter of seconds. First I was inexplicably happy when he said I looked like I needed the sleep, meaning he was looking out for me. Then the mention of all the other girls he'd woken up beside and... Not such a nice feeling. "Where are we?" I asked, instead of the question I was dying to ask— How many girls are we talking here?

I glanced at the clock on the dash, which read almost five a.m. The sun would soon break the horizon.

"Few miles from school."

"Oh." I sat up and rubbed my eyes, trying hard not to imagine what my hair might be doing. As I squinted out of the window, I didn't recognize where we were. All I could see was grass. And trees. Lots of them. There was a lot of forest and woodland areas around our town. A huge wood surrounded my back yard in fact. We could be anywhere.

Archer shoved his book in the compartment in his door and put the car in gear. He drove for a few minutes, until gradually a few streets became familiar and we passed my work.

A swirl of emotion settled in my stomach. A pang of regret laced with wanting—a hard dose of wanting time to slow. Whatever had happened with Archer tonight, whatever made him break the icy exterior, the wall surrounding him would be back up strong the second I was out of the car. And I'd wasted all those hours sleeping!

"I'm not a stalker," Archer said, breaking me out of my reverie.

Um, okay.

"Or psychic." Archer looked at me pointedly.

"Uh..."

"I don't know where you live."

"Oh!" I wanted to smack myself in the head. God, how stupid was I? Another glance out of the window and I realized we were only one street over from mine. "Um, anywhere around here is fine."

"I can take you to your house, it's no big deal."

"Thanks, but it's right around the corner, here's fine. You've done enough tonight."

"Worried about me knowing where you live?" He hid the emotion in his voice, but I heard the disappointment nonetheless.

I frowned, annoyed at myself for having insulted him. "No. I just don't want to be any trouble."

Archer didn't argue any further, just pulled over and stopped the car, leaving the engine running.

With my hand on the door handle, I twisted back to face him. Maybe he would be more likely to give me an answer in a confined space, rather than me trying to talk to him in English class, which, let's face it, hadn't worked out so well in the past. "Why did you stop?"

He raised an eyebrow. "You wanted out here."

"Earlier when you saw me walking," I said, not letting myself be deflected. I wondered how long it had been since he'd answered a direct question about himself. "You could have kept driving. Not many people would stop to pick up a girl walking alone at one in the morning."

"I wouldn't be a very nice person if I didn't, would I?"

"Would you have stopped for someone else?"

"Like who?"

I said the first name that popped into my head. "Kimmie."

His lips twitched. "You wouldn't want her out walking at night, would you? She could fall prey to a big bad wolf."

I snorted. "I'd be more worried for the wolf."

Archer turned away from me to stare out of the front windshield. "I wouldn't have stopped for Kimmie."

"Why did you stop for me?"

Silence.

"Whatever the reason, I'm glad you did. Thank you." I got out of the car, deciding to quit while I was ahead. The second I closed the door behind me Archer took off, tires screeching on the asphalt as he tore away from me.

I tried not to take his sharp exit personally. After all, I had just been in Archer's car. I wondered how many other girls at school could say as much? Actually, after that waking the girls up comment, I didn't want to know.

Chapter Ten

I started the next week at school with my head held high. I'd walked away from Jill on Saturday night, seen the girl for who she really was, and I couldn't *un*-see it. We were done. I didn't search the girls out on Monday morning to suck up and beg to sit with them. I was free from the pressure of trying to fit in. No one was in any great rush to befriend me after I had ditched Jill and the others — not that I blamed them. Thanks to Jill, over the years I had systematically alienated almost everyone from our class who didn't fit her idea of a good type of friend. In other words, no poor people, no ugly people, no dorky people, no person who could not be deemed popular by Ms. Myers.

I told myself it was a good thing I had so few distractions this year. I had a lot to prove academically, and I would not fail.

It wasn't even an option.

To get where I needed to be I had to work hard — harder than ever. So every lunch hour I'd sit outside, sometimes in the quad, other times under a huge tree near the playing fields and study, or read, or…do whatever I had to do to take my mind off the fact that I had no one to talk to.

Fourth period English wasn't scary anymore. Kimmie was apparently satisfied that I'd 'learned my lesson', and pretty much left me alone. Archer sat next to me every day and every day we ignored each other. I didn't take it personally. By this point I realized he ignored everyone. After the night of the party I didn't resent him for his silence. He'd proved he wasn't an asshole. But that didn't mean he wanted to be my friend.

"Listen up, people," Mr. Poole said as he came into the room. "We're working on Shakespeare's sonnets this unit. I want you to partner up and read and analyze Sonnet 116. Find an argument that supports what you come up with — a published one if possible, guys."

I groaned inwardly. Partners in class used to be fun, an excuse to slack off. Now I dreaded it. Unpopularity sucked.

The room erupted in frenzied chatter as people called across the room to their friends. Mr. Poole laughed. "Did you guys really think I'd let you pick your own partners? Yeah, right. We'll go alphabetically. Mr. Archer, you're with Miss Black..."

The rest of the partner assignments were lost on my ears. My face was on fire. He couldn't have paired me with a worse person. Actually, I should think myself lucky that Kimmie and I weren't side by side in the alphabet. I glanced at Archer. Maybe it wouldn't be so bad.

"You're all excused to the library this lesson — but I'll be around, making sure you're working, so don't get any ideas."

Everyone got to their feet, the appeal of the library now gone thanks to Mr. Poole's threat. I found an empty table in a quiet section of the library, Archer dropping down opposite me a few minutes later. I pushed a copy of the sonnet Mr. Poole handed out toward him and started reading my copy. This was why I hated English. I'm awful and have no creativity, making it damn near impossible for me to analyze anything.

"Um, so," I said once fifteen minutes had passed and neither of us had spoken. "It's pretty clear that he's talking about love."

Archer bent over the paper, his fingers laced behind his head. It didn't fill me with confidence that at least one of us would know what the hell to write.

I sighed and dropped my head on the desk. "I suck at this. I've got nothing."

Archer cleared his throat. "It's not just about love — it's

about love in its truest form. Shakespeare is praising the lovers who come together of their own free will with no ulterior motives."

Slowly lifting my head, I stared at Archer long and hard before realizing my mouth was hanging open. I'd never heard him say so much at once. I wanted to hear more.

He huffed out an impatient breath and pointed to a few lines on the sheet in front of me. "See here? He's showing his adoration of love that's strong and will not 'alter when it alteration finds'.

"Um," I breathed. All conscious thought fell from my head.

"Are you getting any of this?" Archer asked, frowning.

I squeezed my eyes shut for a moment before reading the sonnet again. With Archer pointing out how he had interpreted a few lines, the meaning of another jumped out at me. "Like he's saying true love can survive anything? Because it's an 'ever fixed mark'?"

A small smile pulled at his lips. "Right."

I grinned. "I am so kicking Shakespeare butt."

Archer snorted. "Don't get ahead of yourself."

Ruin my buzz, why don't you?

Archer and I finished the assignment during that one class. We had a week to complete it. Either we really kicked ass, or he just didn't want to spend any more time with me than he absolutely had to.

That assignment opened my eyes. It proved that we can judge people and make assumptions about them all we want, but unless they show us a part of themselves, we haven't a hope in hell of actually knowing who they are. Archer had showed me that there was a heck of a lot he held back, that under his harsh and cold exterior was a literature lover who could interpret the great works of Shakespeare.

I think I'm becoming a poetry lover.

Chapter Eleven

That afternoon, I worked at the reception desk in the vet's, fulfilling the glamorous job of chasing the people who had neglected to pay their bills. An hour before closing, I was only at the Fs and my fingers had started cramping. The bell above the door chimed and a little boy around six struggled into the office, lugging a travel kennel with him, wincing as it banged off his shins.

I smiled as I stood. "Hey, can I help you with that?"

"No," he said, frowning. "I got it."

His mother appeared behind him and mouthed, 'Sorry.'

When the boy eventually reached the counter, he set the kennel down and grinned at me. "I got a kitten. Mom said if we brought her here we'd get some free stuff."

The mother flushed scarlet. She touched his shoulder. "Shane, I said she needed her kitten check-up and the vet might give you something for her."

Shane's mouth turned down at the corners as he peered up at me with round brown eyes. "Is she gonna get some stuff?"

I came out from behind the reception counter and crouched in front of him. "Hmm. Let me ask you a few questions. Is she a good kitten?"

All sign of worry dropped from his sweet face. He grinned. "Yeah! She's the best. She always wants to play with me. Sometimes she bites my fingers but it doesn't hurt. Much."

"Hmm." I tapped my chin. "What about you? Are you a good owner?"

He nodded so fast I thought his head would fall off. "You

bet! I feed her and brush her and bath her — she doesn't much like that — and throw her ball, but she prefers this little mouse Mom got her. And I let her sleep on my bed. Sometimes even under the covers."

"I'm not sure." I looked at his mother. "What do you say, Mom? Is Shane a good kitten owner?"

"The best," she said with a smile, placing her hand on her son's head.

I tapped my chin with my index finger as I narrowed my eyes at Shane. "Okay. I've almost decided. One last question and I'll tell you. What did you name her?"

"Spongebob!"

I swallowed a laugh. "Spongebob? That's my favorite kitten name in the whole world!"

"Really?" Shane asked, his eyes wide.

"Of course. Okay, I might have something Spongebob will like. But only if I get to hold her."

"Sure!" Shane said, unlocking the kennel.

"Wait," I said, pausing his eager hand with a laugh. "Let her get checked out first, then we'll have hugs, okay? It'll give me time to find stuff for her."

"Okay," Shane said, locking the kennel again.

Doug, thankfully, had time to squeeze in Shane and Spongebob. She got a clean bill of health and left with three kitten starter packs, two new mice, a ball and a bag of dry food. Shane was so excited he forgot his promise to let me have kitten cuddles. I felt cheated.

"You're good with kids. That boy loved you," Doug commented as we locked up that night.

"Yeah, I'm great with the guys — when they're his age. It's when they get to mine that I can't figure them out."

My boss gave me a lazy smile. "Wish I could say it gets easier, but I don't like lying to you."

"Gee thanks," I said, rolling my eyes.

Concern filled his eyes. "Trouble at school?"

"Not really." I glanced at him. "Hey, Doug, what do you think about poetry?"

All the other partners in English class needed the extra time to work on the assignment. But Archer and I had finished, so instead of sitting together like everyone else in the library, we retreated to our own space and thoughts and left the other in peace. For like a second I expected him to sit with me anyway, but of course he didn't. He sat by himself, book open in front of him. I couldn't help but wonder what he was reading. I daydreamed it was more poetry that he could explain to me in that low, silken voice of his.

I sank lower in my chair, almost burrowing my face in the biology textbook I was attempting to study, hoping if I got low enough I wouldn't be able to see him and the temptation to stare wouldn't be so bad. Nope. If I sank any lower, I'd look seriously strange.

So I gave in and stared.

"Hey, Lo."

I jumped about a mile out of my skin and dropped the textbook on my face. I sat up to see Joel in front of my table, an easy smile on his face.

"Sorry, did I scare you?" he asked, his eyes alight with mischief.

I rubbed my smarting nose. "Only in the literal sense."

Joel pointed to the chair beside me. "This seat taken?"

"Is that a trick question?" Joel was the first person in weeks at school even to acknowledge me.

He shoved his hands in his jeans pockets and gave me an easy smile. "Nope."

"Knock yourself out," I said, waving my hand toward the chair.

Joel eased his tall frame into the chair beside mine, angling it so he blocked Archer from view. It took all my self-control not to move my chair in response. "What are you doing in here?" he asked.

"English assignment, stupid paired thing."

He grinned. "Where's your partner then?"

I nodded in Archer's direction. "We already finished."

Joel twisted around, his face darkening when he spotted Archer. "I don't like that kid. I hope he wasn't rude to you."

"Of course he wasn't. Just because he doesn't kiss ass doesn't mean he's a jerk." I frowned. No one at this stupid school had any idea who Archer really was. I had only been permitted a glance, but it had killed any preconceived notions I'd had.

Joel leaned back in his chair. "Right. Yeah, that was stupid, huh?"

I shrugged. "What are you doing in here?"

"Free period."

"Oh. If you see Mr. Poole, don't talk to me, okay? He's an ass."

Joel smiled. "Sure thing."

* * * *

My routine remained consistent. It only changed one afternoon at six-thirty as I filed some paperwork in the veterinary surgery reception, getting ready to close up for the night. The bell above the door chimed and in burst Archer came in carrying a gorgeous Akita dog. I jumped to my feet and buzzed for Doug, grateful that he didn't have anyone with him. He was in reception the next moment, ushering Archer and his dog into the examination room.

An agonizing twenty minutes later, Doug and Archer came back into reception.

"Like I said, it's just a precaution," Doug said. "I want to keep her overnight to make sure it's nothing more serious. If everything looks fine by the morning, you can collect her tomorrow afternoon." Doug nodded toward me. "Leave your details with Vix and we'll be in touch."

My cheeks warmed at Doug's embarrassing nickname. I handed over a pad and Archer silently jotted down his name, number and address before disappearing out of the door. I couldn't help but be a little surprised at his name as

I read what he'd written. Jack Archer. Jack... Such a normal name. It didn't suit his quiet and mysterious persona. Why did everyone call him by his surname?

"So what's up with his dog?" I asked Doug as we locked up the surgery.

"Most likely eaten something it shouldn't have. The kid said she'd thrown up and seemed out of it. I've given her something for it and that should set her straight. Like I told him, just want to keep her overnight to make sure."

I grinned. "So no full night's sleep for you again, huh?"

Doug laughed. "I think the last time I got a full night's sleep was in high school. Make the most of it." Doug lived in an apartment above the surgery so he could check in on all the animals whenever he needed to throughout the night. I didn't envy him for it.

* * * *

Fourth period the next day was killer. I itched to update Archer about his dog. He probably already knew — Doug would have called him first thing that morning. But I wanted to tell him how great a vet Doug was and how he would take great care of her. Usually in class Archer remained still. That day he fidgeted, tapping his pen and flipping back and forth through the book we were supposed to be studying.

I ached to place my hand on his and tell him not to worry, how Doug would never let anything happen to an animal that could be prevented. I kept my hands to myself.

After Archer...Jack...whatever, had left the night before, I'd gone into the examination room to help get the dog into one of our kennels. I'd stroked her soft coat before shutting the door. Most Akitas are gorgeous in my opinion, but this one was something else. She was almost all white except for the top of her head, down her back and halfway up her tail, which was the color of pale sand. I'd always been a sucker for animals.

Like every other day, Archer disappeared out of the door the very second the bell rang. I couldn't have tried to talk to him if I'd wanted to.

Every time the door chimed that afternoon at work, I snapped my head up to see who'd came in. Annoyingly, my face heated when he eventually did arrive, and I silently hated myself for being happy he'd finally turned up. I buzzed through to Doug's office to let him know he was here.

"Doug'll be through in a sec. I'll go get your dog," I said, stumbling to my feet. The dog was more than happy to be free of her kennel, lapping at my hand and darting bounding around my legs. But it was nothing compared to when she spotted her owner.

I lifted the hatch in reception to go out into the waiting area and she knocked past me to get to him. She caught me off balance and I almost fell on my ass — I would have, had Archer...Jack...whatever, not reached out and steadied me.

"You okay?" he asked, his eyes skimming over me.

Doug laughed. "You've got to be rougher than that to hurt our Vix."

Archer didn't answer, the reunion with his over-excited dog taking precedence. For the first time since I met him, a real honest-to-God-happy smile lit up his already handsome face. Guess something could crack that rocky exterior after all. He clipped on her leash and shook Doug's hand. "Thanks for everything, really." And, like always, disappeared out of the door before anyone could blink.

"Nice kid," Doug commented as the door closed behind him. "He go to your school?"

"Mmm," I answered.

Chapter Twelve

Something weird happened the next day at school. Instead of bolting like normal, Archer took his time getting his stuff together once English class ended. I sneaked a few glances at him, though nothing showed on his stoic face. We reached the door at the same time and he motioned for me to go first. Even weirder was that once out in the hallway, he fell into step beside me. A heavy frown creased his forehead as we walked in silence.

I chewed my bottom lip, a thousand questions on the tip of my tongue. But talking hadn't exactly gone down well for me in the past... Though, he must want something, at least? Why else would he be walking with me?

Oh, what the hell. "How's your dog?"

The corner of his lip pulled up into a smile and the frown smoothed out. "Good. Better."

The sight of his half-smile made my own lips curve upward. *Note to self – the dog is a safe topic.* "I'm glad."

I struggled with what to say next when he stopped at his locker. For a second I stopped too, unsure how to continue. Then I realized I probably looked like a creeper, and started to move away, convinced that whatever had prompted him to walk beside me in the first place had ended. Just as I turned to leave, Archer's voice made me pause.

Without looking at me, he said, "So what's up with you and the vet?"

"Excuse me?" I asked, my eyebrows shooting up.

Archer still didn't turn around. He continued transferring things from his bag to his locker, seemingly uninterested in the conversation he'd initiated. "He calls you Vix. I thought your name's Lori. Or Lo, whatever."

He had noticed that? *Oh God...that's embarrassing.*

"Are you going for some new name reinvention or something?" he asked, breaking into my reverie. "Or collecting names or personalities?"

"Oh, no." A blush warmed my cheeks. "It's a nickname I have there. It's kind of embarrassing."

"Your nickname is Vix?" he asked, still half hidden in his locker.

"Short for, uh, Vixen," I mumbled.

"Vixen?" he repeated, a question in the word.

I swallowed. "Yeah. You know, a female fox?"

"Does the vet have a crush?"

"What? No," I said with an incredulous laugh.

"Then why call you a fox?"

Gee thanks. I didn't entirely want to be called a fox, but I wanted to be not called one even less. "Because I have one."

Archer paused, not moving for a few moments. "You have a fox? Like a pet?"

I smiled. "Kind of. You can't really call him a pet, he's still a wild animal. But he's tame. Most of the time at least." I rubbed the freshest scratch on my arm—this time safely hidden under a long-sleeved shirt.

"And how does one go about getting a tame fox?"

Even though he was still totally engrossed with whatever was in his locker—what the hell was he doing in there, anyway?—I dropped my gaze to the floor. As much as I adored Kit, a pang of guilt still appeared at the memory of our first encounter. "It's a long story. I was helping with his rehabilitation and he imprinted on me. Separation is impossible after that. So now he lives with me."

"Hence the name Vixen."

"Yeah," I mumbled. "You must think it's really stupid."

Archer closed his locker and leaned against it, folding his arms across his broad chest. "Actually... It's pretty cool. Not the nickname, that's lame, but what you did for the animal. Taking it in like that. Looking after something that wasn't your problem."

I glanced at my shoes, my ballet flats that had once again become my staple now I no longer had to impress anyone with my wardrobe choices. "It was the right thing to do."

He considered this for a moment. Archer glanced at me and seemed to debate whether to speak again or not. When he did, his voice lowered to just above a gravelly whisper, as though he was about to confess a terrible weakness. "I was worried about Harlo when I brought her to you guys. I didn't sleep at all that night."

I shrugged, trying to lighten the situation for him. "Understandable. Pets are like family. Sometimes preferable to humans."

He smiled. "Yeah, tell me about it." Archer looked down the hallway—searching for his exit?—before he dropped his eyes to his scuffed sneakers. What a pair of awkward misfits we made. "So who are you—Lori or Lo?"

I laughed. It sounded false and the bitterness in the sound surprised me. "There's a loaded question if ever I heard one." I shrugged and, for the life of me, I couldn't seem to lie. Not even to try to brush off what had unintentionally become a serious question. "I don't know anymore."

Archer studied my face, his rich brown eyes sweeping over every inch and reading me far more intently than anyone else ever had. "Who do you feel like?"

"I don't feel like anyone," I admitted quietly.

There was a bloated pause before Archer spoke again. His eyebrows drew together and I had the impression that he was the kind of guy who chose his words carefully, that he used them so infrequently that he made sure the ones he did use meant something. "Be the person you want to be, then."

* * * *

Another three days passed before we spoke again, as though our semi-bonding whatever hadn't even happened.

The next day in class, things went back to normal — no one, not even Archer, acknowledged my presence. Even though he remained silent, I pretty much had to bite down on my tongue to keep from trying to talk to him.

Most people would write him off and forget about even trying. But there was something about him…something I wanted to get closer to. Maybe because he seemed lonelier than I was, and I felt an almost kinship with him. But more than likely it was because he was mysterious and I couldn't stand not knowing stuff. Sometimes if I was really into a book I'd skip to the back page because I'd need to find out how it was going to end. And if Archer was a book, he would be a big fat mystery stuffed full of bad guys and intricate plot details and would need a decoder to figure out.

It was at work when we did speak again. I was cleaning up in the back and making sure all the animals had enough food and water for the night when I heard the tinkling of the bell above the door.

"Just a sec," I called, wiping my hands on the wrecked jeans I only ever wore to work. My heart sped up double time when I headed back into the reception and saw Archer leaning against the counter.

He turned at the sound of my approach and offered me a small smile.

"Hi," I said, hoping he might miss my blazing cheeks. "What are you doing here?"

Archer held up a sheet of paper and I caught the surgery logo on the upper right hand corner. "Came to settle my debts."

"Oh." Duh! Why the hell else would he be here? "You're lucky you found me. I mean, you're lucky I'm here." *Breathe, Lori. Seriously, just breathe.* "I mean, I was just about to close up. You left it kind of late. In the day, I mean." Note to self, don't say 'I mean' for at least six months due to extreme overuse.

"So?" he said, his voice short and pissed off. Archer blew

out a breath, and his face softened like he regretted being so blunt with me. "I had things to do."

I took the bill and cash from him and rang it up on the register and cleared his account on the computer. When I glanced at the name on the bill, I couldn't help but ask, "Why does everyone call you Archer? What's wrong with Jack?"

"What's wrong with Lori, Vix? You should understand nicknames better than anyone." Archer's lips twitched as if he was trying to hold back a smile.

I rolled my eyes. "Whatever. It's not the same thing and you know it. You don't talk to anyone at school, so why would they make a nickname for you?"

He tapped the counter with his wallet. "Did you pick yours? Sometimes people decide for you what your name is."

"Which do you prefer?"

Archer shrugged. "I don't really care. Like you pointed out, I don't talk to anyone anyway."

"You talk to me."

Archer lifted his eyes and pinned me with his gaze. There was so much in that look that I couldn't interpret. I wanted to question him—get answers to all the thoughts that burned in my mind. Where did he come from? Why was he so quiet? Why, out of everyone, did he talk to me?

"So where is everyone?" he asked eventually, nodding to the empty surgery.

I welcomed the change in conversation. I doubted he'd talk to me for much longer if I gave him the third degree. "Doug is out seeing a horse that took a bad fall during a race today. Mandy, the junior vet, left a few minutes ago, so I'm all alone for closing tonight."

"You don't mind closing by yourself?"

"Not really," I said with a shrug. "I'm here till closing most nights anyway, being alone doesn't really make a difference to me—I've seen all the jobs and done them all often enough to know what to do. Besides, Doug lives in the apartment upstairs and he'll check in here when he gets back, so at least if anything's been done wrong it won't stay wrong till morning."

Archer straightened his tall frame, his stance hesitant. "So you're finished now? You're going home?"

"As soon as we're done here," I said. Oh, God, was that rude? Did it sound like I wanted to kick him out? I would gladly stay an extra three hours if it meant Archer would stay.

"Any plans?"

"You mean besides a shower?" The words had left my mouth before I could stop myself. I'd felt disgusting for the last two hours after a Saint Bernard, a wet Saint Bernard might I add, slobbered all over me when I'd helped Doug do his examination. Smelling like animal is part of the package when you work in a veterinary surgery, but I was extra stinky today.

His lips twitched again. "I meant for getting home. I have my car if you want a ride."

I blinked. Had that just happened? "Um…okay. Thanks. It'll just take me a minute to close."

Archer nodded. He didn't hover as I locked up and checked everything one last time. Familiar tugs of nerves pulled low in my stomach as I followed him to his beat-up car. The passenger door creaked as I opened it, and like last time the smell of food and cigarette smoke hit me as I got in. Only tonight I nearly had a heart attack when something lunged from the back seat and licked my face.

"Hi," I said laughing, wiping my cheek when I realized it was only Harlo. I reached around to scratch her head.

Archer started the car wordlessly. Harlo kept trying to scramble onto my lap but backed off when her master barked an order at her. "Sorry," he mumbled.

"Don't worry about it. I'm stinky anyway." I'd never been more aware of how badly I must smell than I did that entire car ride. The small confined space wouldn't do anything to help my anxiety.

He didn't turn off the engine when he pulled up outside my house. Archer gave the house a thorough examination. "Big place," he noted.

"Yeah, I guess." The house never used to feel big. Now it felt endless...and empty. But I still loved the space it came with. We had around an acre and a half of land around the house, perfect for me and my unusual companion.

"You must get a lot of privacy from your parents and stuff."

I laughed quietly, wondering what it would be like to have anything but privacy. "You could say that."

Archer didn't answer but I sensed his gaze on my face. When I turned to look at him, there was a curious frown at play on his face, as if he were trying to figure me out.

"I should go. Thanks for the ride."

He nodded once.

"See you tomorrow?"

He didn't respond to my question. I gave Harlo one last scratch and reluctantly opened the car door.

* * * *

Archer proved harder to figure out than a cryptic puzzle. The following morning as I sat in the quad poring over my biology textbook, my heart leaped into my throat when a body dropped itself onto the bench beside me.

An Archer-shaped body.

He pulled out a battered paperback and started reading without even a nod by way of greeting. I opened and closed my mouth like a fish before deciding to leave well enough alone and not question his presence.

His presence, as it turned out over the days that followed, grew more and more frequent. Archer didn't talk much, but it wasn't as weird as it had once seemed. Instead it was refreshing. Yeah, the girl who has no friends and no one to talk to found it refreshing when the one person who didn't run screaming in the other direction didn't want to talk much. But there was no pressure with Archer.

I didn't have to wonder whether I'd said the wrong thing or if I would be ostracized the next day if I had. Our quiet moments weren't awkward.

Until I daydreamed, of course. And there was nothing like trying to keep a blush at bay when I looked at muscular forearms and wondered what the rest of the muscles looked like.

And I wondered a lot.

Chapter Thirteen

Every day that passed, my mind was more and more full of Archer.

That afternoon at lunch, he found me at my usual tree and dropped down beside me. He leaned against the rough bark of the trunk and opened his book, reading with one hand as he dug into his sandwich.

Once again we didn't speak, barely even communicated past a brief nod for hello and goodbye.

Not even when Jill walked past and shot us a glare so foul it would have had a lesser person ducking for cover. I had known Jill for long enough that there was only one reason for a look so hateful—jealousy.

Archer was one of the best-looking boys in school—if not the best. Tall with muscles on muscles and a face to make angels weep… And he wanted nothing to do with Jill or her band of merry followers.

Which would surely only earn me more demerits in their eyes.

Like I cared.

I'd take a silent lunch with Archer over anything Jill had to offer any day.

I broke down barriers with Archer every day. Tiny ones, but barriers nonetheless. And with every surreptitious glance I sneaked his way, I fell harder for him.

On my way home from work a week or so after Archer became a permanent feature around me, I ducked into the convenience store. I craved something sweet, and as I pondered my choices, I remembered having seen a box of Reese's Pieces poking out of Archer's backpack. I grabbed two off the shelves — one for me tonight…and, wait — would it be totally lame if I bought the other for Archer tomorrow?

With a shrug, I decided not to overthink it, and bought the two boxes. I turned to leave and bumped into a guy standing close behind me.

"Oh, sorry," I said with a laugh. I sidestepped him, and glanced at his buddy. Hadn't they been outside the fast-food place?

I stuffed the candy in my backpack and headed back out into the night. The bell above the door of the convenience store jingled a moment after I'd left, and I glanced over my shoulder to see the two guys step outside. My skin prickled with unease and even though I told myself that it was a coincidence, I hurried my pace.

They still followed me when I glanced back after two blocks, and I broke into a jog. There was an alley a few blocks ahead that I could cut through. I never took that shortcut because it had next to no lighting and I was too afraid of what dangers lurked inside.

Tonight the danger seemed to be behind me.

Heavy footsteps behind me echoed in the empty streets. My heartbeat pounded in my ears. They sounded right behind me and I forced myself to run faster.

With the alley in sight, I turned swiftly in, crashing into something the moment I did. A shriek escaped my mouth before a hand clamped down over it, muffling the noise.

I wrenched away, stumbling over my own feet and hitting off the side of the building. The side of my face stung, having probably scraped a good chunk of flesh off. My head swam from the impact and I tried to scramble deeper into the darkness of the alley to reach the other end.

I was jerked back against a body, fingers biting into my arm that would surely leave bruises. "Where you running to, Lo?" Cam asked.

Ice-cold dread flooded my veins at the sight of him. He smiled, sure and cocky, and backed me up against the wall of the building. Cam looked behind him and I followed his gaze to see the two guys who had followed me.

He gave them a nod and they disappeared.

They had never been the threat at all... They had delivered me to the real one.

"What are you doing?" I whispered. I had hoped that after these few weeks I would have fallen from Cam's mind, but it seemed I was firmly in the forefront of it instead.

"I've been looking for you, Lo," Cam said. "How have you been? Told anyone about our...friendship?"

Was that why he wouldn't leave me alone? He wanted to make sure I'd keep my mouth shut about the night we met?

I shook my head. "N-no, of course I haven't. I wouldn't—I won't."

"And what about your little boyfriend?"

Archer? God, I wished he was here..."He won't either, I swear."

Cam's lips twisted into a cruel smile. "How can I believe you?" He tightened his grip on my arm and I cried out in pain. "Should I give you a hint about what would happen if you decided to blab?"

"Please," I whispered.

"I could send a message to your punk-ass boyfriend. I could let him know that no one hits me and gets away with it." The grip he had on my arm burned. Tears streamed down my face and I bit down on my lip to keep from yelping. "Should I deliver the message care of you?" Cam chuckled. "He isn't here this time, Lo."

My entire body shook with fear. Whatever Cam had intended on doing that night we met, it seemed he wanted to see it through. This time, no one could help me.

No one but me.

A tin can rattled against the ground farther in the alley drew Cam's attention from me. I seized my opportunity and pulled up my knee. I slammed it as hard as I could into Cam's crotch.

He grunted and stumbled back a step.

I wrenched my arm out of his hold and bolted away from

him. I had no idea if he — or his two friends — gave chase. I didn't dare turn around. I doubled straight back to the convenience store and begged the clerk to call me a cab. God alone knew how long it would take Cam to recover from aching balls.

I couldn't take the chance of him following me and finding out where I lived.

Back in my house, I rocked myself on my bed. Kit curled up with his head on my feet, that animalistic nature of his so attuned to me that he sensed there was something very wrong.

I should call the police.

I had to call the police.

Twice now Cam had been intent on harming me... And he alone knew to what degree. There was something incredibly dangerous and unhinged about him, and I had a sickening feeling that now that I had eluded him, Cam wouldn't relent until he had taken whatever he wanted from me.

I jumped off my bed, startling Kit. I reached for my cell phone — and snatched back my hand.

I didn't even know Cam's last name. I didn't even know if Cam was his first name — who was to say he hadn't lied?

And... I had no witnesses. Sure, I had the proof thanks to my messed-up face and what would more than likely be a bruised to hell arm... But what else was there? Realistically, all I could do was report an assault.

By a stranger.

I couldn't point the cops in the direction where to find Cam, and there was no one to back up my story.

There was the first time, with Archer.

But Archer had hit him. What if Cam somehow turned it around and pressed charges against Archer?

My stomach rolled with nausea. I couldn't use Archer as a witness.

I climbed into my bed and pulled the quilt tight around my body. It did little to comfort me. Every inch of me trembled. There was nothing I could do.

And if Cam had been pissed before, what the hell would he be now?

* * * *

The full effect of last night showed by morning. And it was real obvious something had happened. The skin had turned a purplish-red and was darkening fast, with clear thick stripes from where his fingers had left their mark. Kids already thought I was weird enough, they didn't need to see this.

As I ransacked my laundry pile, I cursed myself for not putting the clothes away. Coarse fox fur coated practically everything. The only other long-sleeved shirt I owned, I had worn to work a few nights ago and hadn't gotten around to washing yet.

A regular T-shirt would have to do, and the only other thing I could find was Derek's old NC State Wolfpack hoodie. It drowned me, and we weren't allowed to wear team clothes to school unless it showed our own mascot. I could only hope that no one called me out on it.

I spent so much time fussing that I didn't make it to the quad that morning, so it was fourth period before I saw Archer. He was the only one who didn't have the decency to appear ashamed when I glared at his questioning look at the hoodie.

"Mr. Poole?"

I gritted my teeth at Kimmie's sickeningly sweet and totally fake voice.

"It's unfair boys have to take their team baseball caps off in class but she can wear that hoodie. Isn't that discrimination?"

My stomach dropped as every head turned to face me. Mr. Poole followed Kimmie's accusing finger and noted the hoodie. "She's right, Miss Black. Off with it, please." Mr. Pool turned back to face the board without waiting for my reply.

I clenched my hands into fists. *That bitch, what's her problem, anyway?* I couldn't take it off. I couldn't handle the stares...the questions. "No," I said in a small voice.

When I denied him, he slowly turned back around. "Excuse me? I said take it off. Now."

"No."

Mr. Poole walked slowly up the aisle and folded his arms across his chest, coming to a stop in front of my desk. "I am the teacher, Miss Black. What I say in my classroom goes. Now take it off."

"I don't hear you harassing any other girls to take their clothes off. Why am I the special one?" My anger at both Kimmie and Mr. Poole fueled my bravado. I couldn't back down. I couldn't let him bully me. I'd happily take the punishment.

Mr. Poole's face turned a weird puce color. "This is your last warning, Miss Black! Off. Now. Or you can go to the principal's office."

I looked down, about to collect my things.

"We're waiting."

"Why don't you leave her alone?" Archer asked quietly.

A low murmur broke out across the classroom. What did they find stranger—Mr. Poole freaking out over a hoodie, or hearing Archer speak?

Mr. Poole swiveled around to shift his death-glare to Archer. "It seems we have two rebels in our midst today. Any particular reason you so gallantly came to Miss Black's rescue?"

Archer pinned Mr. Poole with a glare. "I don't like bullies."

Mr. Poole laughed in disbelief. "I'm a bully? So what would happen if I let Miss Black break the rules? Everyone else would think they could do it too. It always starts with the small things, like breaking clothing conduct, but these things spiral." He twisted back to face me. "Off, Miss Black."

"It's just a fucking hoodie."

101

A collective gasp rang out in the room. Mr. Poole's facial color deepened. "Enough! Get out of my classroom, both of you! Now!"

Archer was on his feet and out of the door before I even registered what had just happened.

* * * *

I got held back that afternoon for detention, so I had to haul ass across town to get to work on time. I had no idea what had happened to Archer—he wasn't in detention with me. But just because he wasn't present didn't mean he was absent...from my mind at least. In detention, I'd tried to make the most of my jail time and get some school work done, but every few minutes my mind would drift back to the awful encounter in Mr. Poole's class.

When I managed to catch him up after we'd been thrown out of class, he'd shot me a glare that stopped me dead in my tracks. He was pissed, and seriously so. Shouldn't he have been mad at Mr. Poole, since he was the one he defended me from?

But no.

I got the brunt of Archer's bad mood. I guess he didn't enjoy getting kicked out of class.

Boys. Go figure.

Even at work I couldn't keep my thoughts from straying to Archer. Thankfully I had a nice boss who didn't chew my ass out for daydreaming. My head was so far in the clouds I opened the wrong kennel to give the animal inside a specialized flea bath. I should have realized that after the cat left my hands a bloody, gouged mess, it wasn't, in fact, the poodle Missy, who should have been getting the bath.

"What's going on with you today?" Doug asked as we locked up. "You've been a space cadet all afternoon. And I'm not even touching the hoodie issue."

I looked at my scuffed sneakers, trying to find a way around the topic without flat-out lying. Not just because

I respected Doug, but also because I couldn't lie to save myself. But I couldn't tell him about Archer and my rapidly growing obsession with him.

"Listen," Doug said, "You're on the rota to come in this weekend, but don't worry about it. Take some time and figure out whatever is going on, okay? And I mean it, Vix. I don't want to see your face back here till Tuesday."

A whole weekend? He couldn't be serious! "But today's only Friday!" I spluttered.

Doug shrugged and looked at something behind me. "You could use a little downtime. Have some fun and remember you're still a kid. Act like it. Anyway, I'd bet whatever is on your mind is standing over there."

I twisted around and saw Archer leaning against a street lamp, bathed in a yellow circle of light.

"See you Tuesday," Doug said before ducking around the corner.

Archer and I faced each other, silently observing for a moment. His face still wore the scowl that stopped me in the hallway earlier that day. He pushed off against the street lamp and moved closer.

"You missed detention," I said eventually.

Archer shrugged. He jerked his head in the direction I usually walked home, and we set off toward my house, walking by silent mutual agreement.

I let him have ten minutes more of silence before I couldn't keep quiet any longer. "Why the hell are you so mad at me?"

He snapped his head round to me. "You think I'm mad at *you*?"

I threw my hands up into the air. "Who else? I don't get you — you keep doing these things for me, like sticking up for me or saving me from something that could have turned into a nightmare...but you get mad at me for it."

Archer shoved his hands through his hair. "I didn't mean for it to come across that way. I was only ever mad at myself."

"Why?" I paused when we were a few yards from my house. "I don't understand why you would be mad at yourself for being kind... For helping someone when they needed you."

He groaned and flung his arm out to the side. "That's just it! I don't want you to need me."

I stepped back as though he'd thrown a bucket of ice-cold water in my face. "I didn't mean in a romantic way, if that's what you're worried about."

Archer looked down. "Neither did I." He blew out a breath. "Look, the last thing I want is for you to trust me... To mistake me for the kind of person who can help you when you need it."

I frowned. "I don't understand. You've already proved you're exactly that kind of person."

"But I'm not. I've betrayed people... Important people. People who made the mistake of trusting me." He turned his back on me, but I didn't miss the flash of pain in his eyes first.

"People make mistakes, Archer, it's what makes us human."

He whirled around to face me, his eyes wild with disbelief. "Betrayal makes us human? Are you serious? Animals have a better sense of loyalty than humans. Don't for one second assume you understand me or what I've done." Archer whirled away from me again and stomped down the street.

Instead of being hurt by his words as I probably should have been, I got a sense of something else. Something hidden underneath his harsh words and icy tone. "It's okay to need people, Archer," I called out to him, stopping his angry exit. "To have people in your life who care about you—who, despite what you think, aren't going to hurt you." I flinched as something hit my head, then my sleeve and when the sound of spattering all around me heightened I realized it was raining. Not hard—yet. But it didn't take long for it to get going around here.

Archer hadn't moved. He didn't turn back around, but

he didn't storm off either. "And what if I hurt them?" he asked, voice still thick with adrenaline.

I moved to stand in front of him. The anger had spread from his eyes and was now apparent all over his face and straight down to his clenched fists. "Someone only has the power to hurt you if you let them. I know—"

"Do I look like I need some stupid, sappy pep talk right now?" he asked in a low, gravelly voice.

"Then why did you come here?" I demanded, losing all patience. The rain poured heavier down us. "Why keep doing this? You let yourself get closer to me before bolting or lashing out like a cornered animal!"

"I don't know, okay?" Archer shouted over the pounding of the rain on the sidewalk, rivulets of water streaming down his handsome face. "You think I like this? Feeling this way? Wanting to get closer to you, but knowing right down to my bones how stupid that is, because I'm not someone you should let yourself trust?"

"Why don't you let me decide who I should trust?" I took a deep breath and tried to calm my racing heart. Both of us angry and clashing like titans wouldn't help anything. "Why do you think that you're not worthy of...of... anything? And I get it, okay? I get you don't think much of yourself. But all I'm hearing from you is reasons why you don't want to be here right now...so why are you?"

Archer stared at me for a long, hard moment. When he spoke again his voice was gruff. "I just knew I didn't want to be alone. I don't want to be alone. And I don't want to be alone...with you."

As I looked into his dark eyes that seemed to plead with me not to make a big deal out of what he said, it was as though I looked into the eyes of the only person in the world who could understand me. How long had I been alone for now? Since Derek had died, at least.

But it went deeper than that.

I'd never been close to someone else, someone just for me. It had become painfully clear on my return that my friends had been more like acquaintances, and never anyone I'd share a secret with that I wanted kept.

Derek's death only made the absence of someone in my heart that much bigger. Sure, I managed to fill the hole pretty well with schoolwork and the surgery and my plans for the future. But it's not the same and it was the emotional equivalent of putting a Band-Aid on a broken leg.

Archer knew loneliness. I didn't know much about him. Hell, I hardly knew anything about him. Except this one truth.

He eyed me warily as I slipped my hand into his and pulled him up the street. At my house he started to head for the front door but I tugged him around the corner, heading for the backyard. The rain made the lawn a soggy mess and the water seeped into my sneakers.

The rear of the house was my domain. Once upon a time our backyard had been littered with bikes, barbeques and the best lawn furniture. Now the yellowed grass showed a neglected place that held too many happy memories.

At the stairs that led up to the deck Archer paused. I shook my head and pulled him farther into the darkness. All at once we were flooded with light. I blinked for a minute as I fumbled in my pocket for my keys. I really had to get a dimmer light bulb for the security lamp above my door. But I guess that would defeat the purpose.

I finally found my keys and unlocked the door. "You ready for this?"

Archer raised an eyebrow. "For what?"

"Keep your eyes down and don't make any sudden moves."

"What, you got an axe wielding maniac in there?" Archer asked.

I grinned. "Something like that." I opened the glass door slowly. There could be no sudden movements in my domain, at least not at first.

For once nothing bounded to meet me.

Then from the darkness came a growl.

Chapter Fourteen

"Hey, Kit, it's just me," I whispered. I flipped on the lights and hustled Archer in, closing the door behind him.

He gave me a baffled look but when he turned and found the source of the growl, his face froze. "What the hell?" Archer muttered, staring at the less-than-happy-to-see-him fox.

"I said don't stare!" I hissed through my teeth. "Turn to the side, hold your palms out a little and crouch down so he can see you're not a threat."

"You have to be kidding me! If I crouch down he can reach my freaking throat easier." Archer swallowed, but followed my orders.

Kit stopped his low dog-like growl, but his ears flattened against his head and he kept his stomach low to the ground. I fished around in my pocket and found a treat and handed it to Archer. When you have a temperamental animal, or even a skittish one, it pays to have something both comforting and rewarding to hand.

"Give him a sec. He's never met a human apart from me or Doug before. He can smell Harlo on you, and can't figure out if you're a threat or not." I didn't hover around either of them, and moved to the side to give them room. Inch by inch, Kit sneaked closer to Archer. He circled him, neck extended as far as he could to smell all around him. Once Kit realized Archer had food, his ears flicked up.

"Hold your hand flat and for chrissakes don't move," I warned.

To give him credit, Archer didn't flinch once. Harlo was easily double—probably triple—Kit's size, but he was still a wild, and therefore unpredictable, animal.

Kit reached slowly for the treat. As soon as he secured it, he darted off and hid in my bedroom.

"Can I get up now?" Archer asked.

I stifled a laugh. "Yeah."

He slowly got to his feet. Once at full height Archer let out a breath and looked around him. "Interesting place you got here. This all yours?"

I nodded. He probably had a dozen questions but since he wasn't one for prying, Archer left it well enough alone. My part of the house was every teenager's dream. I had the entire basement to myself. I had three rooms—bedroom, bathroom, living room with a small adjoining kitchen area. The living room used to be the laundry room, but Mom arranged for an enormous closet upstairs to be converted. Heaven forbid she should have to run into her daughter on laundry day.

A set of stairs went up to the ground level of the house but I kept the door locked. If I needed to go upstairs for anything I always went the long way round outside because I didn't want anyone accidentally disturbing Kit.

The glass doors opened out onto the back yard and when I was home I usually left the doors open for hours so Kit could explore the back yard at his leisure. But Kit hated the rain and he would be too worked up after meeting Archer to be interested in exploring outside when there was something new to investigate inside.

"Do you want a shower?" I asked, to break the silence at last. Archer raised an eyebrow again and I swear I had a full-body blush. "Because of the rain, you must be freezing," I stammered. "I'm going to have one, then you could have one after me. If you want. You don't, you know, smell or anything." *Oh Jesus.*

Archer's lips twitched. "Sure. Thanks."

"I have some clothes that will probably fit, and the radiator down here is pretty good so yours should be dry in no time." I rambled like an idiot and couldn't seem to stop.

"Okay, I'll be back in a few. Kit'll probably come sniffing around. Just remember—no sudden moves, try to avoid staring and there's a bag of treats in that cupboard, if he hasn't found and destroyed them already."

When he gave me another amused look, I figured it would be a good idea to remove myself before I said anything else embarrassing. Like confess my absolute adoration for him. I backed out of the room and smacked my shoulder off the door frame so hard it made my teeth clatter.

God.

In the shower I turned it up so hot it almost scalded my skin. It was heaven after being in wet clothes.

A million thoughts raced through my mind. Archer, Archer in my house, Archer in my house while I was naked, Archer in my house while I was naked and he was with my fox. What if my fox tried to eat him?

I shouldn't have worried. By the time I left the bathroom, dressed in striped pajama pants and a black tank top, Archer sat in the middle of the living room floor with an excited Kit clambering all over him.

From the safety of the darkened hall, I watched way longer than I should have. There was just something about seeing Archer with Kit and the way he played with him. Archer's face was relaxed and open—something I'd never seen before. Whatever troubled him melted away around Kit, and I suspected around Harlo, too. I ached for him to relax like that around me, too.

Archer stroked Kit's ears, the fox's ultimate soft spot, and it warmed me all the way down to my bare toes. I moved into the room eventually, knowing it would be totally embarrassing to be caught staring.

I held out a T-shirt and a pair of sweatpants to Archer. He accepted them with a strange expression on his face. "What?" I asked.

"I can't wear girl's clothes."

"These aren't girl's clothes."

"Oh," he said, before giving me a glance I couldn't

interpret. I pointed the way to the bathroom and when he was gone I realized he probably thought he was wearing an ex-boyfriend's clothes.

Crap. Why was nothing ever simple?

Kit nipped at my ankle and wove in between my legs, desperate for a replacement for his newfound playmate. The thing about playing with Kit was you could never forget what he was. Though domesticated and tame now, he was wild. Roughhousing with him wasn't the same as roughhousing with a dog. If he got too excited, or forgot that it was just play, he could turn aggressive, fast. You couldn't reach out and poke his belly and tease him or tumble around with him since it could bring out his bad side. Instead, it was actually easier if you just let him do all the work. Let yourself be the toy, or, more often than not, the climbing frame.

When Archer emerged from the bathroom smelling clean and warm and really good, Kit had me pinned to the floor attacking my earlobe.

"Am I interrupting something?" Archer asked with way too much amusement in his voice. At Archer's voice Kit bolted, apparently forgetting that he liked him and didn't have to fear him.

I flushed beetroot from the tips of my ears to my toes. "He's got a thing about ears. Lost many an earring this way." I jumped to my feet way too fast and nearly fell back down again.

The corner of Archer's lip tugged upward. "I think I'm taller than your ex."

"What?" I asked, frowning. Archer dropped his gaze to the cuff of his pants, which stopped about three inches above his ankle. I chuckled. "Oh."

"So you have a thing for short guys or what?"

"Um, no. Those are my brother's clothes."

"He won't mind me borrowing them?"

I tried to smile and failed. "I doubt it." And I seriously doubted Archer would want to hear that he was wearing a dead kid's clothes.

Archer nodded and wandered around the living room. He paused in front of the glass door, looking out into the dark night. "This rain isn't easing up. Heard there might be a storm headed tonight."

Great, Kit hates storms.

"Doesn't seem much point in drying my clothes if they're just going to get soaked again."

"You're kidding, right? You can't walk home in that!" I said, gesturing to the rain as it pelted against the sliding door.

He arched an eyebrow at me. "Did you see another mode of transportation I had with me when we walked here?"

"Don't be stupid. Just stay." The words had left my mouth before I had time to consider them. I'd never invited a boy to stay with me before — not even Drew when my parents went out of town for a weekend while we'd dated. In fact I hadn't even told him... He would have invited himself.

And Archer — while enigmatic and mysterious, a puzzle I still hadn't deciphered — had an air about him that made me relax. Of course, now that I had invited him for a glorified sleepover I wanted to keep him forever and never let him go.

I'm becoming a freak...a total, psycho freak.

Archer blinked. "What — the night?"

Full-body blush again, which was fast becoming my specialty. "Yeah, why not? It's stupid to go back out there tonight. And it's no big deal, the couch is pretty comfy."

"And your parents won't mind a strange boy spending the night?"

I scoffed. "Please. I could forget to come home for a week and they wouldn't notice. I doubt a boy is going to show up on their radar."

Archer studied me for a long minute, processing what I'd said. "Don't be so sure," he said quietly.

"Trust me, you don't know my parents," I muttered. A shiver sneaked down my back from my wet hair. I swung it over one shoulder and Archer's eyes flashed as I did.

He moved closer, his eyes flickering between my side and my face.

"What?" I asked, nerves creeping into my voice. Had I flashed some boob or something?

Archer still didn't speak. He reached a hand out to take mine in his. He lifted it and trailed his long fingers down my forearm. At the flare of pain, I realized my error. I'd been so distracted having Archer in my home that I'd forgotten all about the souvenir Cam left me, the bruise that had now turned a blackish purple, and hadn't remembered to put on another sweater.

I snatched my hand out of his and backed away from him. "So, you hungry? I don't have much down here, but I do have a microwave and some popcorn," I asked in a blatant false cheerful voice.

"What happened, Lori?" Archer asked, following me.

I looked at the floor, avoiding his eyes. The last thing I had wanted was for Archer to find out about my arm. "It's nothing."

"You're a sucky liar. What happened?" Archer leaned against the counter in the kitchen area. He folded his arms across his chest and didn't move his eyes from me for a second.

I sighed, realizing he could be just as stubborn as me. He wouldn't let up until I told him what had happened. And because he had already seen the bruise, he probably already suspected the truth anyway. "Fine. I ran into that guy again. You know, the one from—"

"I know who you mean," Archer snapped. He gripped the counter edge behind him so hard his knuckles turned white.

"Nothing bad happened," I whispered, emotion clogging my throat. "I mean, he hurt my arm a little, but that's all. I handled it."

Archer's eyes narrowed. "That's all? Christ, Lori, you can pretty much see his goddamn fingerprints! And what do you mean you handled it? You call the cops? They find him?"

"Um, no," I said, like a stupid little girl who could never get anything right. *God, why am I such a screw-up?* "I got away before anything serious happened, so what would be the point in getting the cops involved? I have no idea who he really is or where to find him"

He gestured to my arm. "So he just gets away with this? Again? Jesus, I can't believe you, Lori."

Anger crept up my throat and stained my face. I was so sick of Archer being mad at me for someone else's actions. "What is your problem?"

"That is my problem!" He stabbed a finger toward my bruises. "Why do you think it's okay for someone to get away with doing that to you? It's sick, Lori. He should pay for what he's done."

All the fight went out of me. I realized deep down that his anger was misplaced, and while I it made me feel better that it got him all riled up because it meant he must care, I just wanted to forget about the whole thing. Wanted to forget about everything and just get through the next few months and I could leave all this shit behind. "Just forget about it," I said, backing away from him.

He didn't let me get far. For every step I retreated, he advanced. "Forget— Are you serious? This is the second time this asshole has come after you! What about next time?"

"There won't be a next time!" I shrieked. He was right, of course, but I couldn't admit it to myself. At least not out loud.

"Of course there will be!"

Kit halted our argument. The fox's coat bristled, his ears lay flat and he was baring his teeth. A low, threatening growl emanated from his throat and he kept his eyes locked with Archer's.

"What the hell?" Archer muttered, glancing at me.

"He's defending me. He thinks you pose a threat."

"Me?" Archer laughed ruefully. "That's rich."

"Just back off a little, slowly, and show your palms."

Archer followed my instructions and slowly Kit relaxed. He still watched Archer like a hawk, but at least he didn't look as if he would rip his throat out.

After a few minutes, when everyone had calmed down, Archer rubbed the back of his neck. "I should go."

"What?" Panic made my heart pound. He couldn't leave... not now. "No, that's... Don't be stupid. The storm—"

"I've been out in worse."

"Please don't go," I whispered, not brave enough to meet his gaze when I said it.

"You want me to stay?" Archer asked in disbelief. "But we were just fighting, why would you want me around after that?"

I shrugged. "It's my fault we were fighting. I should have told you."

He took a single step toward me. "That's not why I'm mad."

"So will you stay?" I slowly lifted my eyes. "Like I said, I've got popcorn. And, like, a million movies."

There was a moment of agonizing silence before Archer answered. "I'll stay."

A smile pulled at my lips and I couldn't have stopped it if I wanted to. "Okay. I'll get the popcorn. Do you want to pick the movie? They're in that closet over there."

Archer nodded and headed over to it. "Little relieved you left the choice up to me."

"Why?" I asked as I started preparing the popcorn and shoved it into the microwave.

"Chicks always pick smoochy love stories."

I snorted. "The only love story I like watching is True Romance."

"You're a Tarantino fan?" The surprise in his voice should have been insulting, but I was used to it. Jill had hated that I owned no smoochy love stories.

"The biggest. I've seen Pulp Fiction about fifty times."

"Is that your favorite?"

"Depends what day it is, I guess. Some days I'm all about the Travolta, other days Michael Madsen in Reservoir Dogs takes the top spot."

Archer laughed and I froze. I had never heard him laugh before, not a real laugh, and it sounded so foreign coming from him. The laugh was everything Archer wasn't—light, playful with a hint of carefree while also rich and full.

The timer on the microwave beeped and I jumped. I spun around to pull the popcorn out of the microwave and dump it in a bowl.

Archer appeared at my elbow, a crooked smile at play on his lips. "Just when you think you've got someone figured out, they go and surprise you."

I swallowed and couldn't help but notice just how close Archer was. "Aren't surprises good things?"

He looked down, giving my question more consideration than I would have figured necessary. My heart gave a little jolt when he raised them again, and they locked with mine. "Not always. Sometimes. I guess you're one of the good ones." Archer reached past me to snag a handful of popcorn. I stared—mesmerized by the motion of his strong jaw as he chewed.

"So what'd you choose?" I asked, clearing my throat.

Archer held up a DVD case. "I haven't seen this in forever."

"*From Dusk Till Dawn*? Great choice." I grinned. "I love that one shot with Clooney and Tarantino in the car, and the camera looks through the hole in Tarantino's hand. Classic."

Archer's smile broadened and he followed me to the couch. I started the DVD and when I turned around I saw Kit had gotten over his anger at Archer. The fox practically sat in his lap, drooling into the popcorn. Archer scooped up a handful of kernels and held it out for Kit. Surprise washed through me when Kit carefully dug into the offered food, and even more surprise when he let Archer stroke him with his free hand.

Food — the ultimate forgiveness.

I sat down at the other end of the couch and Archer caught me staring. "Fickle little beast, isn't he?"

"You have no idea."

Chapter Fifteen

Halfway through the movie, Archer and I got into a really big fight. A serious one. He said that he preferred new horror movies to old ones. We argued back and forth, each driving home the good points of our preferences and the bad points of the others.

"Seriously, how can you even compare the originals to the new shit they make these days? Malcolm McDowell has nothing on Donald Pleasance, he totally killed as Sam Loomis!"

"The effects are cheap and trashy and you know it!" Archer exclaimed. "Just admit it—there's so much more they can do with film these days."

"Smoke and mirrors," I muttered, waving his comment away with my hand. "Back in the day they didn't need all that high tech shit. Filmmakers today think it's all about the carnage and less about the fear. I haven't seen a movie made later than 1990 that has scared me."

"It isn't all about the fear—what about the experience? New releases are more real, you feel like you're right there!"

"Oh please! They couldn't be any more unrealistic if they tried!" I smiled. "Are you trying to tell me you weren't afraid when you saw Michael Myers in the background, and the only music going is the creepy piano score? People today just can't do what they did back then! The scores for most scary movies now are so complicated! I mean, take Jaws—two notes. Done, terror achieved."

Archer shook his head and tossed a handful of popcorn into his mouth. At the movement of food, Kit jerked his head up to hopefully gaze at Archer. And of course Archer gave in to him. Again. I would have one fat fox on my hands if Archer visited often.

"Besides," I said, trying to distract myself from wondering about how often Archer may or may not visit. "There's only one real reason guys like recent scary movies. The girls are trashier and the boobs are bigger."

Archer gave me a cocky smile and leaned closer, making my breath catch in my throat. "And let me guess, you liked Kevin Bacon in Friday the 13th?"

I shrugged. "I didn't hate him, but I didn't crush on him either."

Archer's grin widened. "And you liked him better than Jared Padalecki in the remake?"

Damn, he had me there. Curse my penchant for tall, dark and brooding!

"Didn't think so." Archer leaned back and tossed a kernel into the air, catching it in his mouth.

I rolled my eyes. "Ooh what, you win one argument and you're so slick now?"

Archer winked and caught another piece. "I know I am."

"Whatever." I nodded to the bowl of popcorn. "And like there's any skill involved with that."

He dumped the bowl in my lap. "Prove it."

Shit…

"Are you chicken?" Archer asked, goading me. "I'd hate to lose to me too."

"I'm not chicken," I said, scowling.

Archer folded his arms and gave me a pointed look. Even Kit watched on with curiosity. I looked into the almost empty bowl. Couldn't be that hard, right? I flicked one piece in the air but instead of catching it in my mouth, it dropped on my open eye.

"Ow," I said with a flinch, batting the popcorn away and rubbing my watering eye. "Oh, ow, ow ow…"

Archer howled with laughter, the whole couch moving with him.

"Shut up," I said, smacking him on the arm. I moved the

bowl onto the arm of the couch. "This really kills. I've got popcorn dust in my eye or something."

Archer scooted closer and pulled my hand away from my eye. I couldn't stop blinking and a tear rolled down my cheek. Archer brushed it away with his thumb.

"Hold still, let me see," he said, coming even closer. "Stop blinking."

"Uh, sure, I'll get right on that," I mumbled. "I can't, it hurts."

Archer smiled and held my face, staring into my bad eye. I took another breath and got a huge dose of his heady scent did it hit me how close he was. His rich chocolate-brown eyes focused on me. I swear I stopped breathing and my heart burst out of my chest.

He stroked his thumb below my eye, wiping away another tear. "You'll live."

I couldn't answer. My breath lodged in my throat as his fingers trailed down my cheek to my jaw and didn't take his hand away. A shiver of anticipation tore down my spine. If I hadn't been so crippled by self-doubt I would have mauled him by now.

His Adam's apple bobbed, a breathy chuckle tickling my face. Barely a millimeter separated us. A heartbeat — the longest heartbeat of my entire life — later, his lips pressed down on mine. Archer clasped my face, his gentle touch so at odds with his obvious strength. His other hand delved into my damp hair.

Archer parted his lips, and I followed him, more than ready to experience this with him. A loud clatter had both of us jumping apart, the kiss broken. Kit nosed the upside down bowl on the floor, trying to find more popcorn.

Thanks, Kit...

Archer moved away, running a hand through his hair — the moment, apparently, over. After I cleared up Kit's mess we watched the rest of the movie in awkward silence. Neither of us moved. I'm not even sure I breathed.

When the credits rolled I grabbed a blanket and a pillow

off my bed and placed them on the couch for Archer. "It's usually pretty warm down here. Will you be comfy enough? I can try to hunt down more blankets "

"No, this is great, thank you." Archer gave me a distracted smile.

"Um, okay then. Night." I fled into the safety of my room before I could embarrass myself. Even though physically tired, just knowing Archer was only a few meager feet away was enough to keep me awake for hours.

As did the phantom touch of his kiss.

* * * *

It was still dark out when a crash jerked me awake followed swiftly by a clatter and a curse. Kit and I bolted out of bed at the same time. He hid under my bed and I darted toward the noise. I flipped on the lights in the living room and a yelp caught in my throat when faced with a chest. A bare, hunky chest.

I clamped a hand over my eyes and took a deep breath. In my disorientation I'd totally forgotten Archer was here.

"You okay? You look like you're having a heart attack," Archer asked, his voice rough with sleep.

"I think I am," I admitted. I sucked in another breath. "What happened? I heard a crash or something."

Archer stepped aside and motioned to the couch. A laugh bubbled in my throat as I took in the scene. Archer's blanket was rumpled and various paraphernalia littered the couch. DVD cases, socks, books, a Tupperware tub, mugs... The assortment was endless.

"I rolled over and half that crap fell on the floor." Archer ran a hand through his gorgeously sleep-mussed hair. "You a sleepwalker or something?"

"Me?" I laughed again. "No. But you've officially been welcomed by Kit."

"What?"

"He brought you all that stuff. He does it with me all the

time. I wake up in the morning and find all kinds of weird things in bed with me." Archer chuckled. I folded my arms across my chest. "I'm hurt. It was weeks after he met me he started doing that."

"What can I say? I'm blessed with charm."

"And apparently not modesty."

He smiled again and moved away from me, stretching. The muscles in his back moved under his skin, and a strange, foreign flutter in my stomach took over.

"What time is it, anyway?" I asked, looking away from Archer before I did something reckless...like pounce on him and beg him to kiss me again.

"Little after five."

I groaned and headed into the kitchen area to flip on my coffeemaker.

Archer disappeared while the coffee brewed, so I opened the glass doors to let Kit burn some energy outside. I suspected he would crash soon enough—after all he'd been busy all night bringing crap to Archer. Kit darted out into the not-quite-dark, not-quite-light yard and I poured myself a nice big mug of coffee.

The sky was a swirl of dusty pinks and purples, giving me just enough light to see around the yard. I sat down on the patio with my coffee and stretched my legs out in front of me, mindless of the dewy grass between my toes.

Once I'd loved this yard. When my parents had been happy and my brother had been clean. Now Kit and I were the only ones who enjoyed it. Kit loved to roam, sometimes even ventured into the opening of the woods. He never went far from me and would always check to make sure he could see or sense me. I wished I could do something for him... Make the yard full of fun and adventure for him the way it once had been for me.

Kit, whose nose investigated under a shrub, turned toward me. He trotted over, but missed me completely and stopped just at the door. I turned and saw Archer leaning against the doorframe, watching me with a slight frown on his face.

"What?" I asked, my voice sounding too loud against the silence of outside.

Archer shook his head and dropped down beside me.

"There's coffee if you want some."

"I'm good, thanks." He stretched his arms back, his hands on the patio supporting him up, and eased his legs out in front of him. He had changed out of Derek's clothes and back into his own. The dark denim jeans that wrapped around his strong legs were way more flattering than too-short sweats. "What were you thinking?"

I shook my head. "Nothing, really."

He touched his foot against mine. "I don't believe you."

"Why?"

Archer smiled. "Because, like I said last night, you're a sucky liar."

A smile teased my lips. He knows my face. "I was just thinking how I'd love to do something for Kit out here."

"Like what?"

I shrugged. "Try to recreate the things he would like if he was still wild. Places he'd investigate, places he'd hide in, places he'd make home."

"What could you do?"

A frown pulled at my brow. "I'm not sure. Dig holes and tunnels or something, but I don't know how I'd get them to keep from collapsing."

Archer was silent for a moment. He sat and brought his knees up, the entire time looking thoughtful. "A sturdy cylinder should keep it from collapsing. Dig a long trench, put in the cylinder and cover it back up again, leaving an entrance. If you do it over by those shrubs, it would conceal the entrance a little, make him more secure or stealthy."

I stared at Archer, unable to stop even if I wanted to.

He looked at me, a guarded expression on his face. "What?"

"Nothing," I said, trying to hide my smile. "Nothing."

Archer turned on his trademark frown. Typical.

"So any plans for today?" I plucked at the grass, avoiding his gaze. "I've got the whole weekend off from the vets."

Archer laughed, startling me. "Any other person would be happy to have a whole weekend off work. But you? You say it like they did it just to piss you off."

I nudged him with my elbow. "I did not."

He nudged me back. "So why is having free time a bad thing?"

"It isn't when you have something else to do." I heard the downcast tone in my voice, and snapped myself out of the gloomy mood. "Like take care of a fox. He keeps me plenty busy."

"Except your mind." Archer pinned me with a look. "You hide at the vets so much because it keeps you distracted."

"I don't hide there, it's my job." Lie. Big. Fat. Lie.

"Yeah, and how many other seniors are willing to work four nights a week and all day on the weekends?" Archer shifted his position, his eyes, along with his voice, softened. "I'm just saying I get it. To need to be distracted."

His words hung in the air between us. We both had unanswered questions, and I appreciated that he didn't push me. Because, as he said, he got it.

"To answer your earlier question, I'm on Harlo duty today. I've ignored my mutt for too long and she doesn't appreciate it."

I smiled, grateful to him for changing the subject and surprised that he'd coaxed me out of silence for once. "I get that. Kit's always so happy when I get home, even though he's probably only just woken up."

"Doesn't that bug you, him being on a different sleep pattern?"

"Not really. It was awful when he was a cub, I got no sleep. But now he's in a good pattern. He loves being outside early in the morning, and will sleep from midmorning to around early evening, and again he loves it around dusk. Usually he roams around outside for a while before coming inside and trashing whatever he can get into." I smiled at my fox's little traits and habits. The very things that have kept me, in a lot of ways, breathing. "He always comes to bed when I do and cuddles in so close I almost suffocate. But he only sleeps for a few hours, then he's off fetching everything, like he did with you. Usually he's back on the bed when I wake up, ready to start it all over again."

"How is he with other animals?"

I snorted. "I don't really want to find out. Typically a fox will bolt from anything and everything, especially if it's bigger than they are. But, if it's protecting something or cornered, it could do some damage to its opponent."

"So Harlo wouldn't be good company?"

"I'd say not."

"Shame," Archer said, a smile in his voice. "They'd be great companions."

Before I even had time to ponder his statement, Archer was on his feet and marching off around the house, with barely a farewell over his shoulder. I sat for another few minutes, trying to decide if he had really just done that. Left. Just like that. Five minutes later I decided he had.

Kit broke me out of my spell, his snout worrying at my hand, his sign of wanting to be fed, despite probably having chowed down on a field mouse or two by now. With a sigh I got to my feet and Kit padded beside me back into the house. Once Kit's appetite had been sated, it was just me and the silence.

I eyed the couch that had held Archer's body last night. The disarrayed blanket was the only proof that he been here at all. I pushed all the crap Kit had piled onto the floor and crawled underneath the blanket. Drowsiness pulled at my eyelids and it was just as I was about to drift off that it hit me. The gentle waft of Archer's scent at first teased my senses, then it was everywhere. The pillow, the blanket, my skin.

I groaned and pulled the blankets over my head.

Chapter Sixteen

For the second time that day, I woke to the sound of a crash. It took a moment for my eyes to focus and see that it was only Kit causing destruction and mayhem. Nothing out of the ordinary. Reluctantly I threw back the Archer-scented blanket and got to my feet.

After a quick clean-up on Aisle Kit, and a shower, I locked up the basement and headed around the house to rummage in the kitchen upstairs. Fall had crept up on the summer months, but it was still warm, and I decided on wearing my short denim cutoffs and an orange tank top.

"Hello?" I called as I opened the front door. "Mom? Dad?"

No one answered me. No noise came from the TV, the radio didn't play in the kitchen. Although there was a note taped to the fridge —

Lori,
We're visiting Uncle Dave and Aunt Julie this weekend. Back Sunday night.
Mom & Dad

My Uncle Dave and Aunt Julie had the most obnoxious kids on the planet, and I loathed having to visit. My parents had spared me.

But not even being given the opportunity to turn down the trip stung.

I walked the silent halls of my youth and crept upstairs. The purple flower sticker was still on my door, though the edges were scratched, as if someone had tried to peel it off. I'd stuck that sticker down when I was eleven. Nothing would get it off now.

Dust motes hung in the air, stirring and moving as I pushed the door open. The drapes were open, letting in a thick stream of sunlight. All my pictures, all my CDs, all the furniture... A layer of dust coated it all.

I perched on the end of my narrow bed covered with a purple and pink bedspread. One thing I definitely was grateful for—the double bed downstairs, bought with money my grandma gave me before I left. Same with the TV, coffeemaker and microwave and anything else I'd needed since coming home.

A frown settled on my forehead as I took in my old room. Had I really been this shallow? Posters of cute boys hung from walls, snapshots of old friends and me decorated the edges of a mirror. Nail polish and makeup cluttered my vanity table along with a ridiculous amount of hair product. Who had I been?

More importantly...who was I now?

The only thing I salvaged from my room was a pair of sandals that had taken me forever to break in, and it was a waste not to wear them. When I closed my bedroom door behind me, I clutched the sandals to my chest as though they would create a barrier between me and the place I desperately wanted to go, and the place I desperately wanted to avoid.

Derek's bedroom had been out of bounds to me following his death. My parents had ransacked it in the days leading up to the funeral, looking for the evidence they would never find. They found part of his stash—the stuff he never cared whether they found or not. The good stuff, the stuff that he worried more about the cops finding than his parents, he had taken with him. I knew where the rest would be. Derek never pretended around me, even when I became popular and pretended I was too cool to associate with my stoner brother.

It was at home we were more than brother and sister. We were twins. Derek and I were so in tune with each other it was actually pretty freaky. I would know when to keep Mom busy when all she wanted was to bust Derek's chops for another bogus report card. Derek did the same for me... We protected each other.

With only one wall separating us, we learned to use that as an advantage from an early age. We created secret codes that developed over the years. Last year it had been one knock for cover for me, I'm sneaking out—only I used that one, Derek didn't give a rat's ass about being caught sneaking out, or sneaking back in—two knocks for need smell coverage—that was all Derek. Even when it was blatantly obvious that Derek was a total pothead almost twenty-four-seven, my parents never questioned my weird obsession with incense and how often I burned it, and why I only ever burned the really strong stuff. It covered the smell of pot, but it meant I had to hang my head out of the window for a while, before I fainted from the smoke. Three knocks usually meant incoming. It only bought a few seconds, but those seconds could be precious.

More often than not, the knocks were used to torment. Derek would text me to make him a sandwich, and when I texted back something way too impolite to repeat, he would bang on the wall till I either gave in or stomped into his room to smack him.

We were volatile and fickle, to say the least. We would argue one minute and laugh the next. No one could figure us out... No one ever came close. They didn't understand how Derek could annoy me so much I could've sworn I could cheerfully beat him to death, and the next I would be hiding out in his room, just because it always comforted me—whether he was there or not.

That room would hold no comfort now. I pushed open the door—quickly, before I could change my mind. A laugh bubbled in my throat when I saw the tidy room. Derek never tidied his room. Seriously. Even when I lost a bet and was forced to clean it, two hours in and it still resembled a war zone.

It was pretty barren now. Most of Derek's decent things like his computer, stereo, TV and assorted video game consoles had been hawked in the months before his death. Anything with a price tag had secured his latest fix. I pretended not to notice when my stuff started disappearing. But if I had to brand Derek as a thief, then I would brand him a thoughtful thief. He only ever took stuff I hated. Like the vintage sewing machine some great-aunt once removed on my mother's side got me for my fourteenth birthday. He never, ever touched the stuff that meant something to me.

I curled up on Derek's bed. My blankets downstairs held Archer's scent, but Derek was long since gone from this place. It barely even felt like his room anymore. The ripped band posters still hung from the walls and the graffiti on his closet doors still proclaimed how much he hated conformity and rules, but the life had fled from the room as it had from my brother.

I forced myself to get up before I fell down a slippery, morbid path. For no real reason, I opened Derek's bedside drawer and peered inside at the meager contents. A few scraps of paper, a few magazine and a facedown picture frame. I pulled out the picture and turned it so I could see the image.

A tiny piece of my heart shattered. Derek had me pinned to his chest, grinning manically while I scowled at being forced into such a cheesy snapshot. I'd seen the picture countless times. It used to sit on his cluttered desk — cluttered with CDs and never with books or homework. I always wondered how it didn't ruin his image or reputation when his friends no doubt spotted it at some time or another, having a picture of him and his sister out in the open like that. But whatever his reasons for having it, it had never moved since the day he'd stuck it in the frame and had placed it on the desk.

Not until my mother had shoved it in this drawer. The fact that it was face down really hurt. Really hurt.

I'd always loved this picture of us, and I wondered how

I had forgotten its existence. The picture showcased our similarities. Our hair, the shape and color of our eyes, how we had the same crooked smile. Because even though I scowled, I couldn't help but smile. My brother was such a goof and it had been taken during happier times... Before he used almost every day.

The day was crystal clear in my memory. My parents had taken us to a beach a twenty-minute drive from our house. We'd attempted a picnic but the wind had covered our food in sand pretty damn fast. Derek's shaggy hair and my long locks had whipped around our faces in the picture, making it even more whimsical and even happier.

The picture didn't belong trapped in a drawer for the rest of time. She might not ever want to see it again, but I sure as hell did. It would come with me along with the sandals.

* * * *

Kit emerged from behind the couch when I came back down bearing potato chips, a few sodas for my mini fridge and two PB and J sandwiches — Kit's favorite. We ate in the cool basement before I threw open the sliding doors again. A day this good shouldn't be wasted. It could be one of the last before winter. At the back of the yard, almost concealed by shrubs and overgrown plants, was a wooden garden swing with a thick wooden canopy above.

I brought my soda, a book I had to read for English class and a cushion. Once settled onto the swing, I dangled one foot off the end and lost myself in the book, knowing that I couldn't be spotted by anyone, not even my parents, should they come home any time soon. No one would look for me anyway, except maybe Kit, but he was curled up underneath the swing and no doubt already asleep.

I heard a car door open and close in the distance, and I slid lower in the seat, not wanting to be disturbed by my parents.

Footsteps drew closer, muted on the grass then louder on

the patio. Someone tapped their knuckles against the glass door.

I admitted defeat and sat up. "Over here," I called. I folded down the corner of the page I was on and shut the book. Kit yawned under the swing and a moment later his snout appeared as he sniffed the air.

"Catching the last rays of the year?"

My heart picked up speed at the sound of Archer's voice. I shielded my eyes with my hand and sat up as Archer headed across the yard. "Yeah, seemed a waste not to."

When he reached me, Archer leaned a forearm against the side of the swing. "I didn't see you back here. Pretty well hidden."

"That's kind of the point."

He arched an eyebrow. "Oh? Shall I leave then?"

I laughed. "No, you can stay."

Kit came out from under the swing and stretched before sniffing around Archer. He bent to stroke his head. "I brought you something. But I need your help getting it round here."

Archer had gotten me something? "What is it?"

He looked up at me. "You'd better come see." He led the way back to his car. Strapped to the roof of his car was a huge cylinder...thing. "What the hell is that?"

"Old stove pipe. Found it at the scrap yard."

"Um, thanks?"

Archer chuckled and shoved his hands into his pockets. "It's not for you, not exactly. You could use it for a den for Kit."

I had no words. No. Words. I could only stare at him in disbelief.

Archer was... There wasn't a word to sum up a guy like Archer. He was special and thoughtful and intense all at once.

And I was hooked on him.

He cleared his throat and a frown settled on his brow after my staring became an embarrassment. "So are you going to help me get this round back or what?"

* * * *

Archer set to work digging the tunnel for Kit. He made it look easy…and it was easy to look. After digging for a half hour, Archer took his shirt off and jeez…what a view. The way his muscles moved under his skin seemed to hypnotize me, the way they rolled and tensed. More than a few times I had to retreat into the house to cool down.

"Harlo doesn't mind you ignoring her again?" I asked when Archer stopped for a break and chugged a bottle of water. His torso glistened with sweat in the sun and I could barely tear my eyes away.

"No, my aunt went to visit friends upstate and took Harlo with her."

"You live with your aunt?"

Archer nodded and tipped back his head, catching the last few drops of water from the bottle.

I bit my lip to keep from asking any more questions. Archer had been so great with me, not prying when it was obvious there was more to tell. The least I could do was offer him the same respect. If he wanted to say more, he would.

"Won't you miss her?" I asked. "Harlo, I mean."

Archer gave a noncommittal shrug. "She's in safe hands. My aunt adores her."

I had thought it would take forever to dig the tunnel, a few days at least. But by dusk Archer piled the last of the dirt on top. It looked like a single hole in the ground at a slight angle, but on closer inspection you could see it was a tunnel. Archer even dug a bigger pit at the end of the tunnel so it would be more like a natural fox den.

Kit raced in and out for a half hour. But when dinner time came calling, he soon forgot about his new interest and bolted inside.

"Do you want to stay for some food? It's the least I can

do after everything you've done today." I asked Archer. The afternoon had flown by far too fast for my liking and I wanted more time with him.

Archer smirked. "You can cook food in that kitchen of yours?"

"I wouldn't say I could cook, but I can brew coffee and nuke stuff in the microwave. And" — I fished my cell phone out of my pocket — "I'm a pro at ordering takeout."

His smile widened. "Deal. I've got a change of clothes in my car, you mind if I shower first? I'm ten levels of filthy right now."

I laughed, nerves creeping in, although there would be a logical explanation. "Someone came prepared."

Archer rolled his eyes. "I take Harlo to the beach sometimes. Trust me, when that dog is involved, it pays to carry an extra pair of jeans and a T-shirt." He gave me a small smile before heading around to his car. When he came back I pretended to be focused on the pizza menu. I heard the shower start. My nerves doubled.

I ordered a meat feast pizza, figuring that would be the safe option. By the time Archer emerged from the shower, I had finished tidying up, since I hadn't bothered clearing all the crap Kit delivered to Archer the night before.

We sat on the floor to eat the pizza when it came. Kit switched between us, standing to attention in front of me before moving around to try out his begging techniques on Archer. Archer was a pushover. He even let Kit have the dough ball.

After we ate Archer suggested a movie and he picked again, this time going for The Silence of the Lambs. We moved onto the couch to watch it, and Archer broke the silence about ten minutes in. "Are you okay?"

I jumped at his voice, having been so lost in thought. "Yeah, why?"

"You seem on edge. Something on your mind?"

Yeah, you. Lots and lots of you. "Nope."

"Have I done something?"

132

I frowned. "No, why?" I asked.

Archer gestured to the expanse of space between us. "If you sat any farther away from me you'd be halfway up that wall."

Damn... I'd hoped it wouldn't have been so obvious. There wasn't really a motive behind it, I just wanted to give him room to... I don't even know. Make a move? He hadn't moved an inch. "Just...giving you space."

"For what?" he asked, giving me a trademark Archer glance. He didn't speak for the rest of the movie. As soon as the credits rolled up, Archer jumped to his feet. "I should get going."

My heart thumped double time. I opened my mouth to argue, but what could I say? Beg him to stay the night again? Yeah, because that wouldn't seem desperate or pathetic.

At the door, Archer turned to me. "Do you have any plans for tomorrow?"

I shook my head, not trusting myself to speak.

"Would you come on a drive with me?"

Nod.

"Pick you up around ten?"

Nod.

"Okay then."

Shaky smile.

"God, you're weird."

Frown.

I totally got no sleep that night either. Kit stayed with me most of the night, curled up on my pillow with his head tucked into my neck. Not the comfiest for me, but it kept him happy.

Chapter Seventeen

There were no crashes or boys cursing to wake me up on Sunday morning. Kit slept soundly out next to me and I wriggled farther down in bed, closing my eyes to try to catch a little more sleep.

Then I remembered.

My eyes flew open and I scrambled on the nightstand for my phone to check the time. I still had two hours before Archer would pick me up.

After a mediocre breakfast of a fruity cereal bar thing and a much longer shower than normal, my panic setting reached new levels when I stood in front of my closet. I didn't really have any nice clothes anymore... I saved those for school days. And the rest smelled like animal.

That kicked the panic setting up another notch. Where would we be going anyway? What if we were going somewhere nice and fancy—what if we were going... hiking? Crap...

At five minutes to ten I settled on a jean skirt I hadn't worn to either the vet's or school, so therefore classified as a 'good' item of clothing, a white top and a pair of black ballet flats. I figured if a guy took a girl somewhere like hiking, he should have the good sense to mention it beforehand, since my sex doesn't really do sensible footwear. And I'd take with me a white linen jacket with three quarter sleeves, just in case we ended up somewhere kind of nice. I wouldn't look totally fancy, but at least I wouldn't look like trash either.

Archer showed up twelve minutes after ten.

I agonized for every second of those twelve minutes.

He was clad in his usual dark jeans, dark T-shirt and sneakers. Definitely no hiking, then. He wasn't very talkative during the drive, but then again neither was I. I stared at the passing scenery for the most part, letting the wind catch my hair through the open window and whip it around my face.

He stuck to back roads. After going through dense, forest-lined routes, we came out driving along the coast. Our town was a coastal one with a pretty great beach. So great, in fact, that tourists crowded our small town every summer. If Archer wanted to go to the beach, why didn't he take us to the one closest?

After an hour or so of driving, Archer pulled into a grassy parking lot and killed the engine. When he opened the door to get out of the car I quickly followed suit. He locked up and tucked the keys into his pocket.

Archer nodded his head to an opening in a tall hedge and disappeared through it. I hurried after him along a man-made path, with down-trodden plants underfoot. The plants thinned out and eventually were replaced by sand. A few moments later we stepped out onto a perfect sandy beach. Hardly anyone else could be seen on the long stretch of golden sand. Down the long expanse of beach, a wooded area cropped up to the left. To the right, rocks and a few cave-like entrances rose up from the ground.

It wasn't as well manicured as the one near home. No swim markers, no lifeguard towers. No hot dog stands. But there were dogs. Dogs weren't allowed on our beach. This had to be why it was Archer's beach of preference.

Archer strolled ahead of me until he got to the damp sand near the surf. He turned back to see if I followed. I slipped off my ballet flats and started after him.

"Is this where you come with Harlo?" I asked as we walked along the surf, Archer just out of reach of the water since he still wore sneakers.

Archer shook his head. "Usually I take her to the beach closer to home, to the pathetically tiny area they actually

135

allow dogs. We come here sometimes when I want to get away from everything."

"What are you trying to get away from?"

He cut an unreadable glance my way. "Same thing as you, I imagine."

"And what's that?" I asked as I kicked up the surf, splashing in the water. I'd never grow up. Never. At least not if water was involved.

"Crap at school. Things I don't want to remember." He shoved his hands into his pockets.

"Like what?" I asked. I didn't usually push Archer into sharing so much. The least I could do was try. Maybe Archer didn't have anyone anymore who cared enough to push him.

"Wouldn't that entail me having to remember?" Archer asked with a crooked smile that didn't reach his eyes.

He was trying to be nice and not flat-out tell me he didn't want to answer my question. I shrugged and dropped the subject.

"What, no twenty questions?"

I shrugged again.

"You really aren't like most girls, are you?"

Ha. Total lie. I just had better restraint. "Guess not." I kicked to make a bigger splash and somehow managed to trip myself up. I landed ass first in the water. The shock of cold water on my legs made me gasp and a moment later a blush scalded my cheeks when I realized I would have a completely soaked rear.

Archer let out his too-rare laugh. I muttered something unrepeatable but took the hand he offered. He hauled me to my feet and I tried not to notice the closeness of our bodies.

I brushed in vain at my butt, but only really succeeded in moving around some of the wet sand stuck to me.

Archer laughed again and I decided that I'd fall in a hundred oceans if that was what it took to hear that sound again. "That's what you get for acting like a kid."

I arched an eyebrow. "Oh yeah?" I shoved hard with my

shoulder into Archer's chest, sending him sprawling into the surf. My brilliant plan of payback may have worked better if I'd realized Archer still had hold of my hand. I toppled onto him, our legs entangling as we landed in a heap.

Archer's chest rumbled with laughter as he pushed us into a sitting position. The water lapped around us, swaying me closer to him.

"Cheater," I mumbled as my pulse raced.

He scoffed. "Why? Because your evil plan didn't work as well as you hoped?"

"Something like that. But at least we're both soaked now."

Archer rolled his eyes and laughed quietly again.

I swatted his chest but couldn't help the smile creeping on my lips. "Stop laughing at me!"

He caught my hand and tugged me nearer. Archer drew my face closer to his, his hand coated in gritty sand. He stared at me for one heart pounding moment before he crashed his lips down on mine.

The kiss was hard and fast, like he wanted to prove something, or that he had been waiting far too long and impatience fueled his kiss. He pulled me onto his lap and I stretched my legs out behind him. I shivered when Archer trailed a hand down my back, leaving a damp line that cooled in the wind.

This was nothing like that first kiss in my basement.

This was everything I had craved for months now

This was pent-up emotion and raw need.

I could have stayed in that surf forever. It was warm there, safe…from everything, especially my thoughts. No painful memories or worry. All I could think about was Archer's mouth as it moved over mine. But eventually our kiss broke. Afterward, Archer gave me a crooked smile and hauled me to my feet. He didn't let go of my hand as we set off walking again, and a happy glow bloomed in my very core.

We were halfway along the beach when I realized at

some point during our surf kiss my ballet flats must have washed out to sea. When I pouted over my loss, Archer's gruff exterior cracked as he laughed at me for the third time that day.

* * * *

We walked and walked and when we reached the end of the beach we walked some more. The sand turned harder, with more stones and bigger pieces of broken shells until eventually we reached grass. The wood loomed in front of us, as did a clear path. Once under the cover of trees the heat dropped a few degrees cooler and I shivered in my wet clothes.

Archer's phone broke the silence. He pulled it out of his pocket and looked at the screen. He gave me a quick glance. "I'll catch up to you in a sec."

"Okay, sure," I said, carrying on ahead.

The woods began to thin out, and when they disappeared completely I stepped out on top of a cliff. It wasn't a very high cliff, but it gave an awesome view. A sudden tightness gripped my heart as I peered down to the crash of waves below. Derek would have jumped off the cliff edge. Especially if he was high. But even without the drugs, he had a laid-back quality, an unflinching nature that seemed to make him invincible. I remember he wrapped his bike around a pole once.

He broke a toe.

One.

I dropped to sit and dangle one leg off the edge, keeping my other knee up, hugging it to my chest. The wind blew my hair around my face and I rested my chin on my knee. *God, I miss him.*

Archer returned and sat down next to me. "Sorry about that. Kate—my aunt—likes to check in."

"It's no trouble. It's nice she cares enough to worry about what you're doing," I said, swallowing the lump that rose in my throat.

"Yeah," Archer said quietly. He cleared his throat and touched his foot against mine. "I told her this no-good girl pushed me over into the ocean and wrecked my sneakers."

A startled laugh escaped me and I turned to look at him. Archer flashed a rare, carefree smile and my heart just melted. Before I overthought it, I leaned over to press a soft kiss to his lips. It was chaste, a peck, really, but it sent shivers down my spine anyway.

I put all my thanks into that kiss that I couldn't translate into words. Did he understand how important he made me feel? How him making a joke to take the pressure off what had suddenly become a hard moment was the kindest thing anyone has done for me in a long time?

I hoped so.

I hoped he knew just how special he was.

More than anything, I wanted this day to last forever. Archer relaxed more than I had ever seen him, and that kiss in the surf... I would remember it always. What if tomorrow came and he was different? What if tomorrow he became the other Archer who I couldn't figure out, who sat with a world of space between us on the couch and left the second he could?

Once back on the beach, Archer led us a different way back to the car, which passed a tiny restaurant that pretty much sold burgers, fries and ice cream. We ate our fries as we sauntered back to his car.

Archer took us a long way back, weaving along country lanes where the scenery was so much prettier than anything near where we lived. His detour took so long that the sun had begun to set by the time he stopped outside my house.

The windows were dark, no lamps shone and the place looked as empty as it had earlier. My chest pinched. They hadn't even told me they would be gone all day. I slapped on a happy smile and turned to Archer. "Do you want to stay for food? I'll be ordering out anyway."

Archer scanned me with his eyes, either trying to find a

crack in my façade or stalling for time to come up with a good excuse. "Sure. You don't mind?"

I shook my head and got out of the car before I could realize the thoughts swirling around like hungry sharks were too heavy for me to have company. If I didn't play my cards right this could end horrifically. And Archer didn't seem to type to be able to handle a broken and distraught female.

This time we ordered Chinese and Archer fed Kit dumplings. That fox would going to have a weight issue soon. Once I had eaten my fill, I stood up from my spot on the floor to stretch. A huge yawn nearly split my face in half.

"Glad I'm such good company," Archer drawled.

I laughed. "Sorry. Sea air always makes me sleepy." I walked over to peer out of the glass doors. The yard was hidden in darkness and my own reflection looked back at me. "I wish there was more time in the weekends. Monday always comes around too fast."

"Any particular reason you don't want it to be over?"

I worried my bottom lip with my teeth. I didn't have the energy to come up with a lie. "Honestly? Because I don't want to go to school tomorrow and find out which Archer I'm going to get."

"And what the hell is that supposed to mean?" he asked, incredulous.

"I just can't figure you out. You run so hot and cold all the time. I mean, sometimes it doesn't even seem like you even like me very much." My stomach fluttered with nerves that almost made me want to barf. A part of me didn't care how hot and cold he was, I should have been grateful he was anything with me. It wasn't just because I was desperate for any kind of recognition or friendship, but I desperately wanted his. I wanted him to see me. And I needed to know if he saw.

"What gives you that idea?" Archer asked, his voice softer.

I turned to face him. "You're kind of icy, downright cold sometimes. You would initiate conversations with me then just walk off as if I didn't even show up on your radar anymore. Last night is a perfect example. The second the movie finished you couldn't wait to get out of here, but then you ask me to go for a drive with you. I mean, what the hell is that, Archer? Trying so hard to get away from someone one second and the next you're making plans with them?"

He snorted. "Christ, Lori! You were jumpy as hell last night. You think I was going to hang around for hours, making it look like was I waiting for something? Or expecting it? I left because that was the polite time to, and because I wanted you to know that I wasn't expecting something from you. And the reason I asked you to come for a drive? I wanted to spend time with you."

"Really?" I asked quietly, completely regretting my over-analyzing.

"Yeah, is that so hard to believe?"

I folded my arms across my chest. "Then what about all the times you're so short with me? Like the time at the surgery."

Archer slowly rose to his feet. "I would have thought that was obvious."

"I wouldn't be asking if it was."

"Well, for starters I'm only ever short with you because I'm mad at myself. In a stupid and asshole kind of way, it makes it easier."

"Easier than what?" My heart pounded against my chest. I was sure he would be able to see the frantic thrum.

"Admitting." Archer stalked toward me. His voice was a fraction softer when he next spoke. "That time in the surgery I was angry with myself for being so obvious. I had been there for two minutes and you stamped on my plan."

I frowned. "What plan?"

Archer looked down. "I got there late on purpose, Lori."

In my mind I replayed our exchange that night in the surgery when Archer came in to pay his bill. When I

141

mentioned he'd left it till almost closing time he pretty much ripped my head off with his icy tone. I squeezed my eyes shut, half in hope that he was admitting what I seriously hoped he was admitting, but too many other things stood in the way. "But what about Friday night? You kissed me, then it was like it never even happened."

Archer lifted his chocolate eyes and locked his gaze with mine. "Testing the waters. You gave off some pretty mixed signals yourself."

"I did?" I asked quietly.

He moved closer again, nodding once. "Half the reason I left so fast last night was because it seemed like you couldn't get far enough away from me."

I chuckled to myself and dropped my eyes to the floor. Man, that couldn't have been farther from the truth. Archer's sneakers came into view and my pulse spiked at his proximity. In a weird, detached sort of way I noticed some sand still stuck to his shoes.

Archer touched my arm and the skin sizzled. His other hand caught my chin and gently raised it so I had no choice but to meet his gaze. He kept his eyes on me the entire time it took for him to lower his mouth onto mine. Which was a long time when I waited for it.

Chapter Eighteen

Monday morning came round way faster than it needed to. The night before Archer had stayed late — hot, lazy kisses drawing out his departure. When I finally succumbed to sleep after replaying his lips on mine about a million times, I fell into such a deep slumber that I didn't even hear my alarm. Luck was with me and I wasn't late for school, but I also didn't have time to search out Archer. A part of me was terrified the night before had all been a dream, or he would regret everything and we would be left with a broken, awkward friendship.

My worries would chew a hole in my stomach and a tiny part of me didn't want to see him, just in case my fears materialized, despite his reassurances the night before.

I stopped by my locker before first period. I swung my messenger bag around front so I could load some books inside. Something hard caught my shoulder, knocking me into the row of lockers and throwing my bag onto the crowded hallway floor. Kimmie flashed a sneer at me before disappearing into the crowd.

I muttered something unladylike under my breath. As I picked up my battered bag and turned back to my locker, I almost jumped out of my skin when Archer leaned beside it.

"Oh!" I cried, as I ransacked my scrambled brain for something to say.

Archer stared down the hall with a crease between his eyebrows. "What was that about?"

"What?" I asked. "Oh, you mean Kimmie? Nothing. She's a hag."

"Does she have it in for you?" Archer asked, swinging his gaze to me.

"Oh yeah," I said as I plucked a few books from my locker. "We're, like, mortal enemies or something. At least that's what she thinks. Even after a year away from this place she still hates me."

"Why?"

I shrugged. "Who knows? Sometimes people just need someone to hate."

Archer looked back down the hallway for another few beats before letting the tension fall from his face and shifting his eyes to me again. "How are you?"

A nervous laugh bubbled in my throat. "Um, good. You?"

"You weren't in the quad this morning."

"I just got here — overslept this morning." I paused before turning to face him fully. "Were you worried?"

"About what?" he asked, his eyes tightening.

"Me. And how things would be in the cold hard light of high school."

"Don't be ridiculous," Archer muttered as he scowled at me.

A laugh bubbled in my throat when I realized I was dead on with my analysis. "I'm not being ridiculous. You were nervous about seeing me."

"I was not."

"Liar." I elbowed him in the ribs with a smile teasing my lips. Archer rolled his eyes, and if I hadn't been so used to it, I would have been offended when he left wordlessly.

* * * *

A sense of relief always washed over me when I made it through the wide doors as I left school. Another day done. But uncertainty and anxiety mingled with today's relief. Throughout the day whenever I saw Archer, he acted perfectly normal. And by perfectly normal, I mean pre-kissing, declarations and admission of feelings.

I didn't expect him to turn into a romantic Romeo or whatever and have him worship my every step. That wouldn't have been Archer, and therefore wouldn't have been the guy I was so crazy about. Really, if I looked deep down, I would realize my worries all came from my self-confidence.

Or lack of.

Just because I didn't want him to act any differently didn't mean I wasn't all for publicly showing we were now more than friends. And I was terrified he wouldn't. I didn't care the intents or reasons behind it, but people who have secret relationships, to me anyway, have only one reason for keeping it a secret — embarrassment. Why else hide it? This leads me to my anxiety and uncertainty. Did Archer want to keep me a secret?

I was so absorbed in my inner worrying, I almost walked right past Archer, leaning against his car door with his arms folded across his chest. "Never figured you to be the kind of girl to give a guy such a cold brush-off."

I whirled around to face him, half expecting a scowl to be on his face. Color me surprised when I saw the light, teasing expression. "Sorry," I said smiling. "I was on another planet. So…what are you doing?"

"Waiting for someone."

"Oh yeah? You want me to get out of your way then?"

Archer rolled his eyes and my heart give a little tug at his smirk. He reached out to grasp my hand and pull me toward him. Archer dipped his head and planted a soft kiss on my lips, pulling away too fast. "Any plans for this afternoon?"

"Um…no," I mumbled, head still reeling from the too-brief kiss.

"Good." Archer squeezed my hand and jerked his head toward the car, meaning for me to get in.

I couldn't wipe the smile off my face.

I guess that answered my worries, then.

Archer dropped me at home for a half hour so I could

spend a little time with Kit and change. Like always, I had no idea what Archer had in mind, so I kept it simple with a tank top and faded jeans.

I bounced on the balls of my feet by the time Archer returned to pick me up. We drove for a while and it occurred to me how much time Archer must spend just driving around. He hadn't grown up here, yet some of the roads he took only a local would know.

The lake was familiar the instant I spotted it—glassy and clear. Kids loved the lake. Tire swings hung from the overhanging branches and a few rowboats docked on one side. Archer didn't take me to that side. He took me to the side I'd actually never been before. The tall grass almost reached my hip.

"You want a drink or something?" Archer asked, walking around the car to the trunk.

"Yeah, thanks."

Archer had a cooler in his trunk and tossed me a chilled bottle of water and grabbed one for himself. He tucked a thick plaid blanket under his arm, then slammed the trunk and strode out into the tall grass.

I hurried after him, glad I had worn jeans. My legs would get eaten alive for sure. When I reached him, Archer had laid the blanket flat on the ground and sprawled out on one side of it. I lay down beside him, watching the white wispy clouds slowly dance above me.

"You're not like other girls, you know." Archer startled me by breaking the silence a good twenty minutes after we'd first lain down.

"What do you mean?" I asked, twisting my head around to peer at him.

"Most girls would be blabbing nonstop trying to fill the silence. Not you, though."

"Is that a bad thing?"

Archer snorted. "No. Definitely not."

"So why are you complaining?"

"I'm not, I'm just telling you that you're different. In a

146

good way."

"Mmm. Little ole freaky me."

Archer pushed up on one elbow to peer down at me. "You just proved my point. Any other girl would be all giggly and stuff at a compliment. You act like you're trying to figure out the punch line."

"Maybe I am," I muttered.

"Fine," Archer said with a huff. "Forget I said anything."

I groaned and sat up. "No, I'm sorry. It's just... I guess I'm out of practice with all this."

"All what?" Archer asked, cocking his eyebrow.

I gestured between our bodies. "Like dating and stuff. Intimacy and compliments. I'm not used to it."

"Will I regret asking why?"

A laugh bubbled in my throat. I wrapped my arms around my knees, hugging them to my chest. "I wish you knew me before. I used to be a real girl — one who could just take a damn compliment, or flirt her way out of anything. But then again, if you like me now I'm all weird and freaky, you probably would have hated me."

"Before what?"

"Huh?"

Archer sat up and plucked at the grass beside him. "You said you wish I knew you before. Before what?"

"Oh," I said softly. Damn. I'd really walked into that one. "Um, before I left school. When I started this year, it wasn't my first time at Westbrook, I spent my junior year at a different school."

"I remember."

A frown creased my forehead. "What do you mean?"

"The first day I met you in Mr. Poole's class you said you were the old-new kid."

"You remember that?" I asked, surprised

Archer nodded and pulled up more grass. A moment of silence hung between us. It wasn't as if I had anything to hide with my past. Hell, it was pretty much in the gossipmongers' scandal handbook at school. But Archer was flighty, and I didn't want to freak him out—or, worse, scare him off. "So why'd you leave?"

If it had been anyone else apart from Archer asking, I'd say they already knew and were just fishing for insider info. But he was the one person at our school who talked to fewer people than me. It was possible he had no idea. "My brother died." Even just saying the words seemed to hurt. But this kind of thing was like ripping off a Band-Aid. Best to get it over with fast. "My parents couldn't deal so I went to live with my grandma. I was home schooled and had tutors for junior year. I'd probably still be there if she hadn't had her stroke. Bad luck for my parents."

"Why?"

"They had to take me back." I sneaked a glance at Archer and saw a crease between his brows. "You're not like other boys."

His head snapped around to me. "What?"

I smiled, though it probably didn't convince him. "Most other guys would be full of half-hearted condolences, probably trying to use what happened as a way to get me naked."

Archer snorted. "Now there's an idea." He jerked away to miss me swatting him. "But in all seriousness, I don't really see the point in telling you I'm sorry, or I wish I could have met him, or how rough it must be. Doesn't matter if I mean it or not, it doesn't make a difference to you. It still hurts, no matter what anyone says to try to comfort you."

A thick lump formed in my throat. "Thank you."

He shrugged.

"No, seriously, thank you. When Derek first died so many people told me they were sorry it didn't even sound like a word anymore." I shuddered, remembering the days following his death. "There were always people around me. I couldn't breathe. Guess that was the curse of popularity. All those people trying so hard to be your friend, I don't think they even once tried to actually get to know me."

"Were you happy?" Archer asked. "Before everything

happened."

I sighed. It was a question I'd asked myself countless times. "Honestly? No. I just didn't know any better. Looking back, I can see how shallow I was. I had so many friends, so many guys wanting to date me. But it didn't mean anything. I never thought to question why I didn't confide in anyone except Derek."

"So you guys were close?"

I laughed. "I loved him, and hated him, more than anything."

"Everyone must have wanted to be his friend so they had a reason to visit, secretly hoping to catch sight of his hot sister."

This time he didn't get out the way as I playfully swatted him. "Not even. Derek didn't care about being popular. And he always warned me to stay away from his friends." I couldn't stop the smile that spread across my face. "He used to say it was because I'd break their hearts, but he didn't think his friends were good enough for me. I heard him chewing out one of his friends once who said something about me, saying no way would his sister end up with a stoner loser."

"Stoner? Was Derek a pothead?"

"To start with."

Archer shifted as he took this information in. When he didn't probe further, I figured he got what I meant. "So was he older or younger or what?"

"I've no idea."

"What?"

I grinned. "Derek and I are…were…twins. When we were kids my mom refused to tell us which one was born first. She never showed us our birth certificates. Derek always joked and said I was the younger one. Would even call me little sis sometimes. I guess it doesn't really matter anymore."

"That's pretty cool. Having a twin, I mean."

I shrugged. "It made it worse when he died. I'm not

149

saying if he was just an older or younger brother it would have hurt less, but afterward the absence of him almost killed me. I'd never been alone before, he'd always been there, you know? Even now sometimes it's like I'm walking off balance, like there's something missing."

Archer watched my face, as if trying to find a sign of me breaking down and losing it.

I let out a breath and leaned my hands behind me, supporting myself. "Pretty heavy, huh?"

"What, are you apologizing?"

"Maybe."

"Why?"

"It's not really cheerful, is it? It's a beautiful afternoon, we should be making out or something, not talking about my dead brother."

He arched an eyebrow. "Do you want to make out?"

I blushed.

"Look," Archer said, twisting toward me before I had a chance to get too embarrassed. "Everybody has something that hurts them. Don't apologize for having pain in your life or for talking about it. Whatever you need to say, I can handle it, okay? Stop worrying I'm going to disappear whenever you show some emotion. I wouldn't be into you if you were a robot."

"You're kind of awesome." Wow, that would have been a 'moment' had I had the courage to look at him when I said it.

Archer scoffed. "I'm not so great." For a second I expected him to shut off as he used to. He scanned the sky above us before turning back to me with a grin. "Now what were you saying about making out?"

My breath caught, right before Archer reached for me.

* * * *

It was dark when Archer drove me home. At a stop light, I scanned the darkened streets absentmindedly. We were opposite the Grill and my stomach jolted when I saw Cam step out onto the street. Kimmie followed soon after him, and he draped an arm around her shoulders before they walked off together.

Archer snapped my attention back to him as he squeezed my knee. I opened my mouth to point them out, before thinking better of it. Archer had been pissed when he saw the mess Cam left my arm in. I couldn't guarantee Archer would just leave it alone.

I forced Cam and Kimmie from my mind, scooted closer to Archer and let the heat from his body comfort me.

Chapter Nineteen

I chewed on my nail. Kimmie stood alone at her locker, shoving books into it in a messy heap. Despite being a total bitch and the meanest girl I'd ever had the misfortune of pissing off, I couldn't keep my knowledge about Cam to myself. A cruel part of me wanted to reason that Kimmie was a big girl and more than capable of taking care of herself.

The night before, my conscience had fought a bloody war on what I should, and what I wanted to, do with the information on Cam. In fact, I'd been so distracted, I had started to get out of the car without even a backward glance when Archer had stopped at my house.

Archer had chuckled. "Again with the brush-off. You know how to hurt a guy."

Cringing, I'd turned back around, relieved when I'd seen his lips twitch into a smile. I'd let out a breath. "I'm sorry. I can't remember where I left my brain today."

He'd shrugged. "You've got a right to be distracted."

"I do?" Had he seen Cam too, and not wanted to scare me by pointing him out?

Archer had nodded. "I'm not getting the impression you talk about your brother a lot. It's got to take a lot out of you when you do."

"Right." I'd laughed breathily. "Right."

"Are you going to be okay? I can come in with you if you don't want to be alone."

Wow. Really, seriously, very tempting. But I'd be crappy company. I'd forced a smile. "I'll be fine. But thank you, though."

He had rolled his eyes. "Like I offered completely selflessly."

A laugh had bubbled in my throat. "And here I thought you were a gentleman."

"I am so the perfect gentleman."

I'd arched an eyebrow. "Oh? You won't be wanting a goodnight kiss then?"

He had caught my wrist and tugged me closer. "I'm not that much of a gentleman."

"Didn't think so," I'd whispered, my heart fluttering as his mouth had pressed down on mine.

I took a deep breath and crossed the hall to Kimmie. "You got a minute?"

Kimmie slowly turned to face me. "What?"

I stepped closer, lowering my voice. "I need to tell you something."

"You found your brother's stash?" she asked, deadpan.

"Excuse me?"

"Well, you've got to be high right now. What the hell do you think you're doing? You know I hate you, right?"

I sighed. "Trust me, I don't want to be here any more than you do. But I still have something to tell you."

Kimmie slammed her locker shut and pushed past me.

I swore under my breath and started after her. "I saw you last night with Cam."

She spun to face me. "And?"

"And he's an asshole. He'll hurt you, Kimmie. Bad."

She snorted. "Aw, worried about my feelings? Do me a favor, Lori? Fuck off."

"I'm trying to help you out here. Cam is bad news. Stay away from him."

"You're trying to help me out? Well, let me help you out. Get out of my face, stay out of my business, or I'll break your nose. Got it?"

It seemed Kimmie didn't appreciate my good intentions. She upped her bitch game for the rest of the day—bumping into me so hard I fell into my locker, tripping me up on my way past her desk, spreading rumors I was using like Derek.

I didn't expect Archer to wait for me after school. I had work this afternoon, and while I'd have given my right leg for an afternoon like yesterday, I couldn't help the excitement when I got to the surgery. I'd never been away for so long and I was eager to see Doug and the animals.

At six-thirty, the chime above the door sounded. I was in the back helping Doug, and headed through to reception to see who'd come in. Cam leaned on the reception desk. Cold, hard fear stopped me in my tracks.

"Hey, Lo." He smiled, flashing perfect white teeth. He resembled a wolf baring his teeth to his victim.

"What are you doing here?" I asked. My voice choked in my throat and I had to force the words out.

"Came to see you. I heard something today and I didn't like it. Can you guess what it was?"

"Get out," I choked out past the thick lump of fear.

Cam laughed. "That's not very polite. Where are your manners?"

"I mean it. Get out and leave me alone. And stay away from Kimmie."

Cam's face twisted in rage as he pointed an accusing finger at me. "You keep the fuck out of my business! I'll do what I want, you hear? And no little prick tease like you is going to stop me. You'd do well to listen, Lo. Kimmie isn't happy with you. And I'm very unhappy with you."

The door behind me opened and Doug stepped out into reception. Relief flooded through me so fast I almost lost all feeling in my legs. "Hi," he said to Cam.

Cam smoothed his face back into its charming mask. "Hello." He looked back at me. "I'll be seeing you, Lo." He tapped the desk for a second before striding out of the door.

I had an awful, burning sensation in the pit of my stomach that, yes, he would.

"Friend of yours?" Doug asked.

"No," I whispered.

Doug gave me a quizzical look before heading into the back again.

When seven rolled around, I toyed with the idea of asking Doug if I could sleep in the surgery. If it hadn't been for Kit I probably would have. The last thing I wanted to do was walk home with Cam the Crazy out in the darkness somewhere.

But as we locked up, Doug chuckled. "You've got a regular fixture around you."

For a terrifying moment I though he meant Cam had returned, but when I looked in the direction Doug nodded, I saw Archer parked down the street with Harlo hanging out of the window. "See you!" I cried before bolting toward the car.

I heard another chuckle from Doug, but all I focused on was getting in that damn car.

Harlo barked her greeting and hopped around the front seat. She made room for me to get in, then clambered onto my lap, smothering me with welcome kisses. I pressed my face into her glossy coat, the drum of her heart echoing against my ear. I sighed, safe in the knowledge that Archer wouldn't notice.

Archer ordered Harlo to move. She jumped into the backseat but kept her face close to us.

"This is a nice surprise," I said, relieved to hear my voice sounded normal.

Archer smiled and started the car. "Yeah. Would have been nice if that had been my greeting."

He'd never know it was taking all my willpower not to climb onto his lap right now.

* * * *

I bumped—literally—into my old *friends* the following day at school. I headed out of the girls' bathroom as the trio passed, and walked smack into Jill.

"Walk much?" she asked with a sneer, shoving hard into

my shoulder as she carried on down the hallway.

Sarah swung her gaze to mine. Her purse slid from her shoulder, hitting the linoleum and spilling contents everywhere. "Shoot," she said, trying to hide a smile. "Don't wait for me," she called to the other girls

Rachel, who had looked back at the thud, nodded and carried on trailing behind Jill.

"Sneaky," I said, hiding a smile myself as I bent to help Sarah gather her stuff.

"You would expect anything else?" Sarah grinned. Her face softened as she held my eye. "How are you?"

"Good. You?" I asked, with a more genuine smile than I would have predicted.

Sarah shrugged.

I chuckled. "That doesn't sound like the rehearsed 'Life in the In Crowd Is the Best' speech."

She paused in collecting her stuff and locked her gaze with mine. "You're the only one who wouldn't buy it."

A few yards down the hall, Rachel turned back to us. She lifted her eyebrows at Sarah and me, before rushing to catch up with Jill.

"Uh-oh, busted…" I said in a singsong voice.

Sarah laughed. "I couldn't care less."

"Rebel."

She smiled "So. It seems someone is keeping you company these days."

A blush warmed my cheeks.

Sarah nudged me with her elbow, a grin spreading across her pretty face. "Come on, tell me all about him. No one knows anything about that kid."

I opened my mouth to start rambling about Archer and his awesomeness and how he made me feel special and always listened…but then I remembered who Sarah reported to.

Her smile fell. I had hurt her.

"Sarah—" I started.

"No, don't worry about it," she said holding up a hand. "I get it. If things were different, I wouldn't trust you either."

"I want to, it's just…"

"Yeah, I know." She looked at the ground before lifting her eyes, a smile once again lighting up her face. "Who knows? Maybe one day all this crap won't be here and we can actually hang out, be friends."

I laughed quietly. "Right. When the punishment isn't death by firing squad."

She giggled. "Right."

"I'd better…" I pointed down the hallway.

"Me too…" She pointed after Jill and Rachel.

"Take it easy."

"You too."

Sarah flashed me a sad parting smile. My mind flickered back to when things were fine and normal — in other words, before I left. How had I not seen the true nature of Sarah? How her ditzy persona hid a real person? One who was sweet and caring and saw way more than she let on. Of course, I knew the answer. Because she had her role to play, and I had mine.

* * * *

I was determined to make Kimmie see sense. After my 'whatever that was' with Sarah, I hunted her down. "That hoodie I wore? That was so I could hide the bruises that Cam gave me. He's an asshole, Kimmie. Why won't you listen?"

Kimmie stared me down with a cold, hard glare. "Because you're a jealous little bitch. He told me all about you. How you came on to him downstairs in the Grill and he practically had to fight you off. Are you that desperate for some attention? You're pathetic."

"He threatened me last night." I said, folding my arms across my chest.

Kimmie smirked. "He'll have to make sure you listen next time then, won't he?"

Something in Kimmie's eyes as she walked away told me

that she knew exactly what Cam did last night. Oh yeah, she knew all right. And she did care—about seeing me suffer. So the girl who actively hated me was now in cahoots with the guy who'd loved to cause me some serious pain.

Shit.

Chapter Twenty

Archer kept up his routine of picking me up from work. A week after Cam's threat and nothing had happened so far. No surprise visits from him at the surgery, no abrupt hauling of me into darkened alleys — not that I went near any — and my fear slowly started to subside. It didn't make me complacent. I still scanned the streets before I darted out of the surgery and into Archer's car. The walks from my house to work gradually got scarier with the seasons changing, and the light along with it. Before long it would be dark early in the afternoon and I'd be begging Archer for a ride to work as well as from it — not that I ever asked him, he was always just there… There for me like he always seemed to be. He seemed to have a sixth sense about me and any perilous danger I seemed to find myself in.

Most nights we did something together. I would get into his car, waving goodbye to Doug, and Archer would drive us someplace. A few times we went back to the lake, others hitting run-down diners in the next town over where we wouldn't run into anyone from school.

I wanted to go to the Grill with him, to shoot some pool and laugh and play video games and choose songs on the jukebox. I'm neither a coward nor a defeatist, but there was no way I wanted what could be an awesome time with Archer turned into a night of hell just because of Jill, or Cam and Kimmie.

Friday night after work, Archer and I parked near the woods a few miles out of town, sprawled on the hood of his car, staring at the sky above. Stars always have bittersweet memories for me. Derek and I used to lie in the back yard for hours trying to find our favorite constellations (mine — the one shaped like the dog, Derek — the Milky Way because he liked the ring of it… I never had the heart to tell him that the Milky Way was a galaxy, not a constellation) talking about nothing important and everything that mattered. Then, when he started using more, he got paranoid saying satellites watched, collecting evidence so the feds could do a drug bust on him.

Somehow, with Archer, the bad memories didn't touch me. Out here with him, we made new ones.

"You know, I can't figure out what to call you," Archer said after a few minutes of silence.

His random announcement made me laugh. "Why?"

Archer twisted his head to look at me. "You've got three names. I can't decide what I should call you."

"You can call me whatever you want. You're the one who has to say it."

"You're the one who has to hear it." He smiled wolfishly. "Who do you feel like? Lori, Lo or Vixen?"

"Vixen is so completely and totally humiliating, so no for that one."

"That just leaves Lori or Lo."

I wrung my hands. "It might be nice to be Lori again."

"Why were you Lo in the first place? I've never heard anyone at school call you Lori. Wouldn't you prefer to just go by Lo?"

I shook my head. "Not anymore."

"Is it a Derek thing?"

A laugh bubbled in my throat. Was I that obvious or was he that observant of me? "Yeah. Everyone called me Lori — our parents, relatives, kids at our old school. Derek was the only one who called me Lo. I loved it. It was like it was just for us, you know? Then we moved here and Jill heard him say it. It spread like wildfire once she branded me Lo. No one would dare correct her. I've never been Lori at this school. And now it makes me feel cheap and shallow instead of special."

"It's time for a change, then."

"Sounds like a plan to me."

"Good to know, Lori."

I smiled. "What about you? What do you want me to call you?"

He grinned and shrugged. "Whatever you want."

"I'm serious."

"Archer is fine."

"But everyone at school calls you that. Won't it bug you?"

Archer shook his head. "To Kate, my aunt, I'm Jack, always have been. Then I came here and some jock asshole shouts my surname one afternoon and it stuck."

"So why would you want me to call you Archer when everyone else does?"

"Because I don't talk to everyone else, I talk to you. I couldn't give a crap what the jerks at school call me."

"Archer and Lori it is then."

"Has a nice ring to it, don't you think?"

* * * *

I strolled around the side of my house after a long, long drawn-out goodbye with Archer. The smile was on my face right up until I opened the sliding door and glimpsed the reflection in the glass.

I wasn't alone.

Cam stepped forward and pushed me inside.

Kimmie lurked behind him. She wiggled her fingers at me before darting a glance around the dark back yard. "He's gone. She's alone."

"You decided not to listen then, huh?" Cam asked, his voice soft—completely at odds with the fierce anger burning in his eyes. It made him seem all the more dangerous. "I warned you to keep out of my business but you just couldn't help yourself, could you? Did it never occur to you that Kimmie knew exactly who I was, but just didn't care? Stupid, interfering little slut."

"What do you want from me?" I choked out.

Cam backhanded me sharp across the face. My cheek stung and tears filled my eyes. I lurched backward. "What do I want?" he gritted out through his teeth. "Payback, perhaps? Make you realize that you had damn well better stay out of my business. No one likes it when a prick tease shoots her mouth off."

"I won't say anything, never, I swear," I whispered. Something told me it didn't matter what I said or how I pleaded. Cam followed a script, and nothing would make him falter.

"I don't believe you." Cam smiled as he stalked toward me. He reached into his jacket pocket and pulled out a small flick knife. "How about I cut out your tongue? You won't be saying much of anything then."

"Whoa, Cam," Kimmie said quietly. Her eyes widened as they flickered between Cam and the knife. "You never said anything about—"

"Shut up!" he bellowed. "Shut the fuck up! You told me you wanted her to pay…to suffer. So now she will." Cam turned to glare at Kimmie.

While his attention was diverted I turned and tried to bolt up the stairs. Cam was ready for me. He grabbed a handful of my hair and tugged me hard against his body. I winced as he pulled my hair harder, almost ripped it right out of my scalp.

A low, threatening growl came from the darkness. My heart thudded when I heard Kit. This wasn't like the growl he gave Archer when we argued, he meant business this time.

"What the fuck is that?" Cam demanded. When I didn't answer he yanked on my hair until I cried out. "I said what the fuck is that?"

"My fox, he's trying to defend me."

"Oh yeah?" Cam laughed. "He's not going to like this then." Cam held the knife to my throat and I couldn't help but whimper with fear.

Kit slinked into view, his belly low to the ground, ears flat against his head and teeth bared.

"Kit, shh, it's okay," I hushed, trying to comfort him.

"No, it really isn't," Cam said as he pressed the knife harder to my throat. The skin gave way with a sickening pop, a sharp, sudden pain followed by a warm trickle.

Kit got closer and Cam kicked out with a foot to try to deter him.

Bad move.

Kit snapped at Cam's foot, but missed. Cam snarled at Kit, angry that he wasn't scaring the fox. He kicked at him again, but this time Kit clamped down on his leg with all his might.

Cam bellowed in pain. He let go of me and tried to kick Kit off him. Cam lost his balance and fell to the floor. He swung out with his arm to Kit, but the animal saw and moved his attack onto Cam's forearm.

I'd heard stories about completely docile, peaceful, quiet dogs that wouldn't so much as accidentally nip your fingers while eating out of your hand turning into ferocious beasts to defend their owners. Kit was small, but he had teeth — sharp ones. And he had ancient instinct flowing through him, made more powerful by his need to protect me.

Blood poured from the wound, and Cam clenched his teeth. He punched at Kit and finally managed to pry his arm free. Cam bolted for the door and disappeared into the night. Acting fast, I slammed the sliding door into place before Kit could streak after him. I heard angry shouts from Kimmie, but I didn't care. I tugged on the string for the full-length blinds and tried to breathe normally once the black glass was covered.

Kit still bristled with his teeth bared. I moved around him and fell to the ground, leaning against the couch for support. "Shh, Kit, shh, it's okay," I whispered.

The fox inched closer to me. He finally relaxed and sat down, though he remained fixated on the door, as though expecting Cam to come back at any second. I didn't dare touch him, he was too on edge. Instead I worked on calming myself down.

Mom and Dad would be upstairs. I could go and find them, tell them what had happened.

But I couldn't make myself move.

It took a solid few hours before I had the courage to peel myself off the spot on the floor and take myself to bed.

Usually I sprawled every which way, getting tangled in my covers. That night I slept pressed against the wall, the sharpest knife I could find in my tiny kitchen under my pillow. Every time my eyelids drooped shut they sprang open, scanning the room for possible threats. Kit stayed on guard duty for most of the night, lying by my open bedroom door before jumping up and curling into me, his head on my stomach.

I finally drifted off to sleep somewhere in the early hours, despite the terror still thick in my veins.

Chapter Twenty-One

When I woke the clock read almost eleven. It took a moment to realize someone was hammering on the sliding door. I bolted upright and scrambled up the bed until I was in the corner, knees up to my chest with my hands flattened over my ears, wishing the noise would stop. The hammering continued and the pounding in my chest intensified. Kit leaped from the bed and ran into the living room. I heard him whine and scratch at the blinds.

A shadow cast over my bed through the small ground level window. Someone stared into my bedroom. A scream rose in my throat, piercing the air. I clamped a hand over my mouth, breathing hard.

Archer jumped back from the window as though it had electrocuted him. I swallowed the lump of fear in my throat and forced myself to walk through the living room and open the door for him. He hesitated at the doorway, taking in the scuffed and out of position rug and spattering of dried blood on the floor. When his eyes finally landed on me, looking like shit and still in yesterday's clothes, suspicion was written all over his face.

"What the hell happened?"

I opened my mouth to tell him it looked worse than it actually was, but my lip trembled and I didn't trust my voice. Archer was at my side in an instant, tucking me into his chest and wrapping his arms around me. He held me for the longest time, only letting go when I started to pull away from him.

Archer clasped my hand and led me into the bathroom. He ran a washcloth under the faucet and gestured for me to turn my head. He dabbed at my throat. The stinging reminded me of the knife held against it the night before. The cut was superficial and didn't even need a Band-Aid.

"Can you tell me what happened?" Archer asked quietly, wiping the dried blood from my throat.

The truth came spilling out of me, faster than I would have thought possible. Surprisingly, Archer was calm when I finished telling him every last detail.

"You know you have to go to the cops now, right?"

I nodded, squeezing my eyes shut. Cam had been at my house... In my home. I still had no concrete evidence against him, but I had to do something. I had to. Next time... I swallowed. Rationally, I knew I should have already contacted the police. But rational thought had been on a different planet after Cam disappeared the night before. "I will. Later. I can't right now."

"Do you want me to come with you?"

"You would do that?"

"Of course. Whatever you need."

Archer didn't crowd me the way some people would. He sat beside me on the couch and didn't pressure me to talk, or do anything, really. The day wore on and his mere presence soothed me. Kit stayed closer than Archer did, following me from room to room and standing guard at my feet.

"Hey, did you remember to call your boss and let him know you wouldn't be working today?" Archer call through to me while I tried to find a sweater.

Crap. "No, I forgot. I'll do it in a sec."

"I think he's here." Archer chuckled. "Looks like he's got a cop with him. You're so getting arrested for being a flaky employee."

I straightened. My stomach dropped and the blood in my veins turned ice cold. Somehow I managed to force myself to walk into the living room. I hovered in the doorway, glancing into the room to see Archer at the window on the opposite side. Doug got out of his truck to talk with the cop.

Archer turned to face me, a frown pulling at his eyebrows.

"Did you call the cops? Are they taking a statement here?"

I shook my head and watched as Doug made his way to the screen door. He met my eyes through the glass and gave me an unconvincing smile. Wrenching my eyes away from him, I looked at Archer. "Work stuff. It will probably take a while, you should go."

He seemed unconvinced. "I'll give you some privacy. I'll be outside."

The lump in my throat hardened as I tried to smile. Archer slid open the door, nodded at Doug and disappeared from sight. Doug peered behind him and held up a hand in a stopping gesture. Probably to the cop.

"Um, I forgot to call in sick this afternoon, I'm really sorry," I said feebly, still unmoved from my spot at the door.

"That's okay." Doug's voice was warm and slow, comforting. He took a step toward me.

"Don't," I croaked. "I know why you're here."

He hung his head. "I've seen the pictures. There's nothing I can do."

A sob rose in my throat. "He was protecting me, Doug. The asshole forced his way in here and came at me with a knife. He could have killed me."

"I know," Doug said quietly. "He's never shown any aggression before. It's completely out of character. The circumstances are understandable."

"Then leave," I whispered.

"I can't, Lori. It's only because it's you that it's me telling you this and not the cop."

"It's not fair," I choked. "He was protecting me—it's my fault."

Doug looked down.

The cop appeared in front of the screen door and gave Doug a pointed look. Doug nodded and turned to face me again. He took another step forward.

"No, wait," I said in a hurry. "What about First Bite Free? Doesn't that count for anything? You know his history, couldn't you give a statement and tell them I work with you and I can handle him, and, and…"

Doug's eyes radiated the pain that stabbed my heart. "It's different for Kit, Lori. He isn't some dog that bit a jogger or something. He's a wild animal who did extensive damage to a human being."

"Cam is not a human being. He's a cruel, poor excuse for a human," I hissed through my teeth.

"It doesn't matter. Cam spent four hours at the hospital last night getting his wounds treated and stitched up. By law, the hospital had to report it as an animal attack and this morning Cam went to the station and made it clear he wanted action taken against Kit." Doug sighed.

I shook my head. "No, no, that's a lie, Doug! Can't I tell my side of what happened?"

"Do you have a witness?" When my face fell Doug reached out to touch my arm. "It's done, Lori. I'm sorry. He wants the animal dead."

"The animal," I repeated bitterly. "He is not just some animal."

"I know, believe me, I know. We don't have long. You should get him. Do you want me to get your parents so they can come with us?"

The small, frightened little girl inside of me desperately wanted my mom. Instead I shook my head. "No." They hadn't approved of Kit, and on the rare occasions either of them had been in the back yard or the basement had even seemed afraid of him. I couldn't bear it if I sought my parents out for relief and they acted superior.

"Okay." Doug ducked out of the screen door. I watched him for a minute talking to the cop. At the absence of voices, Kit poked his head out from behind the couch. He sat at my feet, looking up at me with blissfully ignorant eyes. I crouched down beside him, slowly reaching a hand out to brush his coarse coat. Kit leaned forward to lick my ear. He jumped as Doug came back in, this time carrying a large animal travel kennel. Doug nodded to me and went into the kitchen to give us space.

Kit was already beyond curious at the kennel. He sniffed around it and the minute I opened the door he darted inside, padding around in circles. Kit sat down and looked at me triumphantly. I dug around in my pocket and produced a handful of his favorite treats. His ears flicked up and I tossed them inside for him.

Kit didn't react as I closed the door and slipped the lock into place. Standing, I vaguely felt Doug's hand on my shoulder. I nodded and before I knew what was happening, Doug had the kennel by its handle and was out of the door.

I started after him, following close behind as Doug talked again with the cop. We rounded the side of the house and Archer pushed off the side of his car where he waited. His eyes flitted between Doug as he opened the back of his truck and slid the kennel in, and me.

"I'm going with them," I said, nodding to where Kit was in the truck. "Kit might not like it."

Archer's forehead puckered as he tried to figure out the situation, but nodded. Doug held out his hand to help me into the back of the truck. I settled myself in front of the kennel and poked a few fingers through the grate so Kit could see and smell me. I didn't notice Doug close the tailgate, or the engine start, or even the journey. I only came back to reality when Doug touched my arm. Only then did I realize we had parked in the alley beside the surgery.

I hopped from the truck and followed Doug inside. We went in the side entrance. I couldn't stand seeing the concerned and sympathetic faces of my co-workers. In the exam room, Doug wore gloves as he tried to negotiate Kit onto the table. Kit growled, not in menace, but in fear of what he didn't understand. I helped lift him and held him still while Doug gave him the first shot that relaxed him. I encouraged Kit to lie down, and soon he was on his side, lying still though his eyes flickered around him, before always landing on me.

"I'll give you guys a minute," Doug said, his voice thick.

I ran my hand the full length of Kit, trying to force my brain to remember every part of him and how he felt under my touch and smelled. I lowered my face to his and kissed the end of his nose.

Kit blinked.

"You were awesome, you know that?" A tear ran down my face. "You were my best friend. You saved my life, Kit. In every way. I'm so sorry, Kit," I whispered.

Doug came back into the room when I had my face buried in Kit's coat. I didn't look when he gave him the injection that would slow his heart. I didn't look at Kit once he was still.

"What do you want to do, Lori?" Doug asked softly. "We can take care of him, or do you..."

"I don't know," I croaked, my throat swelling as I struggled to force the words out. "I'd like to, myself, you know."

"Of course. Call me in the morning when you decide. I'm sure your friend could help."

I nodded and left before Doug had a chance to utter any condolences. It occurred to me, as I hurried from the surgery out onto the street where Archer stood waiting for me, that I hadn't cried yet. The tears were there, waiting to fall, but I couldn't let myself crumble yet. I didn't want to feel the hurt.

Archer tucked me into his chest and guided me toward his car.

Chapter Twenty-Two

Archer seemed to know what I needed without me ever saying a word. He slowed to a stop outside a small, nondescript two-story house. I'd never been to his house before, Archer choosing to keep that side of his life private. I saw in a detached, seeing but unaware sort of way the small front yard with dead, yellowed grass, the porch that was in serious need of a touch-up.

I followed Archer wordlessly inside. He tossed his keys into a dish in the entryway and led the way into his small living room. I hovered in the middle of the room, unsure what to do.

"I'm going to get you a drink," Archer said.

I nodded and Archer wandered off down the hall. A moment later Harlo's excited barking broke the silence, with Archer greeting her. Harlo's nails clicked on the hardwood floor as she bounded into the living room. She stopped at the doorway and observed me, a soft whine in her throat — a sound that pierced my heart.

As I dropped onto the couch, Harlo slunk toward me. She rested her chin on my knees and looked up at me with mournful eyes. I chewed on my thumbnail, anxious and torn over what I should do and what I wanted to do. Harlo was trying to comfort me, picking up on my distress. A part of me wanted to stroke her for trying to help. Another part wanted to scream and push her away, craving a different animal to be in her place.

The former won out and I placed my hand on her head, stroking her soft ears. Archer came into the room but halted at the doorway. He collected himself a moment later and held out a glass of iced tea for me. He sat beside me as I accepted it, leaning against him as though the contact would be enough to jump-start my body into healing. Harlo jumped onto the couch, throwing as much of herself as she could onto my lap. I sighed before taking a gulp of the cold liquid.

It burned my throat, and I spluttered as Archer tried to warn me. "Uh, I'd take it easy with that."

"You go all the way to Long Island for this?"

He smirked sheepishly. "Figured you could use it."

"Good call."

When I finished the drink, Archer relieved me of the glass. "Can you eat?"

I shook my head.

"I need to walk Harlo. Do you want to come, or you can stay here if you want?"

Being alone terrified me. Surely once alone the floodgates would open and the grief would crash down on me. Not that taking Harlo for a walk was a more appealing option — just the lesser of two evils. "I'll come."

Archer rose from the couch and paused as he looked out of the window. "My aunt's home."

I followed his gaze and saw a woman wander up the front path and fish keys out of her purse. She looked the polar opposite of Archer. While Archer was dark-haired and tan, his aunt was creamy skinned with shining blonde waves.

"Is she a nurse?" I asked, noting her clothes.

"Yeah."

The front door swung open and Harlo bolted to greet her. Archer's aunt tried to walk around Harlo as she came into the living room, which wasn't easy with a dog darting around her.

"Okay, okay! I see you!" She laughed. She looked up and saw me. Her face faltered for a second before regaining composure. "Hi."

I tried to smile. "Hey."

"This is Lori," Archer offered, jamming his hands into his

pockets. At least I wasn't the only one he was guarded with.

"Nice to meet you, Lori. I'm Kate." Her wide and open smile would, in normal circumstances, be contagious.

"We're going to walk Harlo."

Kate's eyes flickered between Archer and me for a moment. "Tell you what, why don't I do that? I could use the exercise."

"You don't mind?" Archer asked. "You just got off work."

"It's no trouble. You guys relax."

We waited in the living room for a few minutes while Kate changed. Once she and Harlo left, Archer took my hand and led me upstairs. He opened one of the three doors and pulled me inside. Archer's room was sparse, but somehow still radiated him. Books were piled randomly around the room. An old model computer stood on an older-looking desk. The chair had a dark T-shirt thrown on the back of it and I spotted a collar of Harlo's tossed on top of the bureau.

Archer closed the door behind him and moved across the room. He turned on his small TV in the corner and picked up a DVD disk to put in the player. I sat on the floor and leaned my back against his unmade bed. Archer picked up a remote and sat beside me.

The Grudge started.

Archer played movie after movie, neither of us ever speaking.

* * * *

Hours later I rubbed my eyes with the heels of my hands. I'd lost count of how many movies we'd watched.

"You should try to get some sleep," Archer said.

I kicked off my shoes and crawled into Archer's bed, not caring that I was fully dressed and being over-presumptuous. I hadn't exactly been invited. I pressed my face into one of his pillows and Archer's scent worked a calm through my body. Lifting my head, I watched Archer take a pillow and a blanket from the bottom of the bed and arrange them on the floor. "What are you doing?" I asked, frowning.

"You look like a bed hog," Archer said, his face serious.

"Oh," I said quietly, hearing the disappointed tone in my voice.

Archer studied me for a minute before sighing. He tossed the pillow back into place on the bed before climbing in bedside me. "I'm warning you, I'm possessive. I like my blankets. Okay? No stealing."

"I promise."

Archer pulled the blankets over our bodies. We lay in the quiet darkness until I could stand it no longer.

"I have to call Doug in the morning. When I decide what I want to do with..."

"What usually happens?" Archer asked, turning his head toward me.

"The surgery can dispose of it," I said monotonously, thinking back to past experiences with other clients. "Or they can arrange for a cremation and I can have the ashes. Or I can take care of it. Do it myself."

"What are you going to do?"

"I don't know. Nothing sounds appealing."

"It never will." Archer let out a breath. "What about that spot under the swing in your back yard?"

"To bury him?"

"Yeah. He liked it, didn't he?"

"I guess." I swallowed the hard lump in my throat. "It's my fault."

"What is?" Archer asked carefully.

"Kit. The fact that he's dead. He'd never have been in that situation if it hadn't been for me."

Archer rolled toward me. "What do you mean?"

"He should never have been reared by humans."

"But you saved him, he would have died without your help."

"Maybe at first." It felt weird saying it out loud. I'd thought it so many times and beat myself up over it for

174

months. I'd figured it would be a relief to admit to someone, to ease the guilt a little. It didn't. "The first rule they teach you when working with wild animals is rehabilitation over adoption."

"What do you mean?" Archer asked softly.

"With all wild animals there's usually a good chance they can be released back into the wild. Except imprinted animals. An animal that's imprinted on a human has two choices—life with humans, or euthanasia. They can't ever return to the wild after imprinting."

"What is imprinting?"

"It's kind of the animal's way of identifying their parent. That's why you have to be careful when handling young animals. If they imprint on you...then it's over. They can't ever leave you." I let out a breath. "I'd been home for a week when I found Kit. I was walking in the woods behind my house and I saw his den had caved in. There was trash and stuff around it, some joint butts. I figured some assholes found it and their idea of fun was to destroy some poor animal's home. There was no sign of his family and he was so small. He was calling for his mother and looked half starved.

"I couldn't stand the idea of leaving him alone out there, so I picked him up and took him home. I gave him some food and by the next morning I could tell he was pretty attached to me. It wasn't until later in the day that I finally got my ass down to see Doug and tell him what had happened. I was due to start working for him the following week, so I knew I could trust him. I took Kit with me and Doug gave him a clean bill of health, but noticed that Kit had imprinted on me. It's easy to do, especially when they're so young. Doug figured Kit to only be four weeks old."

"Did you know it would happen? The imprinting, I mean."

"No. It was after that Doug explained it all to me. We talked about what I would need to do, how to care for him."

"I'm not seeing how this is your fault."

175

I sighed and twisted my head away from Archer, unable to meet his eyes when admitting my ugliest trait. "It's my fault because I was so damn lonely. I was so desperate for any kind of love that I took away a decent life from a poor animal. It wasn't Kit who needed someone, it was me."

Archer reached across for my hand. He laced his fingers with mine and squeezed. "Lori, Kit loved you. Yeah, he would have had a pretty different life if you hadn't found him that day in the woods. He would have died."

"He died anyway," I mumbled, my eyes stinging.

"That isn't your fault. Look at why he died — it was because he loved you so much. He'd have done anything for you. And he did. He protected you because he loved you."

A lump formed in my throat. "He didn't know any better. He would have had a better life if I'd never found him."

"Like I said, it would have been different. How do you know it would have been better? Kit loved his life with you. He was happy, Lori."

I let out a shaky breath and hugged the covers tighter around me. "Do you really think he would like the spot under the swing?"

"Yeah, I do." Archer leaned over to kiss my temple. "Now what did I say about hogging the covers?"

Chapter Twenty-Three

It was late when I woke the following morning. It took a minute for me to remember there wouldn't be any paraphernalia for me to send crashing to the floor. No curious nose nudging my hand to see what I could have tucked into it. With a heavy sigh, I rolled over. The other side of the bed was empty.

Gentle music played somewhere in the house and directly below me I could hear someone moving around. I lay for another few minutes and decided Archer wasn't coming back in a hurry. It took all my effort to drag myself from the bed, and ventured downstairs in search for him.

Kate sat at the small table in the kitchen, munching on toast. Harlo sat at her feet, doing her best to appear sweet enough to snag some for herself. "Morning," she said with a smile.

I smiled shakily in response. She wasn't looking at me as if I was a hussy, but I blatantly had 'I Spent the Night in the Same Bed with Your Nephew' stamped on my forehead. I bit my tongue to keep from screaming that we both kept our clothes on.

"Jack had to run an errand, he shouldn't be long. Do you want some coffee?"

"Yeah, thanks. I can get it, though," I said, not wanting to impose.

She waved her hand. "Don't even think about it. Sit. I'll take care of it."

I sat in the chair opposite the one she'd vacated. Kate moved around the kitchen, fetching me a mug that didn't match anything else on the table then buttering a few slices of toast.

"Do you want some bacon? Eggs?" she asked.

"No, I'm fine, really. Uh, thanks, though."

"You sure? It's no problem. You've got to speak up, though, okay? You want something, just holler. Jack sure does."

I smiled. "I can imagine."

Kate placed the coffee and toast in front of me. I soon became Harlo's center of attention. Kate sighed. "That looks really boring. I've got some bagels too if you'd prefer?"

"No, really, this is great. I never usually bother with breakfast, so this is nice. Really." I enjoyed having someone fuss over me. It was kind of awkward and I wasn't sure how to not offend her by refusing the bacon and stuff, but she was a grown-up and she wanted to take care of me. I'd missed that. A lot.

Kate didn't seem harassed as she busied herself around the kitchen. A lot of parents would shout at the kids to eat up or you'll get what I'm making, nothing else. I guess Kate was one of those rare people who just liked to take care of people and make them happy.

She topped off her own mug with coffee and sat opposite me. Harlo glanced to make sure Kate didn't have any more food and quickly turned her attention back to me. "I wish I could offer you something nice, but my culinary skills don't stretch far. Jack, however, makes a mean batch of pancakes."

"Really?" I asked smiling. I hadn't had Archer pegged as a cook.

Kate grinned. "Oh yeah. Like I need the carbs. But, seriously, they're heaven. I'll tell him to make you some when he gets back."

"Oh no, that's okay," I said in a rush.

Kate winked. "Come on, if I say they are for me I might not get them. You, on the other hand, I get the feeling he'd do anything for."

A blush burned my cheeks.

It made Kate smile wider. "How long have you guys been friends?"

"Not long," I said. "Just since I started back at my old school at the beginning of the semester."

Kate's eyes looked curious for a beat, but she didn't push for information. Guess Archer's trait was hereditary. "I'm glad you guys are close."

"How can you tell?" I asked, squirming a little in my chair. "That we're close, I mean."

She smiled. "You wouldn't be here if you guys weren't. Jack is...cautious with new people coming into his life. He's lived with me for over a year now and this is the first time I've been introduced to anyone."

I nodded. "The kids at school are jerks. I don't blame him for not hanging out with any of them."

Kate rolled her eyes. "I remember well. My high-school days were harsh. But there's obviously something about you he likes. I was getting worried about him. It's not healthy to be so unsocial."

"No, I guess it isn't."

"Has he told you why he lives with me?"

"No."

"You haven't asked?"

I shook my head.

"Aren't you curious?"

I let a breath. "A little. But if he wanted me to know he'd tell me."

Kate settled back in her chair, a funny expression on her face.

"What?" I asked cautiously.

"Nothing. I'm glad he has you, that's all."

Harlo startled me by scrambling out of the room and barking. A moment later, the front door opened and closed. A smile spread over my face when I heard Archer's voice as he greeted an overexcited Harlo.

"Oh, hey," Archer said, smiling when he saw me as he came into the kitchen. "You been up long?"

"Not very."

He leaned over me and snatched my remaining slice of toast. Archer demolished it in four decisive bites before he turned to his aunt. "You didn't force feed her, did you?"

"No," Kate said.

Archer looked down at me. "Did she?"

Kate gasped. "I didn't!"

"I'll bet. Kate has this overwhelming need to feed people. All the time."

Kate rolled her eyes and stood up. "Ingrate."

Archer grinned and dropped into her chair.

"I've got to get to work." Kate shifted her eyes to me. "See you soon, Lori? Take care, okay?" She touched my shoulder as she left the room.

Archer reached for my half empty coffee cup and drained the contents. He waited until he heard his aunt leave the house before speaking. "Sorry I left this morning."

"It's okay."

Archer asked with a frown. "Were you okay being here and everything? Kate can be pushy, but she means well."

"Kate's awesome. You're lucky to have someone who cares so much about you." Archer grinned in relief. "It's a good thing you came back when you did. I was a minute away from asking if I could move in."

He smirked. "Kate would love someone else to fuss over."

"She never wanted kids herself? Not that it's too late, or anything." Damn, how do I walk into these kinds of things?

Archer shrugged. "She was pretty serious with her high-school boyfriend. They only split a few years ago, I'm not sure on the details. But knowing Kate she'd love a house full of people. Who knows? Like you said, it's not too late."

"She'd make a really good mom."

He nodded and shifted in his seat. "I uh, I have something to tell you."

Unease stirred in my gut. "What?"

"This morning when I left... I went to your place."

"Why?" I asked quietly.

"I dug a spot under the swing."

The room suddenly was too cold with my body too hot.

Archer reached forward and grasped my hand, his eyes frantically searching my face. "You have every right to get upset, but I wanted to do it for you. I figured if you still wanted to bury Kit there then at least it was ready and waiting. After you fell asleep last night, I thought it would be really hard for you to watch it being dug. And if you've changed your mind I can fill it back in, no problem."

I swallowed. The lump threatened to return.

Archer's face paled as I stood up. "Lori—"

The tears stayed at bay as I slid onto his lap and burrowed my face in his neck. His arms snaked around my middle and he let out a quiet sigh of relief beside my ear. "Thank you," I whispered.

* * * *

Doug met us at my house once the surgery had closed for the evening. I stood facing the direction of the woods as Archer placed Kit in the earth. Before he filled the grave, I got Archer to drape a blanket over Kit's body. It was one he'd dragged around all over the house, and even outside if the mood struck him. I'd no idea why he formed such an attachment to it, but that was the thing with attachments. They didn't need to make any sense.

When the grave was filled, Archer and Doug shifted some big stones both to mark the spot and to deter any animals that might get curious over the freshly disturbed dirt.

I still didn't cry.

Before he left, Doug hugged me and told me not to worry about work for a week or two. At first I panicked. Surely having so much free time would be worse. But Archer slipped his hand into mine and laced our fingers. I let out a breath.

Chapter Twenty-Four

The cold, unwelcoming sliding doors reflected the yard back to us, a nicer image than the empty rooms beyond.

"You don't have to go in if you don't want to," Archer said. "You can come back to my place."

"No. I need to face it sometime, right? Might as well be now." The silence was the first thing I was aware of. Kit used to greet me with excited yips and prod with his nose all the stuff he collected sporadically through the day. I swiveled around to Archer. "You're off babysitting duty. I don't mind if you leave. In fact, I want to be alone for a while."

He raised an eyebrow. "I'll stick around, if it's all the same to you. You can go into your room if you want to be alone."

It took all my self-control not to throw myself on him. Instead I walked slowly into my room, needing to change anyway. Being alone was the last thing in the world I wanted, but I didn't want him to feel obligated.

I perched on the edge of my bed and hugged a pillow to my chest. What had I done to deserve someone like Archer? He was definitely one of the strong, silent types. The kind who came through for you. The kind you held on to and prayed you didn't mess anything up. I pressed my face into the pillow as my emotions fought a bloody war inside my body. My grief that threatened to spill over at any moment and hold me captive was somewhat diluted by a swell of feelings and gratitude toward Archer. I sucked in a deep breath, trying to get a hold of myself.

And that's when it hit me.

Kit...

How many nights had Kit curled up on this pillow with his head tucked under my neck? Too many to count. His scent was embedded in the pillow and the memory of him slammed into me with the force of a wrecking ball.

I threw it to the side and jumped to my feet. "I'm going to take a shower," I croaked to Archer en route to the bathroom. I barely made it under the hot stream of water before the tears cascaded down my face in rivulets. After a while I sank to my knees as I willed the tears to stop and the pain to ease. The water grew cold and neither happened. It was only when my shivering turned violent that I turned off the shower and wrapped myself in a towel. I clung to the edge of the sink and took deep gulps of air until the sobbing stopped.

When I opened the bathroom door, Archer was there. He reached for me and pulled me into a full body hug, squeezing me every bit as tight as I needed.

* * * *

We went straight to bed. Archer set up the TV in my room. Somehow it was easier to not-watch something lying down than it was to sit up and stare in the living room. I wore a shorts and tank top pajama set and watched with horror as Archer started to get into my bed with all his clothes on.

"What?" he asked, uncertainty in his voice as he caught my look.

Either he was being respectful...or I was so undesirable that he couldn't even contemplate climbing into my bed less than fully clothed. "That's so uncomfortable. If you sleep in your clothes it'll be for the second night in a row."

"So?"

"Take your clothes off." God, I sounded pushy...and like a giant pervert. "If you want."

He raised an eyebrow. "If you want to see some skin you could just say, it's not a problem. You don't have to make excuses."

Any other time I would have blushed so hot it would have set the blankets on fire. There was no energy for it that night. "Fine, I just want to see some skin. It'll make me feel better."

Archer shook his head, though he complied — pulling off his sweater and jeans, climbing into bed in his boxers and dark T-shirt. I followed after him, the only light in the room coming from the glow of the TV as the studio logo came on screen. As we settled down Archer draped his arm across my waist, his stomach to my back. Did everyone fit together this well? Two halves of the same perfect, amazing, wonderful whole?

Halfway through the movie I rolled onto my back.

"What's wrong?" Archer asked, his voice low.

"Nothing. I feel weird."

"Weird how?"

"I'm not sure. Like I'm running on empty. Like there's something else I should be doing. Kind of numb."

"You should be letting yourself feel the pain over Kit." He moved some hair from my face, sending a tingle down my spine.

I shook my head. "I can't. Before... That was — no, I can't. Not yet." Once I stopped the river of tears I'd clamped the lid shut on my feelings again. They rattled somewhere deep inside me, ready to burst free and ruin me again. "I need a distraction."

"That's what the movie is supposed to be doing."

"It isn't working."

"What will?"

I looked at Archer, his flawless face illuminated by the glow from the TV. "You."

His eyebrows shot up into his hairline. "Me?"

All at once it made perfect sense. The warmth that Archer bloomed inside of me would be enough to dispel the darkness in my heart. "Yeah. Make me feel something else, something better."

"Lori," Archer whispered. "There isn't a quick fix for this.

The sooner you start, the sooner you can deal with it and it will stop hurting so bad."

I pushed up onto my elbow so I hovered over him. "Would you stop me?"

"Stop you what?"

His mouth was unyielding at first—shocked at my sudden kiss. I slid a hand under his T-shirt, dragging my fingertips over the hard muscle and sculpted planes of his chest. Archer hissed at my touch, returning the kiss. His fingers knotted in my hair, the other hand on the small of my back, pinning me to him. I lost myself in him. Allowed myself to fall deeper, deep, wanting to melt under his touch, a strange urge to get closer to him. My blood boiled under my skin, heating up our already smoking hot kiss.

Archer flipped me, shifting himself above me. I tugged at his T-shirt until he relented and allowed me to pull it free from his body. His lips were back on me in a heartbeat. I hitched a leg over him, trying to force us closer together. My skin broke out in goosebumps as Archer's hand moved under my vest, his fingers splayed over my ribs. He groaned as I tugged my vest off, a shiver tearing through me at the sensation of being skin to skin with him.

The urgency roared through my veins. My hand traveled down his side and, almost as though he sensed my intention, Archer ripped himself away from me.

"Stop," he said panting, sitting up out of reach.

I was a woman possessed and crawled into his lap. I didn't care that he had rejected me seconds before. All I could think about was how for the first time in two days I didn't feel bad. I felt good. *Felt.* He needed to kiss me again.

He broke the kiss and pressed his forehead to mine. "Lori, I can't do this. We can't do this."

"Why not?" I pulled back to see his face, hoping to see mischief in his eyes as he teased me. Instead, there was apprehension, a little sorrow and a hint of regret.

Archer stroked his finger across my cheek. "It can't be like this—I don't want us having sex to be about anything other than we want, need, for it to happen. It has to be because of us, Lori. Not a quick fix for something else."

"It wouldn't be. I want to do this, Archer. Don't you? Don't you ever think about it?"

He raised an eyebrow. "I'm a guy. I pretty much think about it every time I look at you."

"Then why are we talking?"

Archer let out a breath. "I'm well aware I'm seriously letting down my gender right now, but just listen, okay? I don't want our first time to be about anything other than us. Call me selfish, call me whatever you want, but I won't do this with you now. Not until you want me for me."

I opened my mouth to argue, but he stilled me with a finger on my lips.

"And you'll regret it if we do it now. Because it will always have bad memories attached to it. Can you seriously tell me that doesn't matter to you?"

On that point he had me.

"Told you," he said, a smile tugging at the corner of his lips.

The passion left my blood in a rush, leaving me deflated and empty. Until a new emotion swept over my body, fierce and hotter than any passion. Shame. Embarrassment. I scrambled away from him, dropped my head and covered my face with my hands while drawing my knees to my chest, trying to cover myself.

Archer pried my hands from my face. "What are you doing?"

"Hiding."

"I can see that. Why?"

Did he sound amused? Jerk. "I'm so embarrassed," I whispered, lowering my eyes.

"Don't be. I understand."

I glanced up at him. "What?"

He shrugged. "It's understandable. I mean, I'm hot stuff. I don't blame you for losing control of yourself when I'm around."

A laugh bubbled in my throat and I elbowed him in the ribs. "Narcissist."

Archer grinned. He caught my hand and tugged me down so we lay flat. He pulled the blankets over us.

When his eyes flickered back to the movie, I discreetly tried to root around for my tank.

"What are you doing?" Archer asked, stilling my hand under the blankets.

"Nothing. Trying to find something," I mumbled.

He raised an eyebrow. "Oh yeah? What?"

"My top."

"No."

I laughed. "No?"

"No," he said again. "I voted and you lost. You can't have the top back."

"Fine. Then you don't get your T-shirt back."

Archer snorted a laugh. "Keep it."

"And here I figured you wouldn't approve of so much skin."

He pulled me closer to him, tucking me into his chest. Archer kissed me gently, a kiss that screamed his affection but forbade anything further. "I approve of all your skin. Just not of you using it to get your own way."

I chuckled. "So that's it, huh? You're just going to let me deal with this on my own?"

Archer pressed a kiss to my bare shoulder. "You'll never be alone. But you do have to go through it."

"Mean."

"I can live with that."

For a few moments I let the silence hover around us, content as Archer traced lazy lines down my spine. "Hey, can I ask you something?"

"Anything."

I smiled into his chest. "How long would you have held out if I'd kept on persisting?"

He paused. "If I answer honestly, you promise not to use it against me?"

"I–"

"Or try harder?"

I laughed. "I promise."

"About four seconds."

A sigh blew past my lips. "I always give up on things too early."

Archer shook his head and mumbled something I didn't catch.

When sleep started to creep closer, I clung to Archer like a life preserver. I concentrated on his skin against mine, the thrum of his heart, his fingers on my back. Anything and all of him to keep the dark thoughts from invading. And because he didn't move an inch away from me all night, and because he was simply there at all, nothing bad found me in my dreams.

Chapter Twenty-Five

I didn't realize how angry I was until I saw Kimmie. The day after we buried Kit, Archer went with me to the police station. Just as I thought, there was no proof unless Kimmie came forward about Cam. They told me to keep a journal and write down every time Cam harassed me, so I would have proof if I ever needed a restraining order or something like that. They filed a report and the awful truth of it was, until Cam did something else, I was stuck in a terrifying sort of limbo.

Archer tried to persuade me to stay off school for a few days, but I needed to get back to normal. Sitting around wasn't going to bring Kit back or dissuade any of my fears, and if anything it just made it worse. At least at school I could try to concentrate on something.

I shot daggers at the back of Kimmie's head in fourth period. If Archer noticed he didn't show it. But he did make sure we took our time leaving class, giving Kimmie a few minutes' head start. I needed to say something to her. I had nothing planned and I was pretty sure it would just be a stream of curse words, but I still had to say something.

When the final bell rang, I looked at the door that would lead me out to the parking lot and to Archer, then to the door of the girls' bathroom. Where I'd seen Kimmie entering.

Kimmie met my eyes in the mirror as she applied another layer of lip gloss. She smirked. "Wow, so you made it today, huh? Figured you'd be too busy crying over that mangy animal."

"Why, Kimmie?" I asked, surprised at my stony voice. "What the hell did I ever do to you?"

Kimmie shrugged. "Sometimes people hate each other with no logical reason. I hate you. End of."

"There has to be a reason. What is it?"

She laughed. "What, you think if I tell you some bullshit story of how you kissed my boyfriend in the eighth grade it'll make things all bright and sparkly between us? There is no reason, Lori. I just can't stand you. The way you acted as though you owned this place, how you thought you were doing people a favor just by being their friend. The way you came back here and expected us all to be in mourning because you left. I. Just. Hate. You."

I folded my arms across my chest and glared at her. "You can act like the big, bad bitch all you want, I'm not buying it anymore. You were terrified when Cam pulled that knife on me. What did he tell you? That he just wanted to scare me? Was it a little more violent than you signed on for?"

A flicker of doubt shone in Kimmie's eyes. Maybe she wasn't so sure about Cam after all.

"So you hate me. That's just fine—I won't lose any sleep over it. But you have to go to the cops and tell them about him. Cam… He's dangerous, Kimmie. He's going to really hurt someone, and if you keep running around with him, that someone could be you."

For a second, a hint of fear showed on Kimmie's face. But she smoothed it out, and a wide grin pulled at her lips. "What are you getting at, Lo? You keep peddling this crap like I don't know exactly who he is. He's got big plans for you. That mutt of yours was just the beginning."

I reared back as though she had hit me. "Shut up," I mumbled.

Kimmie took a step closer to me. "Struck a nerve? Finally. It's about time you showed some backbone. I was beginning to think you were nothing more than a rug, letting people walk all over you."

"I said shut up."

"Yeah, I heard you. See, I don't take orders from anyone, least of all you. Why don't you run along, Lo? Don't you have a pet at home you need to feed?" Kimmie laughed and covered her cheek with her palm. "Oh wait, you don't anymore, do you?"

It was as if something flipped in my brain. A part of myself that I'd never seen before was set loose. I was like a rabid animal, and I had Kimmie in my sights.

I flew for her. I grabbed Kimmie by her hair and shoved her back against the row of sinks. Her eyes widened in surprise and I had to act fast before she had a chance to regain herself. I pulled my fist back and slammed it into her face, catching her nose.

"Stay away from me!" I screeched. "Stop messing with me and leave me the hell alone!"

Kimmie's eyes were still wide and blood started to pour from her nose. The adrenaline left my body and my hand throbbed from the punch. Taking a step back, I sucked in a deep breath and turned to leave.

Big mistake.

Never turn your back on a psycho—much less a psycho bitch.

Kimmie caught me by the collar and jerked me back. I saw her fist swing at me and had the fleeting realization that it would hurt before it connected with my face.

I was sure my eyeball exploded in my eye socket and when I looked in the mirror I would see goo dripping down my face.

"Like I said, I don't take orders well," Kimmie said before she left.

My entire body shook. When I finally risked looking in the mirror, I was pleased to see my eye was only really, really red, and my eyeball was not, in fact, dripping down my face. It would swell, no doubt. With my finger I prodded a patch of red.

"Ouch."

I rubbed my knuckles as I walked to Archer's car. He flashed me a puzzled expression. "Something wrong with your hand?" he asked.

"Mmm. Hurts a little."

"You catch it on something?"

"Kimmie's face."

"Kimmie's— You hit Kimmie?" There was a hint of amusement in his voice. "Did anyone see you?"

"No, we were in the bathroom. I doubt she'll be running to the principal and reporting me."

"How'd she take it?"

"Not well. She hit me back."

"Where?"

I pointed to my eye. "It was like my face exploded."

Archer snorted. "Yeah, well, getting punched'll do that to you." With a finger he turned my head so he could see where the hag had hit me. He looked carefully for a minute before letting me go and starting the car. Archer headed to his place. Kate was curled up in an armchair watching TV when we walked into the room. She smiled in greeting at us, but did a double take when she saw me.

"Whoa! Who's been swinging punches at you?"

I groaned. "Oh, God, is it that obvious already?"

"No, I just know what to look for." Kate stood up and peered closely at my face. "No lacerations. Starting to swell."

"Any recommendations?" I asked.

She pulled back. "Ice for about fifteen minutes. No aspirin, Tylenol if you have a headache. And sleep on your back. Do that and it might not bruise too bad."

Archer disappeared from the room and returned a moment later, tossing a bag of frozen peas at me. I sank into the couch, holding the bag to my eye.

"Are you staying for dinner, Lori?"

"Yeah," Archer answered for me.

"Fajitas okay?"

"Perfect." I grinned.

* * * *

Archer tasted spicy. We'd parked outside my darkened house, which looked less appealing than a graveyard, drawing out our goodnight kiss. I had negotiated my body onto his lap so I sat astride him. Archer gripped my hips, as though he was using all his willpower to keep them there and stop them straying.

It wasn't as disgusting as it sounded, Archer tasting spicy. It just made me crave him more.

Archer shifted under me and pulled me closer to him. A soft sigh escaped my lips. He broke the kiss and brushed the hair from my face. "What's wrong?"

"Nothing," I said, closing my eyes and breathing in the smell of him. "You're just making it really hard to say goodnight, that's all."

Archer smiled and kissed me again. "I'm in no hurry."

"I'll bet," I murmured. I cast another glance toward my house, wishing more than anything that Kit would be there when I got inside.

"You don't have to go," Archer whispered in my ear.

I pressed my forehead against his. "Stop making it harder."

"Just making sure you know all your options."

A laugh bubbled in my throat. "I know, thanks. But I can't avoid it forever, or keep taking the easy way out. Things aren't going to get better unless I face them."

"I could come with you," he offered.

"And I can't keep using you as my safety blanket."

"I don't mind. I kind of like it," Archer mumbled as he pressed his lips to my throat.

"I do too. But I need to stop leaning on you."

"Fine," Archer grumbled. "Do I at least get another kiss before you run off and leave me?"

"Why not?" I grinned.

Chapter Twenty-Six

Archer became like my hole in the clouds. My world had been dark since Derek died, a previously sunny existence turned black in the moments it took for me to open his bedroom door and find his still and silent body. Kit had made that better. He'd turned the cold and frigid darkness into varying shades of gray. Death of a loved one changes people in ways they can't even comprehend until they face it themselves. It didn't matter that Kit had chased away the worst of the darkness. However much he brightened my day it couldn't expel the shadows.

When Kit died I was terrified I would be lost in the darkness again, unable to find my way home. Instead of how Kit changed the black to gray, Archer punched holes in the dark like a clear strip of sunlight on a stormy day. My hole in the clouds. Archer brought me out of the dark without me ever realizing it. He didn't intentionally do things to try to cheer me up, or bring me half-hearted gifts. He did something even better. He let me go through the pain, but wouldn't let me wallow in it.

"Pain is human," he told me one afternoon. Usually I stuck with my coping mechanism of avoidance, but even I couldn't outrun it for long. "It reminds us we lost something we loved, so it deserves to be remembered. The pain helps with that—it keeps the memories fresh."

I doubted it would make a Hallmark card for cheeriness, but I got what he meant. And he was right. The more I hurt the more it showed how much Kit meant to me. Archer was like my pain medication, it was always more manageable when he was around. He was my hole in the clouds that let the sunshine in.

A definite black cloud that hovered on the horizon was Kimmie. She glared whenever she saw me. At least she didn't try to dent my face again. Even following Kate's instructions to the letter, I still woke up with a black eye Ali would have been proud of.

I never saw Cam again.

As the months wore on, the weather cooled and so did my pain. It didn't burn in my chest every single day. My parents were still a crater of absence, and I didn't think it would change anytime soon. I was hardly ever home now to let it bother me. Kate became the mother figure in my life, and she willingly took me under her wing, force-feeding me at every opportunity. Never once commenting on my frequent — however PG-13 — sleepovers.

Archer and Kate loved to hear anecdotes from work, and especially when a sneaky raccoon managed to unlock his cage and avoid capture for hours.

Kate drained the last of her coffee and stood. "Twelve hour shifts on a Sunday should be illegal."

I smiled. "I don't envy you."

Archer yawned, leaning back in his chair. "I would have got up earlier if I'd known you were working this morning. Who's going to feed me now?"

Kate swatted him across the back of the head.

He winked at me. "Are there eggs?"

She sighed. "There are always eggs, why?"

"No reason. I might make Lori pancakes."

Kate gasped and I stifled a giggle. "You little punk," she muttered, only half angry. "I'm out of here before I do something I might regret. Besides, it might be weird if I showed up with blood on me."

"Bye, Kate," I said, hiding my smile behind my hands.

"Mmm."

When we heard the front door close, Archer yawned again and wearily got to his feet. We had been up late the night before, watching movies until close to dawn. "Chocolate chip or regular?"

"You don't have to make me pancakes."

"Of course I do. I owe you, remember?"

He did? Oh, right. We'd watched one of his disgustingly over-done modern horror movies last night. I only relented when he swore to be in my debt until I deem him paid in full.

"This doesn't clear your debt, you get that, right?"

Archer rolled his eyes. "I wouldn't presume otherwise."

I smiled and reached for the remote, flicking on the portable TV in the corner to get a healthy dose of cartoons while Archer cooked for me.

A particularly engrossing episode of Scooby Doo had me so entranced I didn't realize the food was done until he shoved a plate under my nose. I came to with a start, looking at Archer then down at my plate. A huge stack of chocolate chip pancakes drowning in maple syrup with a dollop of butter melting on top.

Archer winked and refilled my coffee mug.

God, I love this boy. Shit, where the hell did that come from? A four letter word. One tiny, inconsequential, casual in some cases, word, changed my relationship in a heartbeat. I was so taken aback by the thought that I choked. And if that wasn't bad enough, I had a mouthful of coffee at the time. Yeah... Hot coffee coming out of my nose? One word — ouch.

Archer rubbed my back. "Are you okay?"

I nodded, my eyes streaming.

"Is the coffee too hot?"

For my mouth? No. Nose? Uh, yeah.

I shook my head, frantically rubbing my nose to try to stop it running and to get rid of the weird sensation.

He laughed. "What the hell happened?"

"I think I forgot how to drink," I forced out.

"Oh yeah? You'd better not have forgotten how to eat."

And just to prove I hadn't, I polished off the entire plateful in record time. Let's just say it was a good thing Kate had some Pepto in the bathroom cabinet.

* * * *

I think I'm in love with Archer. I think? Yeah, right. Don't be so freaking stupid, Lori. I am in love with Archer. Like my body wasn't full enough of feelings. And now I needed to worry about keeping that little admission all to myself. And I happened to have, like, the most perceptive boyfriend in the history of attentive boyfriends.

Oh yeah, I'm in love with him. Stupid, giddy, embarrassing, all-consuming, light up when he's around kind of love. Whenever I saw him I had to bite down on my tongue to keep from screaming the words at him.

As much being in love warmed me to the tips of my toes, it also made me sad. I wanted more than anything to talk to Derek about him. If he were alive and I started gushing about my boyfriend he'd look at me as if I was a Martian and kick me out of his room. I wanted to be kicked out of his room. I wanted to bug the crap out of him.

If I needed someone to talk to, Kate would be a willing listener. More than willing, actually. Unfortunately, being Archer's aunt, I couldn't bring myself to tell her. Besides, I'm probably so transparent Archer could have guessed months ago — way before even I figured it out.

I leaned back in my chair and let out a breath. Kate cooking me dinner had fast become one of my most favorite things in the world. "That was awesome, Kate, thanks."

She winked. "Pleasure as always."

Archer piled our plates and put them in the sink.

"I'll get those later, Jack," Kate said.

He grinned. "Don't need to tell me twice." Archer sat back down and linked his hand with mine under the table.

"How was work, Lori? Any more capers from the wily raccoon?" Kate asked, swirling her soda around in her glass.

I laughed. "No. Doug pretty much padlocked the cage

twice and glued the bolts in place."

Kate grinned. "It must be so much nicer working with animals rather than humans."

"I doubt many of your patients take a leak on you."

"You'd be surprised," Kate said dryly.

I wrinkled my nose. "Gross. Today was a good day, though. This lady brought in a box of kittens she found by the river. It's always nice when someone gets there in time and does the right thing."

Kate shook her head. "Yeah, eventually. I don't get people sometimes. How can they be so cruel? If they didn't want them, how hard would it have been to drop them at your work, or the pet store or something?"

"Preaching to the choir. These little guys are amazing, though. Even though they've been neglected and left for dead by humans, they're still so trusting. All they want is a little bit of love."

"What will happen to them?"

I shrugged. "Doug'll put up flyers, see if anyone wants them. He'd take them himself but he promised his wife he'd stop taking in all the waifs and strays."

"Aren't you tempted to take them?"

"A little," I admitted. "Doug asked me the same thing. I think he's hoping I'll cave and say yes. He hates giving animals away, especially if he doesn't know the people personally. Hence all his strays."

"Would your parents not let you have them or something?" Kate asked.

"No, they aren't the problem. They didn't say anything about Kit, so I doubt a cat would make much difference." I shifted in my chair. "I guess if I'm being honest it feels too soon after Kit. It's only been a few months. Plus I've got college next year. I couldn't take them with me and it's not like I can ask my parents to take care of them for me."

"I'd take them for you."

I blinked. "You would?" She'd said it with absolutely no hesitation. Just offered...just like that. Was that what a true parent was like? I couldn't remember.

"Sure, why not?"

"It— Nothing, just generous is all."

"You don't like the idea?" Kate smiled.

"No, it's not that," I said, frowning. "I suppose it might be a little disruptive for the cats. Getting used to me, then coming and staying here."

Kate sighed. "I'll probably regret this. How many are there?"

"Three."

"Neutered?"

"They're too young, but Doug can arrange it when they're old enough."

"Had their shots?"

"Yeah."

"I'll take them."

Despite keeping her face placid, I could tell Kate was excited. I promised I'd take Archer shopping before I started work the next afternoon and get all the stuff the kittens would need, and I'd bring them back with me once I finished work. Oh yeah, there was a definite bounce in her step after that.

Archer squeezed my hand. "I bought something today. Come see."

He pulled me to my feet and I followed him upstairs to his room. "What is it?" I asked.

He produced a DVD case and tossed it to me.

"*The Shortcut*?" I said. "This looks like the lamest movie ever."

Archer rolled his eyes. "Why? Because it wasn't shot last century?"

I giggled. "No. It just looks lame."

He took the case back and shoved the DVD into the player. Turning to face me as the movie started, he smiled slow and predatory. "I can liven it up."

I squealed as Archer reached for me with no warning and backed me onto the bed. I guess the movie wasn't so bad.

* * * *

"No way does one little cat need all this shit," Archer muttered as I added yet another invaluable item into our shopping cart at Petco.

"It's three little cats, and yes, they do."

"What do they need these stupid collars for? They won't be going outside yet, so what does it matter?"

"They're flea collars. Preventative."

"Gross. Do they need a bed each?"

"Probably not, but you can put them in different areas of the house so they always have an option."

"No way do they need all that food. Harlo doesn't eat that much."

"It's cheaper if you buy in bulk."

"Aw, Christ, Lori. Another toy?"

* * * *

Doug was ecstatic when I told him Kate would take the kittens. He gave me a bunch of free stuff from the surgery. He got tons of samples anyway, so it wasn't a big deal. I doubted Archer would see it that way...

Since the kittens were so small, they fit in one cardboard carry box. Harlo was eager as always when I got in the car, but the second she heard the mewling coming from the box her ears stood to attention and her attention zeroed in on the box.

"You know she's probably going to eat them, right?" Archer asked as he started the ignition.

"She will not."

"We'll see."

Kate actually swooned when I opened the box and she saw her new furry friends. One was jet black and had a feisty personality. Another was a gray, black and white tabby that was content to simply be adored. And the last was an indignant little thing, snubbing all attention until he got too curious and came looking for it. He was almost pure white, except for a spattering of stripy ginger on his ears, face and tail.

I lay on my side in front of the fire Kate had set and lit, leaning on my elbow and supporting my head in my hand. The black kitten crawled all over me, biting my chin and attacking my fingers. The second she saw something, she was off like a shot to investigate, and didn't seem afraid of anything.

"I like this gal. She's got gumption." I laughed.

Kate grinned from her spot in the armchair, where the tabby was yet to budge from her lap. Archer was sprawled on the couch, appearing uninterested in any of the kittens. Harlo lay in the middle of the room, watching the kittens. The black one had already investigated her, and deemed her unworthy of her attention.

"What are you going to call them?" I asked Kate.

"I've no idea. How do you choose a name?"

"I chose Kit's name because Kitsune is the Japanese word for fox. Watch them for a while and observe their personalities. The names will come soon enough."

"What would you call her?" Kate nodded to the black kitten, who was trying to burrow her way under my sweater.

"Uh, Indie," I said after a moment. "After Indiana Jones. She seems like an adventurer."

Kate grinned. "Indie. I like it." She looked down at the kitten on her lap. "Sunny. He looks like he's basking in the sunshine."

"And what about your rude cat?"

"How about Jack?"

I laughed. "Good call."

Archer shot his aunt a look before returning his gaze back to the TV. The white cat clawed its way up the couch and onto Archer's chest. They stared at each other for a minute before the cat curled up in a ball and went straight to sleep.

Kate and I both grinned like idiots.

Harlo jerked her head up, not looking impressed that

her beloved Archer now had another animal on him. She slunk over to the couch and Archer dropped his hand on her head. Harlo, content that he still loved her, lay down on the floor. Archer stroked the cat asleep on his chest, and a smile worked its way onto his lips when he started purring.

"Jack it is," Kate said.

Chapter Twenty-Seven

Archer met my parents the week after Christmas. Kate had invited me to spend the holidays with her and Archer, and after a quiet, somber meal with my parents, Archer had picked me up and I'd pretty much spent the entire break from school at their place. Archer had got me a collection of Alfred Hitchcock movies and I'd got him a few more dark T-shirts and a gift certificate for the local bookstore. Like he needed any more, but whatever.

I needed to check in at home, let my parents know I was still alive... That sort of thing. We crossed the street and had stepped onto the lawn when the front door opened and my dad came out. His eyes flickered between us for a beat and he seemed to be undecided on whether or not to speak.

"Hi, Dad," I said. I glanced back at Archer. I'd never introduced my parents to a guy before — any guy. Not even Drew.

"Lori." A tiny smile pulled at his lips. My dad, whose eyes had once crinkled at the corners as he laughed, now had deepset frown lines on his forehead, making him look older than his years.

"This is Archer."

Dad nodded to him. He glanced between us and came down the steps, pausing a foot away from us. "Nice to meet you." He extended his hand to Archer.

Archer crossed the space between them and took Dad's hand. "You too."

"I haven't heard anything about you," Dad said with an awkward chuckle.

"That makes two of us," Archer replied.

"Richard, we need to go," Mom said as she closed the front door behind her. Her gaze flitted between the three of us. "Oh, hello."

"Hi, Mom," I said, folding my arms across my chest.

"Who is this?" she asked, heading down the steps to join us.

"Archer. My boyfriend."

"Oh. How nice." She smiled thinly and touched my father's elbow. "We really do need to be going."

They got in their car and backed out of the driveway. Was that normal? Weren't parents supposed to give a new boyfriend the third degree? Weren't mothers supposed to question their daughters, make sure they were…safe? Not like I wanted to have that cringe-worthy conversation, but still.

Didn't they care?

Archer followed wordlessly as I stomped around back. I paced the length of my living room before dropping down on the couch, hugging my knees to my chest. "I don't know what I did to make myself so damn unlovable," I mumbled.

Archer crouched in front of me. "You aren't unlovable. It's them that have the problem, not you."

"Right."

He tugged on my knees and forced me to move closer to him. "I mean it. Harlo loves you. Kate and those stupid cats love you. I—"

My breath caught in my throat.

A faint blush stained Archer's cheeks and he bolted upright. With his back to me he mumbled, "Sorry."

"For what?" I asked, frowning as I stood up.

"Not being able to say it." He sighed. "You need to hear it, and I want to say it, but…"

"But what?"

Slowly Archer turned to face me. "I've never said it to anybody before."

"Well, neither have I."

"So it's supposed to be special, right? Romantic setting,

over-priced restaurant, that kind of stuff?"

"I'd rather you just mean it than do all that crap."

"I do. Mean it."

"Then that's plenty enough." I smiled. "You know I do too, right?"

Archer smirked. "I do now." He cleared his throat and I saw his Adam's apple bob.

"Wait—" I said, holding my hand up to stop him. "You don't actually have to say it, if you don't want to."

"Why?"

I shrugged. "Saying it out loud won't change anything."

Archer let out a breath and pulled me closer, holding me tight against his body.

"You will one day, though, right?" I mumbled into his chest.

He chuckled. "Yeah, I will."

"Good." A lot of girls would have insisted he spell it out right there and then, made him sign a blood oath promising that he meant the words. A lot of guys would say the words, not caring whether they were true or not. Drew told me a few times, usually when he tried to separate me from my bra. Somehow Archer saying it without uttering the words felt like the truest thing I'd ever known.

It didn't matter that my parents were now foreign and unfamiliar to me. Because I had something pure and unblemished in my life. I wasn't lonely anymore. I was part of something amazing. So, because of that, I could take anything else the rest of the world could throw at me.

Chapter Twenty-Eight

My relationship with Archer shifted. Admitting our feelings changed us into something even more amazing. We moved in sync with each other and seemed to be on the same wavelength. It was as effortless as breathing. The hole in my heart began to fill over. The stab of loneliness or the ache of abandonment couldn't hurt me anymore. Instead I felt safe. I felt loved. His house became my house. I pretty much went back to my place to sleep. Archer stayed a few nights a week also, and I crashed with him and Kate every weekend. Somewhere along the line it stopped being about avoiding my place because everything reminded me of Kit and started being routine. I didn't care. We were happy.

If my parents were aware of my frequent overnight guest, or my frequent disappearances, they never called me on it. I couldn't decide what was worse—that they knew and didn't care... Or didn't care enough to know.

I yawned and wriggled deeper into Archer's embrace. An unimpressed growl sounded in my ear. Indie curled up on the cushion behind me, tangled in my hair.

"You are so not hardcore enough for this," Archer said.

"I so am." I so wasn't, I was already falling back asleep.

"We've only watched one movie and you're already falling asleep. Definitely not hardcore."

I sighed and forced my eyes open. "I'm fine. Really. I can do this."

"You sure? This was your idea after all."

I had no comeback. It had been my idea. With Kate working nights that week at the hospital, Archer and I had decided to make use of the free living room—and therefore big TV—and have a Hitchcock marathon. We'd ordered pizza and pigged out on junk food. The cats curled up in the free spots on the couch, attacking body parts if we dared move and disturb them. Harlo, thoroughly unimpressed, lay on the floor.

All in all, a perfect night with Archer.

Except I was almost asleep.

Archer moved and I ended up face first in the cushion. He tugged on my hand. "Come on. I can't watch the movie if I'm just watching you, making sure you're not asleep."

"I wasn't asleep. Honest." That almost came out coherently.

He detangled Indie from my hair and led the way upstairs. I snatched the T-shirt of Archer's I always slept in whenever I stayed over and woke myself up enough to make it into the bathroom for bedtime prep.

When I returned, I paused in the doorway of Archer's room, frozen to the spot. He sat on the edge of his bed with his back to me. His pale blue pajama pants hung low on his hips and thanks to his lack of upper body clothing, I saw the muscles in his back roll and flex under the olive-toned skin as he moved. Soft thuds hit his floorboards as he tried to find a new book to read. He hated being between reads, and even if he didn't start the new one right away, just the decision made him relax.

I pulled myself out of the daze and forced myself into the room. I grabbed an elastic band I kept on top of his dresser so I could tie my hair up.

I rolled my hair into a messy bun. When I turned to face Archer, his eyes were already fixed on me. I never wanted him to stop looking at me the way he was looking at me in that exact second.

Archer smiled shakily. "No way should you look that hot in one of my old shirts."

I rolled my eyes. "Yeah. I could stop traffic."

"You would if I was driving."

I laughed, more out of nerves than anything else.

Archer stood and moved slowly toward me.

"What?" I asked as my pulse spiked.

"Nothing. It's just weird—you see girls in bikinis and on huge billboards in pretty much nothing, but..."

"But what?"

He let out a breath and raised a hand, his finger plucking at a hole in the T-shirt at my collarbone. A shiver tore through me as his finger brushed my skin. "I can't stop thinking about this stupid hole. When you move sometimes I see a flash of skin... It's the sexiest damn thing I've seen in my entire life."

I opened my mouth to say something but he silenced me with his thumb on my lip.

"Don't say anything. Don't make a joke." He brushed his thumb across my bottom lip and replaced it with his. There was something different in his kiss. His barely contained restraint radiated out of him. I wished he would just let go. Let go and take me.

He broke the kiss, both of us breathing hard. Archer pressed his forehead to mine. "God, you have no idea what you do to me, Lori."

I chuckled. "I'm pretty sure you do it to me." I grasped his hand and held on as tight as I could. Squeezing my eyes shut for a second, I tried to figure out a way to let him know what I wanted without actually verbalizing it. Or making an ass out of myself.

Turned out all I needed to do was look at him. When I opened my eyes the intensity of his gaze knocked the breath out of me. A small smile teased my lips and Archer brought his hand up to stroke my face. I leaned into his palm and saw the smile spread across his face.

Wavelength.

* * * *

It wasn't what I'd thought it would be like. I'd expected the pain, but it wasn't so bad. What I didn't expect was the rush of emotions that hit me when Archer and I took our relationship to the next level. I thought I would burst into a million little sparkles and was so consumed by love and adoration for this boy that it made me dizzy.

Afterward we lay on our sides, legs still intertwined and hands unable to stray from one another. Archer stroked my face, his eyes burning into me.

"Does it always feel like this?" I whispered.

"Like what?"

I smiled. "Like everything I could ever want in the whole world is right here. Like I wish I could freeze this moment in a bubble and relive it over and over again."

Archer smiled slowly and kissed me. "I don't know. I hope so. Christ, I hope so."

"What about before? Did it feel like this for you before?" Hello, my name is Lori, and I can't leave well enough alone.

Archer frowned. "Before what?"

I squirmed, wondering why I had to ruin every good thing in my life. "Before me."

"What are you talking about?"

Despite being on a one-track path to destroying what a second ago had been a beautiful moment in my life, I couldn't stop. The stupid, insecure part of me needed to know that he'd never felt like this before either. I needed for it to be as special for him too. "Um, you...and other girls."

"What other girls?"

This time I frowned. "The other girls you've been with."

Archer rolled onto his back. It was an agonizing wait until he twisted his head around to look at me. "I knew you were too good to be true. You are like other girls after all."

My stomach dropped.

Something in my face must have betrayed my emotion, as Archer pushed himself up onto one elbow and moved his hand to tease my hair. "I mean that part of girls that are always so freaking curious about exes and past conquests."

"Is that what I am? A conquest?" My voice was thick in my throat.

"It would make you my first." Archer chuckled. "There haven't been any other girls, Lori."

I frowned. "None?"

He smiled crookedly. "Do I give off a man-whore vibe or something?"

"No, I just... How is that possible? You're hot. You could have had any girl you wanted."

"I have. You're the only girl I've ever wanted."

"Oh."

"You don't sound convinced."

I never would be. It wasn't as if I thought he was lying about being a virgin, but I couldn't figure out why I was the only one he wanted. What was so special about me? Absolutely nothing. I forced a smile. "I am."

"Good." Archer firmly ended the conversation by bring his mouth down on mine.

* * * *

It was like we had this huge important secret. The day after Archer and I made love, we went out for a walk on the beach, the one he had taken me to all those months ago. The wind whipped my face and I burrowed into my coat to shield myself from the cold. Harlo darted between us and would run barking at the water before dashing away at the last second. We stopped at a little café for a hot drink before heading back to his place. We sat close together in the booth, hands somehow finding each other like we were a pair of magnets. Hardly anyone paid attention to us, yet it felt like I had a huge neon arrow pointing at my head, screaming what we'd done the night before.

Archer killed the engine outside his house. I moved to open the car door, but Archer's hand on my arm stopped me. I twisted around to face him, and he smiled wickedly. He jerked me closer to him and caught me up in a kiss that stole my breath.

I chuckled. "We're going to be inside in, like, thirty

seconds."

"I couldn't wait that long," he murmured against my lips

Harlo let us have about a minute more before her impatience made Archer groan and get out the car. Kate came out of the living room to meet us as we got inside. Though she smiled, it didn't meet her eyes. She looked tired, like she hadn't even been to bed yet. Kate got home from work around eight a.m. and was still up when Archer and I left at ten thirty.

"Some mail came for you, Jack," Kate said, pointing to the table in the hallway. A single white envelope rested against the bowl Archer normally tossed his keys in.

He picked it up and for a minute nothing happened. "When did it come?" he asked, his back still to Kate and me. His voice sounded detached, and nothing like the guy I was so into.

"This morning. I only checked the mailbox after you left."

Archer stared at the envelope in his hands, his back straight and rigid. A few more seconds passed and he marched into the kitchen. I heard the back door open and slam closed.

Kate touched my arm. "You should go home, Lori."

"Is everything okay?"

"Of course. He just needs some space right now."

I nodded. Confused was an understatement, but Kate was right. Archer seemed like he needed space and since he never, ever crowded me, it was only fair that I did the same for him. Nothing else for it except face that I had a long, cold walk home.

Chapter Twenty-Nine

Worry didn't kick in until I lay in bed that night and I still hadn't heard from Archer. I hadn't called him—I'd tried to not push and kept telling myself he'd come to me when he was ready. By Sunday morning, patience was not my friend. To keep myself busy, I called Doug and he said I could come into the surgery to help him out. Since Kit had died I didn't work every weekend anymore, and it was rare that Doug asked me to.

I spent most of the day cleaning out the kennels and cages, topping off food and water and pretty much playing with the animals. We had a beagle puppy staying as a favor for the owners while they were out of town for the weekend, and it was content to hang out with me.

Throughout the day I broke my promise to myself and kept reaching for my cell to call him again. It was agony being ignored, and I struggled to convince myself it wasn't a delayed reaction from our night together, but something completely different that was bothering him. When the surgery closed and Archer still maintained radio silence, I took matters into my own hands and decided to go over there. I knocked and knocked and no one answered. The bottom floor of the house was in darkness so I walked around the side and saw his light on.

I let myself in with the hide-a-key, and a moment later I found myself sneaking up the stairs. A thin strip of light spilled into the dark hallway from Archer's cracked open door and I inched it open farther.

Archer had his back to me, stuffing things into an open sports bag on his bed. Fear knotted in my stomach and it was a long moment before I could force myself to speak. "What the hell are you doing?"

He spun around, a handful of socks in his hands. "What are you doing here?"

His cold voice stung worse than if he had struck me. "I came to see you. I was worried."

"You shouldn't be."

I couldn't read his face. He was back to being the cold and closed-off Archer I had known at the beginning of the year. "Yeah, well, I am. What's going on?"

"Nothing."

"Doesn't look like nothing."

"You don't know what it looks like."

"So why don't you tell me?"

"It's none of your business." Archer turned back around to shove the socks into his bag. He picked the right moment. If he had looked at me for a second longer he would have seen the tears well up in my eyes. "Go home, Lori."

"Why are you doing this?" I whispered.

Archer sighed. "I'm doing nothing more than I warned you about."

"What?"

He glanced over his shoulder at me. "I told you not to trust me. I said I wasn't someone you could depend on. Don't you remember me telling you I'd let you down?"

I started to take a step closer. "Archer, what is going on? Why are you acting like this? It's not you —"

He whirled around. "How the hell would you know what is or isn't me? You don't know me, so stop acting like you do."

A hard lump lodged in my throat. I had a choice. I could break down and let him stomp all over my heart, or I could demand answers. He was speaking directly to my deeply buried fears, but something in my heart told me something else was going on... Something that had nothing to do with me. I folded my arms across my chest and stood my ground. "Fine. You want to act like a jerk? Whatever. But I deserve an explanation. What are you doing?"

"I'm leaving. What does it look like I'm doing?"

"Why? Is it because of —"

Archer cut me off by laughing. And not a warm one. "If you say because of you, then you really will be like all the other girls, Lori. Don't be an embarrassment or a cliché."

"So Friday night meant nothing to you?"

"Guess not."

It was like being stabbed in the gut. Archer watched me for another second before getting back to his packing. "Okay fine. It's not about me, or us. The fact that you said you loved me and that we had sex isn't even registering with you right now. So what is it? What's making you run?"

"Nothing is making me run," Archer said as he shot me a dangerous glare. "I'm leaving because I want to. And, for the record, I never said I loved you. You decided I did."

"Have you any idea what this will do to Kate?" I asked, choosing to ignore his last statement. If I thought about it... I couldn't hold it together. "Obviously you do, or you wouldn't be disappearing when she's at work. You're a coward."

"You don't know what the hell you're talking about!" Archer roared.

"Clearly, I do," I snapped. I stabbed a finger at him. "You're being a fucking coward. You want to pretend everything was fake between us, fine. You can fool yourself all you want. But one day you're going to wake up and feel guilty as hell for what you're doing."

Archer sneered and started to say something.

I held my hand up to stop him. "No, don't worry. I'm not deluding myself that it'll be because of me. I'm talking about Kate. She loves you and what you're doing is pathetic. She would never stop you leaving but you don't even have the decency to say goodbye to her. I don't know what's going on with you or why you live with her or any of it, but I do know that she would do anything for you. So yeah, you're a coward."

Archer's jaw was locked and tense. He pushed past me to his closet where he pulled out random T-shirts.

"So how were you going to do it? Before I ruined your great escape, of course. A note? Just let her find a ransacked room and once you didn't come back for a few days the worry would really sink in? She'd call me after a while. The cops after that. How long would you let her keep you a missing person?"

Once again I was answered with silence. The anger radiated out of him and I wondered how he didn't rip the clothes or the bag. I shook my head. "How can you just leave like this? Doesn't she deserve better?"

Archer groaned and threw the bag across the room. I jumped as it smacked off his closet, making it wobble. "What the hell else can I do?" he yelled. "How would having a long drawn-out goodbye be any easier for her? It would be fucking painful and I'm not doing that to her!"

"And this is any better?" I shouted back. "Having her come home and find you gone? At least if you talk to her she knows you're safe."

"She'd try to talk me out of it."

"She loves you. It's her job to talk you out of it."

"I don't hear you trying to keep me around."

My breath caught in my throat. Archer glanced at me, realizing his mistake. "Doesn't matter what I think, remember? I'm not an influence in your life."

"That hurt, Lori?" Archer asked, moving slowly toward me and narrowing his eyes. "The fact I didn't want to have some dramatic farewell with you? Maybe you didn't even enter my mind until you showed up here."

"You're just trying to hurt me," I whispered.

"So are you! Anyone else hears their boyfriend doesn't actually give a rat's ass about them, they turn around and leave! Why are you still here trying to make me feel bad about Kate?"

"Because you should feel bad!"

"You're just sticking around hoping I'll crack and say the

mere thought of leaving you was hard enough. Telling you about it would be too much." Archer smiled crookedly. "Would you like that, Lori? Do you wish we had a passionate farewell where I begged you to come with me?"

"Would hardly be a farewell then, would it?"

"Yes. You'd say no."

My stomach jittered. I was no stranger to rejection and every part of me screamed for me to get out of there. The ache of his dismissal rang through my veins... But something told me to stay. Something wasn't right. "How do you know?"

Archer paused. "What?"

"How do you know I'd say no?"

He grinned. It was more like a flash of teeth. "After everything I've said to you, you want to follow me like a kicked dog?"

"We weren't talking about now. We were talking about the alternate reality in which you actually had the balls to end our relationship face to face. If you asked me then to go with you, how do you know I'd say no?"

Archer dropped his eyes and picked up more clothing. "Because you're in love with your job. You're desperate for your parents' approval. Leaving would destroy both."

"Maybe you're worth it."

"You would say yes?"

"Guess you'll never find out." I dug my nails into my arms and tried to hear past my pounding heart. "Unless you ask."

Archer watched me carefully. After a few seconds he sighed and retrieved his bag. He zipped it up and headed for the door.

I blocked his path. "Ask me."

"Why?" he asked, narrowing his eyes. "For your stupid revenge? Any girl would try to trap a guy in this position — get him to apologize and beg her on his knees for another chance. Despite what you think I do have balls, and I like them just where they are."

I swallowed. "How many times have you said I'm not like other girls?"

Archer froze. His eyes bore into me.

"Take me with you," I whispered. "Take me with you."

"You're lying."

"I'm not. But I do have conditions."

Chapter Thirty

My first was that he write Kate a letter. He didn't show me what he wrote, but the emotion in his eyes when he finished told me just how hard it was for him to say goodbye. My second was that he come with me to pack my stuff. I was happy I'd stuck to my instincts and figured out he was trying to hurt me for my own good, to make it easier to hate him and therefore make his absence tolerable. Yeah, like life without him would ever be bearable. But it didn't convince me he wouldn't drive off the minute I was out of the car. And my third was that he told me everything.

"I don't know when I realized my father was a monster. Maybe always, and I just didn't know any better."

I perched on the edge of the double bed in the tiny motel room Archer and I had stopped at. We'd driven for hours before he'd dug the heel of his hand into his eyes and pulled into the first motel parking lot he'd found. I wasn't even sure where we were.

Archer leaned against the wall and folded his arms across his chest, avoiding my eyes. "I'm not like you. It wasn't some painful experience that made me shut everyone out. I've always been like this. Maybe not as bad, but I've always preferred my own company to other people's. I had a few friends at my old school, but we never really hung out. Me and my dad didn't have a great relationship. We hardly even saw each other. He owned a few bars so usually worked most of the night and slept most of the day. Which was fine, I didn't really care.

"When I was fifteen I overheard him and his friends talking about this guy and how they messed him up. Being stupid and curious I started eavesdropping on them whenever I could. Didn't take me long to realize they weren't nice guys. If anyone pissed Dad off, or any of his friends, then they'd be in for a world of hurt. They got booze for the bars at knock-off prices and I'm pretty sure there was a drug ring going on, too.

"Dad was big on family. Not in the traditional sense. Anyone who worked for him, or was in the inner circle, got included as his family. He always said family takes care of their own, and a family was nothing if it didn't have trust. I didn't trust him. I don't think he knew… He would have done something if he did."

Archer pushed off the wall and stared out of the window. "Dad had this grudge against a dude who had a restaurant a few blocks from one of Dad's bars. The guy applied for a new license and could stay open later for the bar. I guess Dad figured this guy was trying to steal some of his business or something, because it was all Dad and his friends could talk about. They were going to teach him a lesson.

"I was scared as shit listening to them. I don't know who I was more afraid for—the guy in for a world of pain, or me if they found out I'd busted them. Maybe it was morbid curiosity, but I couldn't stay away. I rode my bike across town after school. The black truck my dad always used was parked across from this office downtown. He saw this guy and grinned at him. The guy looked terrified. He got in the truck and I followed them. Dad drove them to this old isolated warehouse. Some of his family were there, but they didn't do anything. I wasn't close enough to find out what was said but I saw plenty enough."

Archer's voice grew shaky and it caught in his throat a few times. "He beat the guy so bad he nearly killed him. They all just watched as my dad went to town on him. Even when it was obvious the guy was done, Dad wouldn't let up. When Dad finally stopped he was covered in blood. He wiped his hands, got back in his truck and left the guy. They all did. None of them saw me as they drove past. I've never been so scared in my whole damn life. I called nine-one-one on a payphone and left before the ambulance showed up. I had no idea if the guy was even alive by that point. I was too scared to go home... I was sure he would know the second he looked at me.

"Dad was big on betrayal. He talked all the time how a family never betrays each other, and if someone did then it would be them who bore the consequences. Did I really believe he'd kill me or something? Maybe. But it was the guy I couldn't stop thinking about. He was a person and he belonged to someone. It was dark when I got up the courage to go to the cops. They kept me most of the night, first going over what I saw and how it was me who called nine-one-one. Then who did it and what else did I know? I refused to say anything other than what I saw that day.

"I knew Dad was a bad guy. I knew it. But I felt a nark and I couldn't say anything more than I had to."

Archer sat beside me on the bed, his shoulders slumped and his head down. "The guy nearly died. Died. My father almost murdered someone. The dude with the restaurant — it was his brother that Dad beat on. He didn't even have anything to do with that mess. Dad just wanted to send a crystal clear message.

"The next day the cops wanted to pack me off with social services, but somehow someone found out I had other family. My mom died when I was a baby. Car accident. I never knew she had a sister."

"Kate," I said, speaking for the first time.

A ghost of a smile teased Archer's lips as he nodded. "Dad didn't want anything to do with her, I guess. She told me later that when my mom died, he packed us off and moved without telling Kate where we were. She didn't know me. She hadn't seen me since I was a few months old, but she came anyway. She came for me.

"Kate got a leave of absence from her job so she could move down to Chicago and stay with me for a while. We rented this tiny apartment and I went to the same school, but there were always cops hanging around, protecting us, I guess. Dad's family would protect him, and I guess I was a target until the trial was over. I had to go. To the trial, I mean. I sat in the courtroom barely hearing a word. When I had to give evidence against Dad, I couldn't look at him. My testimony put him away.

"The judge found him guilty and he screamed at me that it was my fault and he should have taught me better to keep my mouth shut and he'd find a way to teach me a lesson soon enough. He called me a coward and said I was no son of his."

Archer's body shook as he recalled the bitter memory. "That day Kate drove us to her place and we've never looked back. Until a few days ago. That letter that came, it was from the prison. He's getting out next week."

A shiver tore through me. "Out? But he must have only been away for…"

"Twenty-six months," Archer answered. "He was sentenced to six years for assault. The evidence was circumstantial and it was only my testimony that put him at the scene. He should have got longer. He should have got attempted murder."

"Why is he getting out so early?"

"Good behavior. Fucking good behavior."

I rested my hand on his shoulder and his body stiffened. "This is why you said you couldn't be trusted. Why no one could depend on you."

"It's true," he mumbled. "If I can betray my own father, I can hurt anyone."

"Archer, you did the right thing. Doing the right thing is never easy, that's why it's hard and that's why it's the right thing. You didn't betray your dad—you probably saved some other families from pain. If you hadn't come forward, how do you know that lesson would have stopped with the brother? And what about the next guy who pissed him off? He could have gotten worse. You stopped that. You can't punish yourself anymore."

"How can I not, Lori?" Archer whispered.

I stood up and knelt in front of him. Archer was bent with his elbows on his knees. I clasped his face between my palms, forcing him to look at me. "Listen to me, Archer. You're a good person. What you did... That was heroic."

He snorted. "You said yourself I'm a coward. And you're right."

"I'm not. And you're not. It was heroic, what you did. Heroic and brave and good. You had to do it."

Archer tried to speak but nothing came out. He blew out a breath, his Adam's apple bobbing.

I pressed a finger to his lips. "No, don't say anything. I can't stand to hear you beat yourself up anymore. You don't deserve it. I know it's hard. Life isn't easy. So stop hating yourself. I wouldn't love you like I do if you were a bad person. And I do love you. More than anything. So stop it, okay?"

Archer crumpled. I pulled him toward me, both of us landing in a heap on the floor. Archer clung to me as the sobs wracked his body. I cradled his head to my chest and whispered that it would be okay, that I would make it okay.

* * * *

It was almost dawn when I coaxed Archer into bed. He slipped into a restless sleep, so much so that I didn't even attempt to sleep beside him, opting for the rock-hard couch instead. When I woke I had an ache in my neck that was overshadowed by the dread in my stomach when I saw the bed empty.

I jumped to my feet and ran to the bathroom. Empty. No. He wouldn't leave me here, would he? I wasn't even sure where here was. Archer wasn't in a great frame of mind. Who's to say what he'd do? If he panicked he might have taken off before even remembering me.

The parking lot! Archer's car would either be there or it wouldn't be. If it was, then he was obviously out getting breakfast or making calls or something. Relax, Lori. Don't panic until you have to.

I bolted to the door and threw it open, dashing out as quick as I could. Turned out, not that quick. Archer sat on the floor with his back to the door, and fell backward into the room. In my haste I stumbled over him, landing on my ass. Hard.

"Ouch," I groaned.

"What the hell are you doing?" Archer asked as he sat up looking dazed.

"Looking for you!" I snapped.

"Well, you found me," he muttered. He stood up and brushed himself off. Archer cupped my elbow and gently helped me to my feet. "You okay?"

"I thought you'd left," I mumbled, staring at the ground.

Archer stepped back from me. "Guess I deserve that."

My head snapped up as I rushed to reassure him. "No! I wasn't trying—I didn't mean to make you feel bad, it's my issue. My insecurity. I'm sorry."

"I went out for some air," Archer said, rubbing a hand over his head.

"Why didn't you wake me?"

He shrugged. "Figured you could use the sleep."

"Have you eaten?"

Archer flashed a brief smirk and bent to pick up a paper bag I hadn't noticed. A smooshed paper bag. "I brought muffins. You killed them."

A laugh bubbled in my throat. "Whoops. What kind were they?"

"Triple chocolate."

"With white and milk chocolate chunks?"

"Yup."

I groaned.

Archer shook the bag. "Want to eat some crumbs with me?"

"Yeah," I said with a giggle.

We left as soon as the flattened muffins were finished. I

didn't recognize any of the signs and Archer stuck to the back roads. He drove in silence, and gave no warning when he stopped. Archer stopped the car on a grass verge and in front of us was a left or a right turn.

Archer got out of the car and paced the length of it.

"What are you doing?" I asked, getting out after him.

"You need to make a choice, Lori."

I frowned. "Okay. What kind of choice?"

He jerked his head to the right. "About a half mile down that road is a town. There's a bus station, you can get home."

My stomach dropped. "I can get home," I repeated.

Archer's eyes drifted to the left. "I'm going that way."

"You...don't want me to come."

An eternity passed before his gaze met mine. "You have to make the choice."

I shifted my weight. "I already did."

Archer stepped closer. "Lori, this isn't some act of rebellion or stupid need to get away from my life for a few days. You're missing school right now, do you get that? When I left, I knew I wouldn't be going back. I can't face my dad if he decides to come looking for me. When we left, I knew I wouldn't go back. Ever. Did you?"

I paused. Now that I thought about it, the time frame never really occurred to me.

"I didn't think so." Archer ducked his head. "I don't expect anything here, okay? I won't blame you for going. I won't even make you feel bad."

"But you said I had a choice."

He frowned as he looked up at me.

"I'm only hearing you telling me to go home. That doesn't sound like a choice. If it was a choice I should have an alternative." I swallowed, trying to dislodge the lump forming in my throat. "Are you telling me I don't have an alternative?"

Archer eyed me skeptically. "Do you want one?"

I folded my arms across my chest. "You've told me a million times I'm not like other girls. This is crunch time.

I'm not going to make a scene. I won't pitch a fit. I won't even cry. But you have to tell me." I took a deep breath. "Do you want me?"

Archer looked uncertain.

"Do you want me to go home? Do you want me to stay with you? Do you want me?"

He dropped his gaze. "I said you have to make the choice. I won't influence you one way or the other."

"This is ridiculous," I mumbled. "It's real simple. I'm not going to beg and plead for you to take me with you. Not if you don't want me. If you really want to see me walk away and go home, then tell me. Tell me and I'll go right now." I stepped closer to him. "I already made my choice. The only way that is going to change is if you tell me to leave."

"Lori, I'm never going back. Do you understand that?"

"Yes."

"Even though your parents could list you as a runaway?"

My parents... I forced them out of my head. "They don't care. And even if they did... We could outrun them until my birthday."

Archer let out a breath. "And your choice is still the same?"

"Why is this so hard for you to get?" I exclaimed, throwing my hands up in frustration.

"Because I've only ever been let down by people before! So yeah, I'm finding it hard to believe someone would give up everything for me!"

I frowned. "I'm not."

Archer groaned and rubbed his hands over his face. "Lori—"

"No, it's just..." I sighed. "For the record, I'm well aware how corny this is going to sound. You said I would be giving up everything for you. That's impossible. You are my everything. I wouldn't be giving up anything."

Archer kicked at the dirt with his shoe.

"But like I said. If you don't want me, you need to tell me."

After a moment Archer reached for me and pulled me to him, enveloping me in a tight embrace. "I don't want you to go anywhere I'm not," he whispered.

Chapter Thirty-One

We had been gone for two weeks. We ditched our cell phones and drove wherever we wanted. I had a ton of money saved up thanks to my salary from the vets. Archer had a small trust fund his mom had left for him that he'd got when he'd turned eighteen the previous month.

The sense of freedom was intoxicating.

Some nights we stayed in motels, other nights we simply pulled over when Archer was too tired to drive anymore and slept in the car. A couple of times it was even warm enough to sleep outside, thanks to winter finally giving way to spring.

We bought a tacky tourist guidebook that listed all the obscure sightseeing stuff dotted off the two-lane highways that we preferred. Archer and I pored over the book, picking out the stops we most wanted to see. Archer loved places like World's Largest Six Pack in La Crosse. After visiting said six pack and learning that when full it could hold seven million real-life six packs, we took in the views at Granddad Bluff and a sense of rightness washed over me that I was exactly where I was supposed to be.

Sometimes we would drive almost nonstop to get to some of the attractions, only stopping for supplies or bathroom breaks. But when we got there we stuck around most of the day, staying in a disgusting motel that tried to make money off the tourist folks stopping for the sights. At Dubuque, we decided to stick around for a few days, spoiling ourselves at the Grand Harbor Resort.

Our second night there, I browsed the guidebook and couldn't help but notice how close we were to Chicago.

"Why would I want to go to Chicago?" Archer asked when I brought it up.

I shrugged and hoped to hell I hadn't made a huge mistake. "You haven't been there for a while. Don't you miss anything about it?"

"Like what? A bunch of assholes who probably want to kill me?"

"I was thinking more along the lines of a diner that made your favorite milkshakes."

The tension left Archer's shoulders. He sprawled next to me on the bed, plucking the book from my hands. He sighed. "Tomorrow good for you?"

Though driving through the city was an absolute nightmare, and he cursed more than I'd ever heard him, the look on Archer's face as he pointed places out to me was so worth it. He became more animated the more he saw — his old school, the park where he used to spend most of his free time and, of course, Wrigley Field.

When we finally stopped, it was outside Millennium Park.

We strolled through the enormous park, hands loosely intertwined. Archer led the way, having spent a lot of time there in the past. He told me about the Bean, otherwise known as the Cloud Gate sculpture, and couldn't wait to show me the Crown Fountain. Kids darted in and out of the spray of water, shrieking and laughing. I wanted to stay longer, to be a part of that strange world where a giant video was a fountain. But Archer was impatient, so unlike him. He tugged my hand, rushing down the path and only slowed when we reached the Lurie Garden.

We found a quiet spot on the lawn under the shade of a tree where Archer leaned against the trunk with me between his legs, my back to his chest. As I settled against him I was glad he'd wanted to leave the Crown Fountain when he did. This was so, so much better.

Archer and I stayed under that tree for hours, talking about nothing and everything important. Mostly we named places in the guidebook we wanted to see and teased the other on their choice.

When my stomach announced its need to be fed, Archer laughed. I swatted his leg. "I can't help that you're starving me."

"You should have mentioned you were hungry."

"I was enjoying this too much to worry about little things like eating. But, now that you've brought it up, I need to eat. Right now. So what do you feel like getting? That grill looked amazing back there."

Archer shifted behind me and stood up. He offered me his hand. I took it and he pulled me up. "I have a better idea."

He took me to Little Al's Italian Beef BBQ, and I swear I could eat there for the rest of my life. We sat at the counter and Archer ordered for me when he insisted there was nothing better than the shredded beef. He couldn't have been more right. Seriously.

It was a total mess with the juicy beef that was soaked with garlic gravy. It was heaven and, even though I was stuffed beyond the point of full when I was done, I could have eaten it all over again.

The walk back to the car was a long, slow effort and as soon as the engine ran I was promptly asleep, only waking when Archer stopped the car outside an isolated motel on a strip of the highway.

"I have never been so tired in my entire life," I mumbled past a yawn.

Archer held my hand, pulling me forward otherwise I'd fall flat on my face. "Come on, your bed is a few feet away, I promise."

"Better be," I mumbled. "Where are we anyway?"

"Somewhere special. I think you'll like it."

"Where?" I asked again.

Archer pulled back the sheets for me and sat me on the edge of the bed, crouching down to take off my shoes. "Route 66."

A sleep smile spread over my face. "Yeah?"

He kissed the side of my mouth. "Yeah."

"Cool. Can we go to St. Louis?"

Archer chuckled and lifted my legs, covering me with the sheets. "We can go anywhere you want."

* * * *

Route 66 was awesome—lined with tourist attractions and diners, gas stations and motels with huge, neon signs and middle of nowhere truck stops. A lot of the places we passed had a fifties feel to it, completely kitschy America. I could have stopped in a dozen small towns, but if we had it would take us years to travel the road. Instead we only stopped at Lincoln and Springfield to eat at Cozy's. We spent the night at the Henry Mischler House B and B before starting early the next day for St. Louis.

The Gateway Arch was incredible to see as its steel body glinted in the sun, dominating the skyline. We went to the Museum of Westward Expansion underneath the Arch, grateful to be out of the humidity. After being in St. Louis for a few hours, it was pretty obvious why tourists didn't visit in the height of summer.

We got a room at Hampton Inn at the Arch and I had the best burger of my life at Blueberry Hill.

I was sad to leave St. Louis, though I'm not sure why. Maybe because I knew, along with it, we were leaving Route 66 to head west. But to cheer me up, Archer got us a couple of the frozen dairy and egg custard concoctions at Ted Drewe's as we headed out of town.

They were so worth going back for a return visit for.

Missouri and Kansas passed by in a blur of small towns, water towers and railroad. When we started on the Million Dollar Highway, the winding road took us through the rugged peaks of the Colorado Rockies. It was like being in another world.

Archer had his back to me when I came out of the shower, this one with an 'under the sea' themed bathroom.

I made a note to my future self to insist—borderline whine if necessary—on a power shower in the next motel we stopped at. A leaking drainpipe would have been quicker than that piece of crap.

"You look different now," Archer said in a quiet voice.

I froze to the spot, unable to decide what had gotten him sounding so mournful, so uncertain.

"Did you know you look different?"

Uprooting myself, I made my way over to him and saw he clutched the framed picture of me and Derek. I'd stowed it away in the bottom of my bag when we left and hadn't brought it out yet. It wasn't one of those pictures I needed on display, just its nearness helped.

"It's nothing obvious," he continued, "it's something so tiny I'm not even sure I'm really seeing it."

"I don't understand," I whispered.

Archer looked up at me, a sad smirk on his lips. He tapped the glass above my cheek in the picture. "This Lori is different to the one I know. This Lori doesn't have grief in her eyes, or fear."

I frowned at him. "Fear?"

He nodded. "I never really got it until now. I mean, I've always noticed it around you, but only now I get what it is…what you're afraid of."

"What am I afraid of?"

"People leaving you." Archer placed the frame beside him on the bed. His eyes lingered on my picture for a minute before bringing his gaze up to mine. "That girl doesn't look afraid of anything. Why don't you talk about him?"

I folded my arms across my chest. "I do."

"No you don't. It's always when Derek died or after Derek died. Never when Derek was alive."

"What's your point?"

"I want to know about him."

"Why?"

"Because he's a part of you. And I'd like to think that so am I."

I let out a sigh and perched on the edge of the bed, out of Archer's reach. "Derek was... Derek was more alive than anyone I've ever met. He was the kind of kid who could walk up to a total stranger and get their life history within five minutes. He, um, he didn't give a crap what anyone thought about him.

"He wasn't interested in popularity. Or school, which was stupid because he was really smart. Derek saw something and instead of thinking how hard it would be or how impossible, he looked at it and did it anyway. He never tried to be someone he wasn't. He was just Derek.

"I don't know why he started using. I think it started as something to do, something he knew was stupid but he wanted to prove he could do whatever he wanted. However much he changed, whatever new drug he experimented with, he was always Derek to me. He could be an asshole and he even hit me a couple of times, but he was still Derek.

"Sometimes when it was just the two of us, I could pretend nothing was different. I could ignore how skinny he'd gotten and how awful his skin looked. I pretended not to notice when stuff started disappearing from my room. Because when it was just us, he was the same as always."

I let out a shaky breath. "Derek was so much braver than me. I spent my life trying to hide in plain sight, to tread water so I didn't make waves. Derek jumped in at the deep end, to hell with anyone who got splashed. It was the one thing he criticized me on—how I let other people dictate my life."

"He didn't approve of Jill, then?" Archer asked.

A laugh bubbled in my throat. "He did, just not as my friend. He was such a perv. He adored all my friends."

"I bet he would be proud of you this year, not taking any bullshit from Jill."

"Are you kidding?" I asked, my eyebrows shooting up. "They tossed me out, not the other way around."

"You didn't trail around after them."

"I did. For a long time," I admitted quietly, as though it

was a terrible sin.

Archer moved closer, his warm hand on my back. "And look at what you're doing now. You're doing what you want to do, not what anyone expects from you. All this... You're braver than you give yourself credit for."

"He'd have hated you."

He snorted a laugh. "Oh yeah?"

I nodded. "You're too alike. He would have hated you because you aren't the kind of guy who would suck up to a girl's brother or try to get him to like you. He would have made life difficult for you."

"Good thing I don't scare easy then, huh?"

"A very good thing," I said with a small, happy smile. God, I was so lucky I had him in my life. So, so lucky.

He kissed my cheek. "Thank you for telling me."

"Thank you for listening."

"And you are."

"I am what?"

"A part of me."

Chapter Thirty-Two

As we crossed into Utah, a bubble of excitement started in my belly. Ever since I'd seen it in the guidebook, I'd begged and pleaded with Archer to head for Moab so we could to go see the Hole 'n the Rock. Archer had successfully distracted me from whining about Utah with promises of other, more obscure attractions.

He stopped teasing when he checked the guidebook and realized we could stay in the same motel Clint Eastwood stayed in while filming Rio Bravo. While the Hole 'n the Rock was awesome, I will always remember Moab for the breakfast we got at the Jailhouse Café. Their pancakes were almost as good as Archer's, who eyed me with contempt when I dug in.

"You notice we're close to Vegas?" Archer asked as he unlocked the door to yet another crummy motel, Moab a day behind us.

I snorted. "Four hundred plus miles is close?"

He shrugged. "Closer than some places."

As I dropped down on the bed, I flashed him a smile. "Okay, I'll bite. Why Vegas?"

"It might be interesting. It could have some opportunities for us. We're going to have to get jobs eventually."

"And you want to get jobs in Vegas?"

"I think we *could* get jobs in Vegas."

I thought about this for a minute. "Can I be a showgirl?"

Archer grinned and knocked me onto my back, pinning me down with the weight of his body. "You can be my showgirl."

"Deal." I laughed.

* * * *

The first thing I noticed about Vegas was, wow, big. The second was, wow, hot. I was kind of bummed we'd arrived in the middle of the day. Whenever I pictured Vegas, I imagined it brimming with neon brilliance, twinkling against a black sky. After ditching the car at a motel, we hit the strip. I looked the definition of white trash in my tiny denim cutoffs and white vest, but I didn't care. Hot after all. Archer was in dark jeans and T-shirt. I was terrified he'd sweat himself into oblivion. I wanted to see everything all at once, but ended up spending the entire day at Mandalay Bay, laughing like a kid at the brightly colored fish, marveling at the gators and watching in awe at the stealth of the silent shark predators. I was in heaven.

We got jobs at a little diner off the Strip. The owner, a plump woman called Nina who was in love with love, hired me and Archer after a five-minute interview. Archer used every bit of his charm and convinced her to let us work the same shifts.

The truth of it was, rather than feel the strain of spending twenty-four hours a day together, it brought us closer together. There was always touching We couldn't be within reaching distance from each other without at least one of us brushing the other's arm, squeezing a hand or kissing a cheek. I needed Archer like I needed air to breathe. And the only thing that didn't make me terrified? He felt exactly the same.

"You know what I think we should do?" Archer asked as he kissed my neck, trying in vain to coax me out of sleep.

"Grmmmff," I mumbled, wriggling closer to him.

"We should use one of those coupons," he murmured against my skin.

"Mfff."

He chuckled, his breath warm against my flesh. "For a chapel."

Hello, wide awake.

A slow smile pulled at Archer's lips. "That got your attention."

I sighed sleepily and stretched. "Jerk. You could try to find other ways to wake me up."

He laughed. "I'm being serious."

It's bad if your heart stops beating, right?

"You don't have a whole lot to say," Archer said, his voice holding an unusual note of unease.

"I'm trying to figure out how to tell if you're still dreaming."

"What would your answer be in the dream?"

"Yes."

"Would it be different if you were awake?"

"No." The word was out before I even thought about it. No chance to wonder if he was bored and just playing a weird game, getting me to say I wanted to marry him then him laugh and say good to know. Nope. There was no taking back that word.

"So you wanna?"

"Do you?" I asked, sitting upright and pushing a mass of hair out of my face.

"I wouldn't have brought it up if I didn't."

"So you do?"

He nodded. "Of course I do. The only problem is we can't do it right away. Vegas rules — minors need parental consent first."

My stomach, and ecstatic mood, plummeted. "Oh," I said, quietly.

Archer leaned over to kiss me. "It's not long, Lori. I just couldn't stand to spend another day without that promise."

"It's something you thought a lot about?"

He grinned. "Sometimes it's all I think about."

"You're serious, aren't you?"

"Why wouldn't I be? I love you, Lori. I want to spend every day till I die then every day after that with you. If we're going to be together forever, what's the difference if we get married soon or in ten years?"

I blinked, scratching my eye with some leftover sleeping dust. Weren't marriage proposals supposed to be over the top and corny as hell? That wasn't what I wanted, I realized. I wanted what Archer had promised. The promise of forever.

I couldn't wait for my birthday.

Chapter Thirty-Three

Thank God our boss at the diner had a forgiving nature, since my mind was totally elsewhere for the duration of our shift. When trying to take an order, my eyes would drift to Archer, and I couldn't stop the goofy grin from spreading across my face.

We left work around four-thirty, in a bigger daze than when we started. Nina scolded us, laughing the whole time, and warned we'd better have the stardust out of our eyes before our next shift.

Archer slipped his hand in mine, keeping me close to his body. He turned to me with a smile, and he kissed me, twice in quick concession, before giving in to a long, hungry one. A happy bubble grew in my stomach at having a kiss like that every day for the rest of my life.

Archer laughed against my lips. "Come on."

Almost as soon as we started walking again I stopped. "Did you hear that?"

"What?"

I tilted my head, trying to figure out what it was I heard, if anything at all. But then it came again. A low, barely even there whimper.

Ripping out of Archer's grasp, I ran around the diner to the customer parking lot, separate from the tiny employee one. Then I saw it. Near the chain-link fence in a broken crumple lay a bloody dog.

Archer skidded to a stop beside me as I dropped to my knees.

"Go get Nina—find out where there's a vet around here. Hurry!" I shouted.

I unbuttoned my blouse, grateful for the camisole I wore underneath. Without moving the dog too much I managed to get the blouse under him, and waited for Archer to return.

It couldn't have been more than three minutes, but the wait was agonizing. Archer scooped the dog up in his arms, no doubt remembering when he'd carried Harlo into Doug's surgery. This dog was smaller, both in weight and build. It was vaguely familiar — a stray that hung around the back door of the kitchen begging for scraps.

"Nina says vets around here will charge a fortune if you take it to any of them. She knows of this chick who runs a shelter or something."

At the word shelter my blood turned cold.

Archer caught my expression. "Relax — she won't put him down, not unless he needs it. Nina says lots of people take stray animals to her since she won't euthanize unless she has too."

I sat in the back, hushing the dog while Archer sped through the streets, all the while frantically checking the slip of paper bearing directions.

Archer screeched to a halt outside a one-story wood cabin. Without wasting a second Archer got the dog out of the back and rushed it inside. The receptionist jump to her feet at our frantic approach. Seconds later a woman in a dirty T-shirt and jeans with wild blonde hair came out of a room and ushered us inside.

I gnawed on my fingernails during the entire examination and when Archer saw blood he clamped his hand over mine and squeezed so hard I was sure I'd be the one needing an x-ray, not the dog.

"It looks worse than it is. I'd say a broken leg and some minor cuts, but we'll monitor for internal bleeding. This guy is lucky you two were around."

Archer nudged me. "Doolittle here you need to thank. I've no idea how she heard the dog, but she did."

The woman smiled. "Have you ever considered working with animals? Most people think it's easy, but it takes a certain kind of person, someone with a sixth sense, or a Doolittle inclination."

I blushed. "Yeah, actually. I'm going to veterinary school but I always imagined myself in the kind of set-up you have here… I'd love to work with wild animals and set up a rehabilitation center to reintroduce animals into their natural habitat and take in strays if I needed to."

She smiled. "You remind me of myself at your age. I was exactly the same. Sure, the pay might not be as good as if you did teeth cleaning for the mutts of Hollywood, but the rewards for doing something like this are so much more. I'd say you have a promising future ahead of you." She filled out a form and handed it to her assistant before giving the dog an injection and wrapping his broken leg.

The dog pressed his muzzle into my hand, and I stroked him absentmindedly. "How do you not fall in love with every animal that comes in here?"

She laughed. "Trust me, you do. A lot of vets distance themselves and train themselves not to care, but I'm not one of them. I'm a big softy, I can't help it. So what makes you interested in rehab?"

"I had a fox once," I said, ignoring the lump threatening to lodge in my throat.

She nodded. "I was that kind of kid. It drove my parents nuts, taking in every animal that wandered into our yard. Well, with your attitude I don't need to wish you any luck."

I grinned.

"Okay, I'm going to get this little guy cleaned up. You two should be proud of what you did today."

"What will happen to him? When he's better, I mean."

She sighed. "I can see him being a permanent fixture. If it turns out I can't keep him, I'll arrange for him to be adopted."

I nodded, relief flooding me.

Archer wrapped an arm around my shoulders as we walked back to the car.

"I'm wiped," I said.

"Me too."

My mind buzzed with images of myself in a place like this, with animals everywhere, an emergency rushing through the door. I slid across the seat to snuggle closer to Archer. "Feel like a nap before...?"

"I'd love a nap."

I was out in seconds, but when I woke Archer lay in the exact same position and wore the same crease between his eyes. It was dark when I sat up, but this was Vegas, and opening hours of chapels run from early to late or twenty-four-seven. I had noticed Archer was quiet when we left the shelter, and it was more pronounced now I was aware of it. For this reason I didn't push to run down to the chapel. He had something on his mind, and I'd always prided myself in leaving him to his thoughts when he needed me to. When we had forever, there was always tomorrow.

* * * *

Archer wasn't in bed when I woke up in the morning. I didn't panic as I had that first time, and instead rationally got dressed and looked for him. He wasn't hard to find, sat hunched over a picnic bench in the courtyard outside. Wordlessly I dropped down beside him. He didn't acknowledge me, but we didn't always need words.

"I never thought about how you become a vet," he said, still not looking at me.

So not what I was expecting. "Huh?"

"I never realized you had to study science — biology and stuff. And that's just college. You've got to do four years before you can even get to vet school."

"Yeah, so?"

"So when are you going to do that, Lori? Or, rather, when were you going to do it?"

"When I finished high school," I whispered, already seeing where his point was headed.

"How are you going to finish high school now? You were

241

all set for your big planned-out future. Until I came along at least," Archer said with a bitter laugh.

"It doesn't matter."

Archer hit his palm off the bench. "Damn it, Lori! Yes it does! It matters. You had a future, one you planned and dreamed about. I've ruined it for you."

"No you haven't!" I cried. "I don't need a fancy degree or whatever to work with animals and do what I love. I could work as an assistant like I did for Doug."

He turned to face me and I almost wished he hadn't. His face was resolved, like it didn't matter what my argument was. "But you wouldn't be, would you? To do what you love you'd need a fancy degree or whatever, to open up that sanctuary or rehab center. That's what you would love, Lori. Nothing more, nothing less. I can't believe I forgot about it."

I shook my head, trying to figure out a way to get him to stop talking like this. "No—being with you, that's what I'd love."

"I was selfish, Lori. I knew I was selfish when I persuaded you to come with me...but I didn't realize just how much you would be giving up."

"No, I told you I'm not giving up anything."

"Yes you are. And I won't allow it."

"What are you saying?"

"We're going back, Lori. Today."

Chapter Thirty-Four

No amount of pleading or crying helped my cause. Archer moved around the motel room like a robot, ignoring my plight. He ducked when I threw things, but otherwise it was as if I wasn't even there. When the psycho behavior didn't work, I went for the stony, silent approach. I ignored him. He loaded the car with our stuff and I got in the passenger seat and lasted six hours before speaking.

By nightfall I hated the deathly, hollow silence that clung to the air around us. Archer rubbed his eyes and pulled into the first motel parking lot he came to. This whole time I hadn't even considered Archer. When he sank onto the bed and hung his head, looking every bit as emotionally exhausted as I felt, I knew I wasn't being fair. He suffered too. And in that second I didn't care what tomorrow would bring.

We had tonight.

Deep down, I hoped if I seduced him he would change his mind. Nope. As soon as daylight broke the horizon we were in the car again, every second taking me closer to the life I'd turned my back on for good. Four weeks had passed since we had left, and it felt like everything and nothing had changed all at once. It felt like we had been gone forever. It felt like we hadn't been gone long enough.

There was no distance between us on the second day of driving. Archer kept his hand intertwined with mine, his arm firm around my waist whenever we got out of the car. We clung to each other when we stopped for the night, and for good reason. We would be home the next day.

It had taken us four weeks to get to Las Vegas, but it only

took twenty-seven hours of driving to make it back. Even though I expected it, the dread when we reached the town limits still raced through my veins.

Without warning Archer pulled off the road and stopped the car.

"What are you doing?" I asked, speaking for the third time in as many hours and hating the hope that sparked within me.

He gripped the steering wheel, his knuckles turning white. He swallowed. "I've tried putting these thoughts out of my head but I can't. I can't do this, Lori."

"What?" I asked, my belly stirring with unease.

He turned to me, a world of tiredness and sorrow in his deep chocolate eyes. "I can't keep you numb anymore. I can't be the reason you don't have the future you want."

"What are you talking about?"

Archer sighed. "I think we've been substituting a lot with each other. You with your parents, with Derek, with Kit. You needed something to love, and pushed all that love onto me."

I sat back, unsure what he was trying. Whatever it was, it didn't sound like a compliment.

"It's not your fault," Archer said quickly. He touched his chest. "I did it too. With what happened with my dad, it was like I needed to prove there was part of me capable of being loved, and loving in return. But I think we've been hiding in each other. And if we're not careful we could wake up one day and realize everything we've missed out on because we were too afraid to look beyond each other."

"What exactly are you saying, Archer?"

He tapped his fingers against his knee. Archer, as a rule, didn't fidget. And the fact that he did now set me on edge. "I'm saying that we're too caught up in this thing to see anything else. I think…we need to take some time."

"So why now?" I asked with a lump in my throat. "Why go through all this and say it now? When it's too late."

Archer whipped his head up to look at me. "No, don't

244

say that."

"What the hell else do you want me to say, Archer? It sounds like...like you're breaking up with me because I fucking love you!"

He dipped his head. "I didn't want to do it like this."

"So what made your mind up?" I asked, folding my arms across my chest and glaring at him as hard as I could. "What did I do?"

Archer reached for my hand but I jerked it away. "You didn't do anything," he said softly.

"I must have because four days ago you proposed to me!" I cried. "How do you go from wanting to spend the rest of your life with someone to deciding that loving that person too much is grounds for a break-up?"

"It was that stupid dog, okay?" Archer yelled, losing that thinly held control. "It was seeing you with that stupid fucking dog and how naturally it came to you, then hearing you tell that woman all your hopes and dreams."

Oh, God, I had...

"You realize they won't let you graduate now, right? You'll have to repeat your senior year. You can kiss college goodbye." Archer shook his head and blew out a breath. "If I had let us go home without saying any of this, then I doubt either of us would have even finished high school. We'd have ended up being fixated with each other and nothing else. Add a couple of kids to the mix and that is your future. A loser future with a loser like me."

Something inside me broke. I hated hearing him put himself down, even more putting down a future that didn't sound anything close to losing. "You are my dream," I whispered past the emotion lodged in my throat. "That loser future you mentioned? It sounds like heaven to me. All the rest... I don't care. The rehab center, it's just one of those dreams I never expected to happen—like when you're a kid and you want to be a rock star."

"You're lying," Archer said quietly.

"I'm not," I whispered.

He pushed the heels of his hands into his eyes. "We can't keep going like this, Lori. It isn't fair."

"I don't care. I told you once before, if I have you then I'm not losing anything."

"That's what makes this so hard," Archer said. When he reached for my hand this time I let him squeeze it. "It doesn't matter what you say now, Lori. It's already done."

And that was it. He started the car and ended the discussion. The boy who had fixed my heart had broken it all over again.

* * * *

I didn't get angry like I had back in Vegas. I guess because Archer's face and the way he held his body told me he hurt as badly as I did. He'd done this because he cared, because he wanted to put my future before his own wants and needs. Instead of taking me home, he headed to his own house. Maybe he thought I'd like to say goodbye to Kate and the animals. The thought broke my heart all over again. How could I say goodbye to them? How could I say goodbye to Archer?

When he stopped the car outside his house he jumped out but I couldn't make my legs work. I didn't trust them to hold me up.

Archer opened my door. So that was it then... Now or never.

He held my hand as I rose from the car. But instead of the stony Archer I expected, I got a version I'd never seen before. I expected the Archer I caught packing his things without warning — the Archer who could turn off his feelings if he had to...be a good liar if needs be. But this Archer crushed me to him and took deep gulps of air, smelling my hair and knotting his hands in it.

It was too much. I collapsed against him, thankful that the car was behind my back to keep us from going ass first onto the asphalt. Archer's breath was unsteady and his body shook.

"Christ, Lori. I'm sorry. I'm so, so sorry." He burrowed his face in my neck, hands gripping me even tighter than before. "I've never loved anything like I love you. Never."

I wasn't sure if his words were meant to be a comfort or an apology. They could have been an explanation. But they didn't help me any. Bit by little bit my heart disintegrated. So I did the only thing I could to get him to stop talking. I smashed my lips against his, our teeth grinding and tongues crashing, all the while salty tears staining the brutal kiss. The kiss of death. The kiss of heartache. The kiss of loss.

"Don't do this… Please don't do this." I couldn't help my last ditch at pleading.

He released a heavy breath. "We need to. I'm so consumed by you that I can't think about anything else. When you're not around it feels like an itch under my skin, like I'm a junkie or something. We need to figure out a way to live a life and have each other in it, not a life where all we live for is each other."

"That doesn't make any sense. People kill for this kind of love," I whispered.

"We're on self-destruct mode, Lori."

"So you're saying to have you in my life I need to prove I don't need you at all?"

"No," Archer whispered and pressed his forehead to mine. "We just need a life outside of this. Figure out who we are on our own. I want you to be brilliant, Lori. Have that future you dreamed about. And I want to be a part of it."

"Can I still see you?" My voice cracked and a single tear ran down my cheek.

"Do you think that's a good idea?"

"I think not seeing each other is a terrible one."

He chuckled, though the sound held no warmth. "I don't know if I can. I don't know how to see you and not touch you."

"So touch me, I don't mind."

"There should be some distance... At least for a while."

"Is this forever?"

"Christ, I hope not."

"Yougoddamnselfishlittlesonofabitch!"

Archer and I both jumped at the slamming of a door and the torrent of angry words. He broke away from me as Kate hit him with a rolled up newspaper as if he'd had an accident on her carpet.

"Jesus, Kate!"

"Yougoddamnselfishlittlesonofabitch!" she repeated, whacking him a few more times. I wish it had been more, because she turned her wrath on me. "And you! You were supposed to be the mature one! The level-headed, thoughtful one! How could you let him leave me a note?"

I flinched at her words, and wow, newspaper stings.

She threw her weapon on the ground and pulled Archer and me into her right before she started crying. When she let us go she took a breath and touched Archer's cheek. "There's someone here."

He gave her a puzzled look before heading for the front door.

Kate guided me after him. "He's going to want you around for this."

"Oh, I don't..."

"Trust me... He'll need you."

I found Archer in the hallway greeting an excited Harlo. Absence had done nothing to dilute her love for her master, and it was obvious how much they'd missed the other. It had cut Archer to pieces having to leave her behind, but he knew a scattered and hectic life on the road wasn't good for her, and she'd be happier in her own surroundings.

Archer looked back at Kate and she nodded toward the living room. My eyes followed him and saw him stiffen in the doorway. I stepped closer and peered around him. An older guy rose from the armchair.

"Jack."

"Dad."

Chapter Thirty-Five

Archer slowly turned to face Kate, the skin over his knuckles taut and white as he clenched them. He swallowed hard as though trying to contain barely restrained rage. If he looked at anyone else that way, I would have sworn blind he would have laid into them. The sting of betrayal in his eyes broke my heart.

"He arrived yesterday. I didn't promise you would see him, but it's your choice. I'll be in the kitchen if you need me," Kate said in a calm voice. I'd never seen Kate with such an apologetic expression on her face. She touched my shoulder on her way past.

Archer twisted back around to his father, his jaw clenched and the muscles twitching in his forearm.

"I just came to talk," his dad said, his eyes flickering to my face. "Alone."

Archer grasped my hand before I could even consider leaving. "Anything you have to say you can say in front of her."

"Fine." He gestured to the couch and sat back down in the same armchair.

Archer tugged me forward, never once loosening the grip on my hand.

"David Archer," he said to me, extending a hand. "Who are you? You must be important to my son if he's letting you be here."

I opened my mouth to speak but Archer beat me to it. He tugged me back and out of reach of his father. "You don't need to know anything about her," he growled.

David sighed. "How's school?" he asked after a long

silence.

"Fine," Archer answered, deadpanned. "How was prison?"

David's lips twitched. "Strict."

Archer's face didn't move. "Why are you here?"

"I came to see my son and—"

Archer laughed. "Oh, so now I'm your son? I seem to remember you saying something different the last time we saw each other."

David's face clouded over. "What did you expect? What kind of kid narks on his own father? You think I'd be happy about something like that?"

"What kind of father acts like a banger?"

"I was making a better life for our family!"

Archer tightened his hold on my hand, so much so I feared for the small bones.

"You were a selfish prick, beating on anyone who got in your way!"

"Now you listen here—" David said through his teeth.

Archer cut him off. "No, you listen." He jumped to his feet, stabbing a finger at his father. "I'm not afraid of you anymore, old man."

"You should damn well respect me!" David yelled, getting up and moving toward Archer.

"Respect? Are you kidding? To get respect you have to earn it!" Archer shouted.

I tugged on Archer's hand to try to force some distance between the two men, but when he didn't move I slipped in front of him. "Don't," I whispered. "He can't get to you, not anymore. Don't let him."

My voice somehow penetrated the anger that smothered him and the adrenaline left Archer, who this time let me nudge him back to the couch.

"I didn't come here to argue with you. Or to give you shit about what you did," David said, hostility still radiating from him as he stayed standing.

"So why did you?" Archer demanded.

David shook his head, some of the anger leaving him with the motion. "I heard you skipped town when you heard I was getting out. I may not be the best father in the world, or even just a good one. But I'm not something you have to worry about."

Archer snorted his disbelief.

"I came to tell you that you'll never hear from me again. I'm staying out of your life. For good." David held his hands up. "You can keep out of my business, and you're free to go about yours. No catch."

"Is that it?" Archer asked after a moment. "May as well start now."

David nodded, searching his son's face with his eyes. He gave a short nod again and wordlessly left the room.

Archer didn't move after we heard the front door close. I couldn't read him. "I'm really proud of you," I whispered in his ear as I wrapped my arms around him.

Archer let out a long breath and pulled me into his lap. I sank into his embrace.

It was beautiful and it was agony.

Part of me never wanted him to let me go.

"I know…" Archer started. He cleared his throat. "I know what I said outside but, could you? Would you — stay for a while? We could go upstairs and watch all those prehistoric horror movies you love you so much." He tried to smile.

I sighed. "I want to. I really want to."

His hold faltered. "But you won't."

"I finally understand what you've been saying." I took his hand in mine and squeezed it as hard as I could. "I love that after something happens it's me you want around. But you aren't going to face up to what you're feeling if you have me to fall back on. And Kate needs you right now. It would be selfish if I stayed."

Archer dropped his head on my shoulder. "I wish I could take back everything I said."

I swallowed the hard lump that formed in my throat. "No you don't, it just feels that way right now. I need you in my life, Archer. And if I have to figure out a way without you for a while, fine, I'll do it. But I have faith that we'll make this work one day. I just hope I don't have to wait too long."

Archer chuckled, a bittersweet noise. "Impatient to the bitter end."

"Would you expect anything else?"

"Nope."

I pressed my lips to his cheek. "I'm going to leave now."

His hold tightened for a fraction before he released me altogether.

"I'll see you?"

"I'll see you."

Walking away from that boy was the hardest thing I've ever done. Harder than watching Kit get put to sleep. Harder than finding my brother dead. Harder than accepting the lack of love from my parents. So hard I wish I'd die for a little while, just for a reprieve from the pain.

* * * *

The walk home did nothing to clear my head. Words buzzed around, never forming whole sentences or even any logical pattern. I concocted arguments and lies for Archer that I'd found a way to live my life without him and therefore could be with him again. None of them sounded plausible. Mainly because I just couldn't see a way where I'd be okay not seeing him every day. Not kissing him. Not anything with him.

What I said to him was true—I did finally understand what he meant. Our love had become obsessive and unhealthy. He had struggled over losing the parental love of his father, and the same with me and my parents. When Archer and I came together we'd desperately needed to be loved by someone—anyone. But it had to be each other that we fell for. No one else could even imagine the loneliness in our hearts.

I did need to find a way where he was part of my life, not

the only reason for my existence.

But couldn't we have found a way to figure it out without actually, I don't know…not *not* seeing each other?

I couldn't breathe without him…but I guess that was the problem. We had to find out who we were again without each other, so that when we came back together, it would last. We were like a blazing inferno, red-hot and all consuming. But fire burns oxygen and if we hadn't made the decision to take some time apart, Archer and I would have sucked the life right out of each other.

It didn't occur to me to worry about going home until I'd actually arrived. The minute I shut my sliding door, the connecting one to the upper level of the house jerked opened and my mother stormed down the stairs.

"Where have you been?" she demanded. "Do you have any idea how — We had no idea if you were safe! No idea if you were— We had the police! Where have— Lori Black!"

I blinked. "What?"

My dad appeared behind her and touched her shoulder. "Go upstairs, Susan."

Mom studied me with her eyes for a long moment. She quickly crossed the room and threw her arms around me, squeezing me so hard it took my breath away. The scent of the fabric softener she used worked its way into my heart. She smelled like every hug I'd received as a child. She smelled like my mom. "I could kill you," she whispered, her voice choked. Mom let me go. She turned and stomped her way back up the stairs.

Dad faced me, giving me a hard glare as familiar as my own shadow. "Upstairs, Lori. Now."

The last time he'd used that look on me had been way before Derek died, on one of the rare times I'd been caught sneaking in. Derek's fault, of course. He'd been high and thought I'd been a dealer coming to make good on a threat and tried to stop me climbing into the house by pelting dirty socks at me.

The three of us sat around the dining table. My mother

and I, mirror images of the other, sat back in our chairs with our arms folded, looking like petulant children. Dad sat at the head of the table acting as mediator, albeit a pissed-off one.

"You have no idea how irresponsibly you acted, Lori. Why didn't you tell us? You thought so little of your mother and me you couldn't even leave a note?" Dad asked, rubbing a hand over his knuckles.

Their reaction to my disappearance, while furious, made me happy in a weird, twisted sort of way. Because it was the most passionate reaction I'd had from them for so long. But now something a lot like anger bubbled to the surface. I slowly twisted to face him. "How long until you noticed?"

He dropped his eyes.

"Seriously." I pressed. "How long? A few days? A week? Two?"

"What does it matter?" Mom demanded, breaking her silence. "We are the parents, we lay down the rules. You are the child, you obey our rules."

I scoffed. "Parents? Really? When was the last time either of you acted like my parents?"

"Lori, your mother and I are not the issue here, you are," Dad said.

I slammed my hands on the table, making them both jump. All at once I'd had enough. I was so done with all this bullshit, of them bailing as my parents. "Of course you two are the issue! Why do you think I left? You made me feel so damn unwelcome in your house I hated every second I spent here!"

"You came back from Gran's and hid in the basement! We tried to give you space," Dad said, his eyebrows pulling together.

"Space?" I laughed. "Is that why you shipped me off in the first place?"

Mom looked down. "It was too hard here for you."

"Hard for you more like," I spat out. "You couldn't even look at me after Derek died."

Mom leaned forward. "I lost my son! Did you think I'd be skipping around picking flowers?"

"You lost your son but you still had a daughter," I croaked, all the emotion welling up in my throat. I'd been angry for so long. I just didn't realize exactly how much until all my pent-up feelings came spewing out my mouth. "You just didn't want me."

Mom shook her head. Her eyes welled up and she reached a hand across the table. "You withdrew into yourself because of Derek's death — you didn't let anyone find you."

"That isn't true," I said, struggling to speak past the emotion in my throat. "Someone found me. He just tried harder than you."

"You wouldn't let us find you," Mom said. "I tried so hard after the funeral, but you wouldn't let us. We thought if you stayed with Gran for a while the change would do you good, but when you came back you set up camp in the basement and refused to even look at us."

"You made me feel like I wasn't even here! Like I was Derek's ghost!" I cried. "It's why I worked so much and studied my ass off in school. I needed to get into a college far enough away that you wouldn't have to worry about dealing with me anymore!" I stood, breathing hard and looking at the stunned faces of my parents. "I cannot wait until I can leave this house forever. And it will be forever. I'll never look back. Never."

Mom didn't say anything, just pressed her fingers to her lips as though trying to hold the words in her mouth.

"This will always be your home, Lori," Dad said, his voice gruff. "Always."

I shook my head as a tear slid down my cheek. "This stopped being my home when you and Mom started blaming me for Derek."

"What?" He frowned. "We never blamed you — "

"You did," I croaked. "You blamed me every time he got high. Every time he got worse. You both thought it was my fault because I didn't stop him."

"Lori, that is ridiculous," Mom said quietly as she rose to her feet.

"Ridiculous?" I laughed as the tears poured freely down my face. "Lori, for chrissakes talk to him! Lori, why can't you get him to stop? Lori, where's his stash? Hide it from him. Lori, find a magic fucking cure and stop letting him embarrass us!"

"That's enough!" Dad roared, slicing a hand through the air.

"No it isn't!" I cried. I stabbed a finger at my chest. "You hate that I found him dead. You blame me for it happening."

"It was an accident!" Mom's voice cracked. "He didn't mean —"

"Of course he meant it! He killed himself! How can you both be so delusional?" I screamed. "How could you have been so oblivious to how much pain he was in? He knew exactly how much would be too much."

"It could have been accidental," Dad mumbled, staring at his hands.

I wiped my face and stared at him. "Then why did he leave me a note?"

And I did it.

I handed my parents the exact amount of pain I'd carried because of their treatment of me since Derek died. Served it up on a nice platter and watched as it destroyed them.

It was as if two hands clamped around my neck and squeezed so hard I thought my throat would be crushed. I couldn't breathe. Backing away from the table, I barely recognized the faces of the people who used to be my parents. The walls closed in on me and if I didn't get out that second I'd die.

I bolted from the house and jumped down the steps outside.

I ran.

My lungs burned and my legs screamed at the force required of them, but I didn't stop. The town rushed by me in a blur and I only screeched to a halt when I realized

I was outside the surgery. It was closed—must be evening now, then. I doubled over, trying not to wretch. My throat burned and I thought my legs would collapse but somehow I stayed standing. I wrapped my arms around me and sloped forward, no idea where I headed, just knowing I had to keep moving.

Darkness sneaked up on me like a bogeyman from the shadows. An odd, detached part of me realized there was no guilt anywhere inside me. My parents hurt me and I hurt them right back. The pressures and residual emotion from the fight made me unobservant and careless. I was at the mouth of the alley beside the Grill before it occurred to me it might be unwise for me to linger in this part of town. Casting a glance into the black alley, I swallowed a hard lump of fear. When nothing happened I chuckled and continued forward, walking smack into someone in the process.

"Where have you been, Lo? I missed you." Cam grinned down at me, a malicious glint in his eye that was different from all the other unfortunate times I'd run into him. "Seriously, I missed you. I thought about you every day. Your little boyfriend hasn't been around either. You didn't run away with him, did you?"

At my silence Cam laughed. "You did, didn't you? What happened? He get sick of you and clicked 'return to sender'?"

I looked around me, trying in vain to spot some escape... witnesses...anything. The street was deserted and no one for me to hope would come and save me.

Cam's hand shot out. He wrapped his fingers around my wrist, holding on to me so tight I knew he didn't mean to let me go any time soon. I didn't care—I still tugged against his vise-like grip. I had to try...no matter how grim the reality looked. "Easy now. I just want some privacy. Al fresco hasn't worked out so well for us in the past, has it?" Cam grinned and pulled me toward a car parked a few yards down the street.

Oh God…ohGodohGodohGodohGod…

When we reached the car I kicked his shin and tried to run. He wrenched me back and slammed me into the side of the car. His fist whooshed toward me and I held my breath, waiting for the exploding pain that would come.

Cam stopped at the last second and pointed his finger at me instead, bringing his face so close to mine his breath was hot on my face. "This is a warning, Lo — do not fuck with me. Do. Not. Fuck. With. Me." He grinned and trailed his finger down my face, my throat and hovered at my chest. He opened his palm and slid it down my breasts and only stopped at the top of my jeans.

A whimper escaped my throat and I squeezed my eyes shut.

"Now, now," Cam crooned. "I want to see the fear in your eyes, so be nice and keep those open for me."

A sob rose in my throat but I only opened my eyes when I heard Cam exclaim in shock and I felt his body jerk away from me. There was a scuffle in the shadows, muffled talking and fists connecting with flesh. A scream readied itself and I shook uncontrollably when a figure slunk out of the shadows.

David Archer stopped in front of me, blood dripping from his knuckles.

"You — But…" I breathed.

"It's time to go home, Lori."

Chapter Thirty-Six

"I don't know how much my Jack has told you about me, but I have connections. More than you could imagine," David said as he led me away from Cam's bloody and groaning form. David was the unlikeliest of unlikely saviors and although it was uncomfortable as hell to be alone with him, I was grateful. Good timing must run in the Archer blood.

David Archer had saved me from... I don't even want to think about what he'd saved me from. Some kind of hell I doubted I ever could have escaped. And because of that, I could never be afraid of him.

"He told me a lot," I said, finding my voice at last.

"I have ways of finding things out." He looked at me. "How did you enjoy Moab?"

I gasped. "How did you—"

"I always knew where the two of you were. I knew when you left town, I knew when you stopped at a motel and I knew when you got jobs in Vegas. I was surprised when you came back."

"It was Archer's idea," I said bitterly. I wrapped my arms around my body as we walked the darkened streets back to my house.

David cleared his throat. "He would never have come back. Not for himself, anyway. Must have been because of you."

"You don't know everything then, do you?" I said.

"I didn't bug your car," David said with a wry smile.

"We came back for me," I said, glancing at him, deciding I owed him that truth, at least.

He slid his eyes toward me. "You don't sound too happy about that."

"Might be because I'm not." I studied him, but, like his son, found his expression unreadable. "How did you know I was in trouble?"

He chuckled. "Like I said, I know things. And in a town like this it's not hard to hear gossip. Especially if someone has a mouth as big as the piece of shit back there. It wasn't until I saw you and my boy together outside Kate's today that I got how much you mean to him. My kid would have killed that son of a bitch if he knew half of what he wanted to do to you. I'm protecting both of you. Cam—when he wakes up—will find himself confessing all his sins to the cops. He'll do time, and he will never bother you again."

That was a lot to process. If David Archer really could get Cam to go to the cops then he was a force to be reckoned with. "Thank you," I said quietly.

"Like I said, I did it for both of you." David said, his voice low and rough. "I care about my kid. He cares about you."

"So why go see him just to say you're leaving him alone?"

"I'm a bad guy. Nothing is going to change that. It doesn't mean I'm a bad father. And if what makes me a good one means staying away, then fine." David blew out a breath and ran a hand over his hair—an action so achingly familiar it made a lump lodge in my throat. "I really hurt Jack. So bad that it will stay with him for the rest of his life. I put him in a position he should never have been in, and in the heat of the moment I said things I'll regret forever. I figured if I could save him or protect him from something that would hurt him, it would help with the hurt I caused in the first place. Something happening to you would be the end of Jack. He'd never get over it. My boy loves you. He doesn't let that happen too easy."

As I pondered what David had said, I only noticed we'd gotten to my house when he stopped walking. He nodded toward the house. "Go easy on them. Speaking as a parent who lost a son, it's something not easy to get over."

I looked up at David, wondering how it was possible to be so kind and so hard all at the same time. "It's not easy being the one left behind, either. I lost him too."

David nodded. "Parents aren't perfect. There's no manual for any of it—especially this kind of thing. Parents are human, they screw up. There is no right or wrong way out of this situation. But allowances have to be made."

"Why can't you do this for Archer?" I blurted out. "You're all guru and wise with me. Shouldn't he hear some of this?"

"Jacky doesn't need anything from me. He's adapted and there's no need to go confusing him." David turned to stand in front of me. "You have my word that neither Cam nor his little whore will ever bother you again. But Jack will never find out what has happened tonight."

"Why not?" I couldn't help but ask. "Don't you want him to forgive you?"

David forced a smile. "I want to make life easy on him. Being mad at me makes it easier. He will forgive me. One day he won't be angry anymore, but he won't feel guilty about lost time either. It's better this way."

I nodded. I got where he came from. And at the end of the day, it was his call to make.

"Good luck, Lori." David turned on his heel and disappeared into the darkness.

I found my parents in the same position that I'd left them in. Mom's eyes were rimmed red as she stood to face me, and Dad looked far older than his years. My heart thumped and it cracked and splintered, as it had so many times before.

But this time, it had to break a little more before it could be healed.

"I— I'm sorry," I choked.

* * * *

I went back to school on a Thursday. Four weeks of missed classes guaranteed I was far enough behind and had missed too many days to pass my senior year. Not that I accepted that, of course. I had mad negotiation skills.

The principal, Mr. Kemp, folded his hands above his desk and pinned me with a hard look. "You understand the seriousness of the situation, Lori."

"All due respect, sir, but I do," I argued.

He sighed. "It isn't like you were out with mono. You chose to miss that much school."

I pointed to the piece of paper in front of him. "My mom has explained my absence. We needed time to try to get our family back on track after my brother's death. We were healing."

Mr. Kemp glanced at the letter Mom had written me that morning. "I understand the problems and troubles that come along with the death of a loved one, Lori, but Derek died—"

"It must seem ridiculous that we're playing this card so long after his death. But if you had known what it was like, not just for me, but for my parents, too, then you would understand. It took a lot to get our family back together. We needed those four weeks." Wasn't that the truth. Okay, so most of it was a flat-out lie, but a lot of it was truth. When I returned home after David Archer saved me, we sat up until the small hours of the morning talking. I showed them Derek's note, and only then did the guilt of what I had done hit me. Mom hugged me so tight, whispering reassurances and apologies to me for carrying the burden of the truth for so long.

It was a Band-Aid over a broken leg, but we were starting to heal. Our family was slowly coming back together again.

Mr. Kemp rubbed his temples. "Even if it was up to me, which it isn't entirely, there's no guarantee you could even catch up in time for graduation."

"I'll do whatever it takes. I don't want to sound rude, but I know exactly where I want to be in ten years. I've worked my butt off to get to this point in my life, and I'll be damned if I fall behind now. I can do the work. I will pass my finals and I will graduate with the rest of my class. Just give me a chance." I studied him, but couldn't decide if my speech had helped my cause any. It had to. It had to. I meant every word I spoke, and I was determined to get back on the right track.

And not just for Archer…but for myself too.

He sighed. "Get a list of every piece of homework and assignments you've missed. And I mean every piece. I'll speak to the school board but I can't guarantee anything."

"I will, I'll get everything completed, I swear." I twisted my fingers as I nodded. Getting back into senior year was only step one. I had a major favor to ask my principal. "I don't know if you know, but I got accepted to N.C. State."

Mr. Kemp nodded. "They will find out about this. It could affect your place there."

"Not if you give me a recommendation," I said with a hopeful smile.

He scoffed. "Lori, I'm hardly likely to give you a recommendation after all the time you've missed."

"But if I catch up, which I will, you could."

There was a long, heavy pause before he spoke again. "If you catch up and if the school board backs you, then maybe I will write a recommendation." Mr. Kemp signed a slip of paper and placed it in a tray on his desk. "But you still better pray and keep your fingers crossed for the next few months."

"I will," I said, trying to suppress a wide grin.

Mr. Kemp sighed, but couldn't stop his lips from twitching into a smile. "Then good luck to you. You're going to need it."

"Well?" Mom asked as I slid into the car after leaving the school. I'd left Mr. Kemp's office and went to every single one of my classes to collect all the work I had missed.

I waved the dozen or so sheets of paper in my hand with a smile. "They didn't give me homework just as punishment."

"Are they letting you graduate?" Mom had wanted to be in the meeting with me. I figured it would show how

263

serious I actually was if I did it on my own.

"If I finish all the work in time and ace all my finals."

"You'll just have to then, won't you?"

"Better believe it."

* * * *

Of course my confidence had drained by the following morning. Not in my ability to graduate, but in having to hold my head up while walking the torturous halls of high school. As I hid behind the tree across the street from school watching my happy, carefree peers, I couldn't help but hope I'd see a familiar tall, dark and handsome person that day.

I'd see him standing at his locker. He would glance up and see me. For a second nothing would happen, neither of us would move... I probably wouldn't even breathe. Archer would give me his crooked smile that to anyone else was barely even a smile at all, but to me it was understated and perfect—just like him. At the sight of that smile my heart would lurch and without realizing it, I would be pulled toward him. We wouldn't kiss. We hardly ever kissed in the hallways, preferring to save it for the privacy of his car, or if we really couldn't last that long, then the parking lot. He would slip his hand in mine and that would be it. All the confidence I needed I would get from him.

Which, of course, was why we were doing this stupid-ass separation crap.

There would be no Archer in school today, of that I was sure.

Would he ever be back?

The first bell sounded—the steps in front of school slowly emptied as kids ambled inside the building. I pushed off the tree and joined the last of the kids who least wanted to be there, mostly stoners and underachievers. A few were old friends of Derek's. None of them spoke to me anymore. A nod here and there by way of greeting was about it. They saw me and knew how quickly their own lives could be turned to shit. Unlike my brother, they weren't stupid enough to move up the drug use totem pole.

I made it out of my first day back at school alive. More importantly, whole. I wasn't noticed by anyone...except Kimmie. She saw me in fourth period English. Her eyes almost bugged out of her head and I waited for the physical attack, or the verbal one, but neither came.

The desk beside me in English remained empty for the rest of the week... A perfect representation of the emptiness inside me. It didn't stop my heart from pounding as I approached the doorway each time, hoping that today would be the day he would surprise me and he'd be there, waiting for me with that crooked smile. Even after the final bell rang my hopes would be high, determined that if I wished hard enough, I could will him to walk into the room.

The let-down was worse every single day.

Finals were six weeks away and I had more than enough on my plate to keep me busy. Every time I stopped, even for a second, my thoughts would be flooded with Archer. His smell, the press of his lips on mine, what he was doing, was he thinking of me? Did he miss me the way I missed him? How the absence of him was like a bitter winter that wouldn't end — with no hope for spring?

I spent free periods and lunch in the library, hunched over whatever I was working on...trying desperately not to let my mind drift to the afternoon Archer and I had worked on the poetry assignment together. In the evenings I sat at the dinner table that held more books than plates, while Mom or Dad, depending on their specialty, helped me or brought me fuel to burn the evening hours.

I wasn't alone anymore.

My relationship with my parents was a long way from being fixed, but it was being repaired. And even though we hadn't talked in weeks, Archer was still mine and I was still his. Because of that, I'd never be alone again. Right now I just had to be patient. Not my strong point, but if I wanted him back sooner rather than later, I had damn well better learn.

Chapter Thirty-Seven

"Hey, Lo."

I turned at the soft voice. Even though I knew who it belonged to, I couldn't help the surprise at seeing Sarah standing beside my locker. I shoved the rest of my books inside. "Hi."

"How are?"

"Peachy. You?"

Sarah blew out a breath. "Can we talk? Like, really talk?"

I closed my locker door. "Why?"

She blinked. "I figured..." Sarah stepped an inch closer. "I figured you could use a friend right now. You and Archer disappeared, and only you came back."

So she wanted the gossip to take back to Jill. Like there ever could have been another reason for Sarah to break out from Jill's fascist regime. "You seem to know enough without me telling you any more."

"I'm not going to report back to Jill, I swear," Sarah said, her big eyes filling with pain. She glanced to the doors letting in a stream of sunshine. "Take a walk with me, let's get some air."

And, for whatever reason, I nodded.

Sarah pushed open the door and led us into the warm afternoon. Neither of us spoke as we ambled along on our loop of the school.

"What do you want from me, Sarah?" I asked eventually.

"A chance to be a real friend to you. I'm not asking for a chance for things to go back to the way they were — for us to form our own band of whatever the hell that was with Jill. I'd like to just be Sarah, and you just be Lo. No agendas.

Just friends."

"Why now?" I asked as I paused, kicking up a clod of dirt with the toe of my sneaker. "How can I trust anything you say?"

"Well… You can't." Sarah sighed. "This is all probably too little too late, but it's only *too* too late if I never do anything at all. I miss you, Lo. And I'd like us to be real friends. I'm done with Jill. So, so done."

I glanced at my feet. "I want to believe you. I really do. I'm not sure I can trust you. Just… Let me think, okay?"

Sarah nodded. "I can do that. But I'm not going to stop trying."

Before I could argue any more, Sarah flashed me a smile and disappeared through a side door into the school.

* * * *

A few days after our exchange, morbid curiosity drew me to the cafeteria. It was no secret I didn't eat there anymore. No one—Sarah included—would have any reason to keep up a front in there.

But Sarah wasn't at Jill's table. She sat with a few kids from the drama club, talking animatedly and laughing at their jokes. Once in sophomore year, Sarah confided in me that she wanted to try out for the school play. Jill overheard. Something to do with the fact that we were at a party and Sarah was totally wasted and thought she was whispering. She really wasn't. Jill teased Sarah for a week and she never tried out for the play. She never mentioned anything about acting again.

"Look who's out of the library," a cold voice said, snapping me back to the present. Jill rose from her place at the table in the center of the room, now looking more empty than full.

I rolled my eyes. "And?"

"I didn't think you liked to be around normal people anymore, Lo. Isn't that why you hide from everyone these days?"

There was no comeback for her. And for once I didn't care. She could have been a metaphorical fly in my ointment for all I cared.

"Wait, you need to spend all your time around the books, don't you? Why is that again? Oh, right, you missed some school. Just what were you and that freak boyfriend of yours doing for all those weeks?" Jill smiled as she crept toward me. "Shooting up?"

A hot roll of anger manifested in my stomach.

"I guess even under the influence he couldn't stand you. It's why you came back, isn't it? He figured out what a loser you were and ditched you on the side of the road? Can't say I blame him."

"Stop talking about things you don't understand. It makes you sound stupid," Sarah said, folding her arms and standing beside me. In my angry haze at Jill I hadn't seen her approach.

Jill's eyes narrowed at me. "You think you're such hot shit? She only came to you because school is practically done. She had nothing to lose. You still have no one, Lo, don't forget it. No one wants you. No one ever will."

"And they want you, Jill? Forgive me, but I'd rather be alone than hated," I said.

"Tell me, how did it feel when Archer left you? Like when your brother finally hit his limit of Lo and took a little too much of his pain relief? Or when you went from being best friends with the popular girls to being pitied by the freaks and losers?" Jill radiated a hate that lit her up from the inside. I knew most of her anger came from being powerless. She'd finally realized there was nothing she could do to me.

"Why don't you tell me, Jill?" I asked. "How does it feel to have people only want to be your friend because they're afraid of you? Or how Daddy would rather buy you a new Vuitton clutch than spend time with you?"

Jill's face turned a violent shade of puce.

"Don't ask me questions unless you're ready for me to ask you." I chuckled. "I feel sorry for you."

Jill choked out a laugh. "Excuse me?"

"We're not so different, Jill. Both trying to find something to take away the pain. Both lonely. The real difference is that instead of fighting it, I accepted that it was just the way it was. And now I'm happy. You don't even know what the word means."

"I could destroy you."

"So could I. But I won't." I gestured around the room. "Look around you. School's done. It's done. We're done, Jill."

There was no point in hanging around to hear what her response was. I didn't need to. The words that came out of that girl's mouth no longer held any power over me.

Chapter Thirty-Eight

When I handed in my last piece of missed assignments, Mr. Kemp told me the school board had voted and I could graduate along with the rest of my senior class. Mr. Kemp never showed me what he'd written to the admissions department at N.C. State, but the day before my first final I got a letter saying that all the letters from my principal and teachers backed their initial decision to let me start in the fall semester.

None of it meant anything without Archer. It had been two months since I'd seen him at Kate's. I didn't call. He didn't visit. I never even saw him around town.

Finals week came around sooner than I would have preferred. I've always been good at retaining information, but around testing time I hated over-preparing in case it had the opposite of the intended effect. Instead of driving myself crazy, I forgot about the exam I'd just taken and concentrated on the next one. It took a long time, but I found a philosophy that worked well for me — no point worrying over things you can't control. And the past, yeah, that was one thing I couldn't control.

Archer's doing fine on his own without me adding to it.

With a sigh I dropped the highlighter onto the open page of the book that was now more yellow than white. I cradled my head in my hands and bit back the irritation. Longing had given way to anger in Archer's absence. Every day that passed found it growing stronger. I would argue with myself, insisting it was because he cared for me that we were doing this. I argued back that that was bullshit, that if he really cared he would be here. He wouldn't have left me to face Jill and her pack of feral bitches alone.

Only in moments of absolute clarity did I make myself see reason. I was tired, under huge amounts of stress and approaching the worst day of the year. All I wanted was the one thing that made me feel better. And I couldn't have it. No wonder I was cranky.

Shoving the book away, I folded my arms atop the desk, laid my head on them like a makeshift pillow and went to my happy place.

My happy place was the only thing that chased away the rain clouds these days. The only thing at all that reminded me of why I was doing this in the first place. My happy place was more a memory than a place – a memory so alive in my mind it was known to block out the here and now, only letting me feel the before.

We were at the spot Archer found for us, a mile walk from the beach into the woods where the sandy floor petered out to soft dirt. We lay in a clearing, Harlo beside us, panting in the warm afternoon. Archer would get a fine if any authorities caught him with Harlo off her leash, but for the time we didn't care. She was well-trained. We didn't need to worry about her running off.

My head was on Archer's stomach, one of his hands running through my hair, teasing the strands until I shivered, the other laced with mine.

"What do you think of the Black Clinic?"

Archer's chest rumbled with laughter. "What, in general, or is there a context to the question I'm not aware of?"

I laughed. "For the name of my animal center."

"Did you forget to tell me something?"

"We're quite the smart ass today, aren't we?"

"You know what I don't get? When people insult you then ask you to agree with them."

I squeezed his hand in warning. "Seriously. What do you think?"

"Seriously? Seriously as in what do I think about you having your own...what? Vet surgery? Or seriously do I like the name?"

"Either. But it wouldn't be a vet surgery. It would be a

272

rehabilitation center for wild animals, like Kit."

There was a moment before he spoke again. "Seriously? It's an awesome idea."

"Seriously?"

"Seriously." His stomach dip as he laughed silently. "But you can't call it the Black Clinic. It sounds like somewhere you go if you have the plague or something."

I snorted a laugh. "Thanks for the honesty!"

"Would you rather I lied to you?"

"I'd rather you liked my idea."

"So get a new last name. The Archer Clinic has a great ring to it."

"Sure does. Too bad my name isn't Archer."

"It might be."

"What?" His tone had been light, uncaring or unaware of the seriousness of what he'd just said.

"You're not going to open the center in the next few months, are you?"

I shook my head.

"Then how do you know it won't be your name when you do?"

"How do you know it will be?"

There was a smile in his voice. "A hunch."

"A hunch?"

"A hunch."

My pulse spiked as his words swam in my head. "Anyway, it sounds like somewhere you'd go if someone shot you with an arrow. And since this isn't Sherwood Forrest, and I'm pretty sure Robin Hood is long since dead, there wouldn't be much of a call for it around here."

He tugged on my hair gently. "Now who's being a smart ass?"

I forced a giggle.

"Why not name it after who inspired you to do it in the first place? Kit's Animal Rehabilitation Center."

"And rescue. Kit's Animal Rescue and Rehabilitation Center."

"Sounds like a gold mine to me."

"What about you?"

"Me?"

I laughed. "Yeah, you. If you're so sure it was going to be your name above the door you must plan on sticking around. How were you going to earn your keep? Or did you plan on mooching around the center like the bum you are?"

"Of course. I'm a feminist. You go out to work and I'll stay home cleaning."

I snorted.

"What?"

"I've seen your room, remember?"

"I'll be cleaner by then."

"You'd better be. Can't have you sitting on your ass all day reading."

Archer sighed. "Sounds like heaven. Too bad you can't get paid for it."

"Who says you can't?"

"What do you mean?"

"You could do a literary degree at college, get a job as a reviewer. Oh! Or get a job for a lit agency. You could find all that untapped American talent."

"You're serious."

"Why wouldn't I be?"

He shrugged. "Sounds too good to be true. Hobbies shouldn't be careers."

A laugh bubbled in my throat. "So for it to be a career, it has to be something you hate? Get real, Archer, your future can be anything you want it to be. You just have to work to get it. What did you ever envision for your future? What did you want for yourself?"

"Just happy, I guess." After a moment, he sighed. "Deal."

"What do you mean, deal?"

"Deal. You can have your animals and I'll have my books. Perfect."

"Where will you go to get the degree?"

He squeezed my hand. "I hear N.C. State is good."

My heart skipped a beat. "I hear it's very good."

And that was all we had ever talked about our futures — mutual or otherwise. I didn't even know if he applied. Any time I'd tried to ask he'd dodged the question in that way of his that didn't feel like he was dodging, and had distracted me before I'd been able to call him on it.

With another sigh, I left my happy place. Lifted my head and reached for the book.

Chapter Thirty-Nine

I'd never been so tired as the day my final final was finished. I slunk home to a huge dinner Mom had spent hours making. Things weren't perfect with my parents. It still hurt like hell most of the time, but it was bearable and we all tried to move forward.

My mind couldn't relax as it should have done now that finals were behind me. There were two other important dates, side by side, that hooked my attention and allowed me no rest.

The cemetery where my brother's still body lay brought an odd mixture of peace and unsettled feelings. A graveyard had never been a fearful place to me, somewhere to cringe or scurry from. In the days following Derek's funeral, I'd spent most of my time in the cemetery, lying flat on the ground beside his grave, talking to him in my thoughts, imagining his response.

It was a place that was restful and brought me peace. It was a place that was peaceful but held my dead brother's body in its soil, and that was unnatural to me.

I didn't bring flowers. Derek never saw the point in them. Sometimes, when the mood struck him, he would walk with me between the headstones. He commented on all the graves with dead or dying flowers, saying it was as though the ground leaked death, infecting the memorials. I asked him what he would want it if was his grave. He snorted a laugh and shoved me, saying he'd be dead, what did I think he'd need?

Derek was in the newer plot, down the hill from the church and surrounded by people whose dates of death outranked his own by decades. Decades and decades of years my brother never got to see.

He was between Martha Caldwell, beloved sister and friend, born June 3rd 1936, died September 17th 2002, and Sid Jacobs, brother, father, comedian and friend, born January 25th 1945, died December 9th 2010. Derek would have liked Sid. Anyone with 'comedian' on his headstone would have been someone Derek would have respected. If he had seen it, he would have laughed and said comedian was code for jerk, but his family were too polite to tell the truth.

I didn't bring Derek flowers, but I did bring him a gift.

Turning it over in my hands, I tried to expel the chill in my bones when I knew I couldn't call it a birthday gift.

My eyes skimmed over Sid's and Martha's headstones, a smile in particular for Sid. I always avoided looking at Derek's until the last moment, knowing what I would see. The dark, black marble slab jutted out of the ground, pale gold writing etched into the stone.

Derek Jonathon Black
Born 29th May 1993
Died 28th May 2008
Beloved son, devoted brother, loyal friend.
It is not length of life, but depth of life.
He jumped into life and never touched the bottom.

Only today, something was different. Derek's engraving was partially obscured. By a person. Rushing forward, I stumbled in front of the person who was sitting cross-legged on top of Derek's grave.

Sarah blinked in surprise before jumping to her feet, mouth open but no words came out.

My breath caught in my throat. "What are you doing here?"

"Same thing as you. I came to see Derek."

I narrowed my eyes at her. "Why?"

She shrugged. "Why not?"

"You didn't last year."

Sarah flashed a small smile. "I did. I watched you leave, actually. Want me to prove it? You brought an iPod and tiny speaker set. You played Green Day. A lot."

I took an involuntary step back, my arms falling from my chest. "I don't get it. You barely even spoke to Derek when he was alive."

"I did," she said softly. "You just never saw."

A surge of anger rose in my blood. "Are you trying to tell me I didn't know my own brother? Derek hated liars, he would never have had a secret girlfriend without telling me."

Sarah laughed. "I wasn't his girlfriend. We never got that far."

Something in her words struck a nerve. I blinked, shocked at the sensation of a tear rolling down my cheek.

She touched my arm. "You should sit down."

"What are you not telling me?"

She nodded and sat opposite me, talking animatedly about my brother. I forgot how he could make other people feel. I forgot how enigmatic he could be when he wanted to. Sarah told me about how she came to our house looking for me and found Derek instead. Baked, obviously, in the back yard sitting in an old paddling pool we used to horse around in as kids. He shared his cooler full of orange flavored ice-pops with her and she sat beside him with her feet in the pool.

After that Sarah kept finding excuses to go see him, to stop in the hall at school and ask him something. Her face darkened when she spoke of what an ass he could be when he was using the hard stuff, when he was cruel and inconsiderate. How lonely and how desperate he seemed right at the end. How deep down, she wasn't surprised when she heard he was gone.

A part of me wanted to scream and shout at her. If she knew it was coming why hadn't she done something to try to help him?

I didn't.

The words I wanted to fling at her I'd already flung at myself.

Derek's suicide wasn't a shock to me, either. I told myself I had tried, I had tried to get him help and convince him to talk to someone. The truth was, Derek didn't want help.

I read sometime after his death that most suicides have evidence of past attempts. Derek didn't have any.

When he was low before, I'd always managed to pick him back up, helped him shake the dust off and start again.

This time he hadn't wanted help so he didn't accept it.

My brother had wanted to die and I hadn't been able to help him.

I didn't realize I was sobbing until Sarah pulled me into her arms, hugging me so tightly that in other circumstances it would have hurt like hell. Then she was crying too and we were holding each other up.

We cried for the wasted time.

We cried for the things we couldn't do.

We cried for the things unsaid.

We cried for her friend.

We cried for my brother.

* * * *

"Why do you have a CD?" Sarah asked once our tears had dried.

"It's for Derek. It has his favorite song on it." I tried to smile. "He would have wanted it played at the funeral, but my mom wouldn't let me. She went with some hokey number the priest recommended. I played it last year, but I think he'd rather have it with him."

"You're going to put it in the ground?"

I nodded.

"What was it? The song."

"*Good Riddance.*"

She smiled. "I love that one."

"So did he." I rolled my eyes. "It drove me crazy."

Sarah giggled.

"I got him this for his birthday one year. I still want to do that. Buy him a birthday present. That's stupid, and fucking awful. He'll never get older but I still want him to know I'm thinking of him."

"It's tomorrow, right? You guys' birthday?"

I nodded.

"What did he like to do on your birthdays?"

A laugh bubbled in my throat. "Nothing—in the literal sense. He liked to be treated like a freaking prince, being waited on hand and foot."

"Did he enjoy it?"

I shrugged. "For a while. Then he'd get bored."

Sarah chuckled. "Sounds like Derek."

"Why didn't you tell me you were friends with him?"

Sarah looked me in the eye. "Would you have believed me?"

"No. I wouldn't have believed there weren't other motives behind it."

"That's why I didn't tell you."

"Why didn't he?" I wondered aloud.

"Maybe he did and you just didn't hear him."

I was about to brush off her suggestion when his voice popped into my head, making comments about Sarah. It wasn't uncommon, he used to talk about how hot all my friends were. But he was different about Sarah. Now that I knew to look for it, there was a gleam of hope and truth in his eyes. "Asshat," I mumbled.

She smiled and I couldn't help but smile back at her, as the giggles started.

I dug a hole in the grave with a trowel I had found in the garage before I left. I dropped the CD, wrapped in a plastic baggie, into the shallow hole. Derek used to call Green Day food for his soul. I hoped it was true.

"You want to do something?" Sarah asked as we got to

our feet, brushing off the seats of our pants. "I don't mean like go to the Grill or someplace else. I mean like sitting somewhere and not caring that it shows on our faces what today is." The uncertainty must have shown on my face, because her expression softened a touch more. "Please, Lo? I'm trying, okay?"

I let out a breath. "I get it. But... I guess I'm a little sore about when I left, especially now I know how much you cared about Derek."

Sarah's brows furrowed. "I'm not getting what you mean."

"You couldn't even come say goodbye to me," I said quietly. "You couldn't give me a five minute farewell when my world fell apart around me."

"Okay, now I'm *really* not getting what you mean. Lo, what the hell are you talking about? You were already gone when I found out you were even leaving."

I sat back, a confused frown creasing my forehead. "What? But how?"

"Jill said she came by your house and your folks told her you'd left town the day before." Sarah glanced at the ground before lifting her big blue eyes to mine. "I was sore about that. Jill made a big show about how selfish you must be to not even tell us."

"I told Jill. I texted her and told her exactly when I was leaving."

We stared at each other for a long minute, the depth of Jill's treachery sinking in.

"What a bitch," Sarah mumbled.

I snorted a laugh at her candor.

Sarah grinned. "Right? I just want it all to be done, you know? Forget about Jill and school. Make real friends who actually like me."

"Real friends, huh? Think we could manage it?"

"Without Jill playing us off against each other? I think we could try."

"Okay. But what about college? What's the point when

I'm leaving soon?"

"You aren't the only one leaving. I'm going to Meredith next year."

"Meredith? As in Meredith College in Raleigh?"

Sarah nodded.

"And I'll be at N.C. State? Sarah!" I exclaimed. "How could you not tell me you got into a college in the same city as mine?"

She grinned. "I didn't know until I saw it on the board outside the guidance office."

"Okay. So I guess distance won't be an issue for our friendship."

"Come on, friend, we have some lost time to make up for." She winked and left me alone at Derek's grave, as though knowing I needed time by myself to say what I needed to say to him.

When she was safely out of earshot, I crouched down and placed my hand on the grass. "I forgive you."

Until I told Mom and Dad the truth about his death, I didn't realize how much anger I had been carrying around inside me. I hated that he had made me keep his secret. I hated that he had put me in that position. But most of all I hated that he'd left me. His death had made me selfish. I was angry with him for being weak. It took a lot for me to let it go and forgive him, and to remember it wasn't me he was trying to hurt. He was trying to stop hurting himself.

Chapter Forty

I woke on the morning of my eighteenth birthday, a little lighter than I had the day before. I stared around my purple bedroom, my eyes drifting over posters of actors with curled edges and the empty places where pictures used to be stuck in the edge of my mirror. A few days after the relationship with my parents had begun to heal, I'd moved back into the house. By move I mean bring a few changes of clothes. The rest of my crap was still in the basement and until yesterday I'd had the excuse of studying for finals to put off moving the rest.

Swinging my feet out of bed, I yawned and made my way downstairs, the cool floorboards delicious on my bare feet.

There was no school to dread or get ready for, nothing ahead of me but a long, empty day. Well, not that long. It was already past eleven.

"At last she wakes," Dad said, smiling over the rim of his coffee cup.

I blinked. "Why aren't you at work?"

He shrugged. "I took a personal day."

"And Mom?"

"She's in the dining room."

"For what? Little early for lunch, isn't it?"

Dad snorted a laugh. "Actually it's a little late for breakfast." He jerked his head for me to go investigate.

I found Mom pouring a glass of fresh orange juice, the tastiest smells coming from the dining room.

Pancakes.

"Oooh, awesome," I said, smiling, breathing in the scent.

She smiled. "Dig in, they've been waiting for hours. Good

thing they kept fine."

"These are perfect," I mumbled past a mouthful of food, actively not thinking about the last time someone made me pancakes.

Somewhere between pancakes four and five, Dad came into the room and sat beside Mom at the table. Neither spoke until my plate was clean.

Letting out a breath, I slumped back in my chair, unable to move.

"That's a relief. I thought you'd chow down on the plate too." Dad laughed. "You feel like coming outside for a sec?"

"Uh, no. Not for at least ten years, which is how long these pancakes are going to take to digest."

Dad looked at Mom. "Guess she doesn't want her present."

I sat up. "Present?"

Mom recovered first. She smiled. "Well, if you can't move…"

"I can move," I said, jumping to my feet.

They exchanged a smile and led the way outside.

Parked behind my dad's SUV was a gleaming blood-red Chevy Aveo5. I stared at it in a daze, the pessimist in me not wanting to believe it could be mine.

Mom held out a set of car keys. "Happy birthday, Lori."

I threw my arms around her. "Thank you."

She laughed and I moved to hug Dad next.

"What did I do to deserve it? Not that I'm complaining," I added in a rush.

Dad's hand landed on my shoulder. "We all screwed up, Lori. Not just you, but your mother and I also. The way you handled yourself when you came back…it proved to us how responsible and mature you really are. A lot of other kids would have shrugged and let the chips fall where they may. You took charge. And we couldn't be prouder."

My eyes welled, and rather than turn a happy moment into a morbid one, I turned so they wouldn't see.

"So," Mom said, nudging me. "Where are you going to

go?"

I opened my mouth to answer, and realized I had nowhere to go. "Nowhere right now."

* * * *

Once I was dressed, I took some of that responsibility Dad said I had, and made a start on clearing out the basement. So far our trashcan overflowed and there were several boxes of junk for Goodwill stacked in the garage. When the last box of stuff I was keeping was in the house, I was covered in a fine sheen of sweat and completely exhausted. I dumped the box in the middle of my room and collapsed on the bed.

"Knock, knock."

I bolted upright, heart pounding.

Sarah stood grinning the doorway.

I threw a pillow at her, which she dodged.

"What are you doing?"

"I've been lugging boxes around all day. I didn't realize I had so much crap."

"Everyone has crap. Need some help?"

"Thanks, but I'm done."

Sarah held out her hand, brandishing a hot-pink envelope. "Happy birthday."

I blushed. "You shouldn't have, thank you." I accepted the envelope, a smaller cream one fluttering to the floor as I did. Opening the pink one, I laughed at the card from Sarah—a picture of two little girls hugging the life out of each other, the caption reading 'to my bestest friend'.

"Thanks."

She smiled. "That one was on the front step when I got here."

A frown worked its way onto my forehead as I reached for the next card. The card itself was simple, a creamy ivory with a sketch of a present on the front. Something dropped out onto my lap as I opened it. A shiver ran down my spine as I saw the postcard from Moab. Jerking the card back up to read the inside, all that was written was a simple 'A'.

"Where did you say you found this?" I demanded, jumping to my feet.

"Outside. A car pulled away as I got here."

I pushed past Sarah and rushed outside.

"I thought I'd find him in your room. I was sure I saw someone around back when I got here."

I frowned as I turned to face her. "What do you mean?"

"Someone came from around back when I pulled in. I went there first before coming upstairs thinking that's where you were."

"Oh. No, it must have been my dad or something."

"Was he helping you lug the boxes?"

I shook my head. "He's got a bad back."

"But I thought you said you were finished."

"I am."

"There's still one there."

I stared at Sarah for a minute before getting to my feet. She followed me as I made my way around the side of the house. Sure enough, the sliding door was open just as I'd left it, but instead of being an empty room, there was a single cardboard box in the center. As we approached it, the box moved, making us scream and jump back.

"What the hell was that?" Sarah breathed, a hand on her chest.

I laughed. "I have no idea."

As I moved to get a closer look, Sarah pulled me back. "What if it's hungry?"

I snorted. "I'll take my chances." I pulled back the cardboard flaps and a pair of wide, blinking eyes stared up at me, a pitiful meow following.

Sarah and I 'awwed' in unison as I reached in for the tiny kitten. It was trembling and I held it to my chest, letting it hear my heartbeat to try to soothe the poor thing. A piece of paper in the box caught my eye and I handed the kitten to Sarah.

Six weeks, found near the hospital. No other cat around —
abandoned or dumped.

"Cheerful," Sarah said, reading over my shoulder. "Who
is it from?"

I would have known the writing anywhere. "Guess I have
somewhere to go now."

"Huh?"

"Feel like a ride in my new car?"

Sarah didn't need to be asked twice.

* * * *

Doug wasn't surprised when I brought the kitten to him.
He claimed I was the animal whisperer and somehow drew
the waifs and strays to me. He gave the kitten a clean bill of
health and asked if I was taking it home. A few weeks ago I
would have, in a second flat. Now I knew better.

"Why didn't you want to keep the kitten?" Sarah asked as
we stopped outside my house.

"What would be the point? I'm leaving in a few months. It
may as well go to someone that can take care of it properly."

"You've got stronger willpower than me. I swear I nearly
took it."

I smiled. "I never used to be that strong, trust me."

"Doubtful, Lo."

I bit my lip. "Please don't call me that."

Sarah frowned. "It's your name, isn't it?"

"Not anymore."

She studied me for a minute before smiling in that carefree,
happy way of hers. "Okay. Sorry, Lori."

And that was it. I didn't need to give a big long explanation.
She took me at my word. Maybe this was the start of a great
friendship.

"Graduation soon."

"Ugh, don't remind me," I moaned. Elated as I was
that I was actually getting to graduate, the thought of the
ceremony filled me with dread.

287

"I know. I bet Jill can't even say teal is her color."
I snorted a laugh. There were small mercies, at least.

Chapter Forty-One

The morning of graduation was set to be a beautiful one. I woke early, morning doves cooing like owls and the sky a burst of hazy pinks and oranges. I couldn't fall back asleep no matter how hard I tried, and in the end, I gave up. Mom and Dad still slept when I crept outside. I curled up on the swing in the back yard, listening to the world around me wake up.

Graduation.

It was a dream so far away and so distant it was hard to believe it had come around so quickly.

I reached into my sweater pocket and pulled out the folded square of paper. Blowing out a breath, I tipped my face to the sky, a single tear sliding down my face and cooling in the morning air.

Graduation. Another milestone my brother would never see.

The ache of his absence had never subsided, had never faded, not even a smidge. He was a part of me, and that part could never heal without him, no matter what I did.

Mom had given me back his note a few days after I'd shown her and Dad. She said it didn't belong to them, that it was mine from Derek. I hadn't re-read it since the day I found it, though the words were committed to memory.

Derek's chicken-scratch scrawl on the paper had changed my life in a way I never could have predicted.

I unfolded his note, and read his words for the second time.

Lo –

I'm sorry you had to see this.

I didn't want it to be you...but I know that it will be.

I'm done, little sis. I need off this ride, and it's time I paid the ferryman.

Your screw-up brother can't embarrass you anymore. But before I go, there are a few things I need to tell you.

Get rid of those bitches. Seriously. They are not your friends, and you're turning into one of them. One of these days you're gonna wake up and realize you've become someone you wouldn't even recognize a few years ago. Or maybe you won't...and that'll be worse.

Ditch the Abercrombie model. He's a dick.

Cut Mom and Dad some slack when all this is said and done. They'll need you, even if they don't show it. More importantly, you'll need them.

Stop bringing strays home. Go out and find some(one) decent to love.

That time you caught shit from Dad for scratching his car? Totally me. Sorry.

Our birth certificates are in Dad's filing cabinet in his office at home, under Audits – 1993. I am so your big brother.

That's it, little sis. Please don't hate me forever.
Be brilliant.
Shine.
I'll see you.

– D

P.S. Sorry for stealing your old lady stationery. Again.

I tucked the note back into my pocket.

I would see Derek again. And, man, would I have stuff to tell him.

* * * *

With Black as my surname, I was one of the first handful

290

of students to receive my diploma. During the speeches, I couldn't help but look at the chair beside me. The chair that should have had Archer sitting in it. It wasn't fair that he wasn't there, wasn't sitting with the rest of his class to get a piece of paper saying he had graduated from high school. They shouldn't give diplomas. They should give medals for bravery and endurance at having survived four years of hell.

Someone was looking down on me as I walked up the steps to the stage, shook hands with the principal, took my diploma and walked down the steps on the other side without falling over my own feet. Maybe there was such a thing as miracles.

When it was done and the cap tossing was over, it all felt somewhat anti-climactic. Apparently I was one of the only ones. The rest of my class seemed overjoyed, or suicidal given the tears some girls were shedding over the event.

As everyone around me wept or laughed and grinned, were hugged by friends and relatives, I stood on the sidelines, like the girl at her birthday party that no one knew. I was saved a moment later as Mom and Dad approached me...Dad with camera in hand.

"Oh no, no more pictures, seriously," I said, frowning at the damn thing.

Mom hugged me, totally ignoring her camera-shy daughter. "Congratulations, sweetheart."

When she let go, Dad moved in for a hug, but was knocked out of the way by hurricane Sarah.

"We're done! I can't wait to say good riddance to this place!" She laughed, hugging the life out of me.

I laughed with her, my spirits finally rising.

"Hey, take a picture of us, Mr. Black," Sarah demanded, keeping one arm thrown over my shoulders.

He didn't need asking twice and clicked the camera in quick succession to get a few shots.

"We're going to go say hello to the Myers," Mom said, tugging on Dad's sleeve.

Sarah and I exchanged a glance but didn't comment.

"So," Sarah said, fussing with her gown, trying, and failing, to get it to sit somewhat flatteringly. "Are you going to the party tonight?"

"Uh, that would be an emphatic no," I said, grinning. "What would be the point?"

She looked at the ground. "A few guys asked if I'd be there. We could do something else, you know, if you wanted."

I nudged her with my elbow. "Sarah, don't be a dork. I don't care if you go to the party. Just because I don't want to doesn't mean that you can't. You have a hell of a lot more friends at this place than I do. It makes sense for you to want to say goodbye."

"You don't mind?" she asked with a confused frown.

"I wouldn't be a very good friend if I did."

Her expression smoothed out and she smiled and hugged me again, looking at something over my shoulder as she stepped back. "I'd better go find my parents. I'll see you tomorrow?"

"Definitely."

Sarah gave a little wink and danced off in the direction of her family.

I watched her go for a moment, wishing her happiness was infectious. She and I were both part of Jill's circle, had both made the same enemies with our popularity, and yet Sarah had turned her back on Jill too, but escaped the outcast syndrome that had befallen me. But that was just Sarah, I guess. Anyone would have a hard time disliking her.

Someone coughed behind me and I turned to see who it was.

A jolt went through me, visibly shocking my entire body.

Archer shifted his weight, hands jammed in his pockets. He looked so uncomfortable I was surprised he didn't turn around and disappear into the crowd. "You did better than me, it seems." He smiled crookedly.

"What do you mean?" I asked, as my heart rate went into overdrive.

"Not wondering why I'm not sporting teal like the rest of you?" He kicked up some dirt with the toe of his sneaker. "I'm summer school bound."

Summer school? Then that had to mean he still had a chance of graduating late. "That's good, though, right? At least you could still finish this year."

He shrugged.

I cleared my throat and took a small step closer to him. "How — How are they not making you repeat the whole year? You missed finals and stuff," I said, dropping my eyes.

"I enrolled in classes online. I took my finals here. You just didn't see me."

How in the hell was that possible? That we were in the same building, let alone the same room, and I didn't notice?

"I didn't want you to see me," he added, a flush darkening his cheeks. He caught my expression, probably horrified, and shrugged. "I didn't want to distract you."

"But if you took your finals why aren't you graduating too?"

"I said you did better than me," Archer said with a wry smile. "I didn't get enough credits to qualify, but they're letting me make it up in summer school. Doesn't really make much difference to me."

"Are you still planning on college in the fall?" How was it this was the conversation we were having? I'd dreamt about what Archer and I would say to each other when we finally saw each other again. College was so not on that list of things to talk about.

He shook his head. "Might travel some." Must be really interesting dirt down there. It was the only place he could look.

"Oh." Whatever hope still lived inside me that we would still be going to college together burst inside me like a delicate bubble.

"What about you?"

"Seems N.C. State still wants me."

"Excited?"

"A little." I blushed. "Scared mostly."

"Don't be. You'll kick ass. You always do." He rubbed a hand over his hair. "Kate wanted to be here, but she had to work. She said to say congrats."

"Tell her thanks."

He nodded.

I turned at the sound of my mom shouting my name.

Archer looked toward them. "How's that going?"

I shrugged. "Slow. Getting there."

"I'm glad."

"I got your birthday card. Thank you."

Archer shrugged. "No problem."

"Why didn't you stay?"

"I wasn't sure if we were ready yet," he said after a long moment.

My heart thumped. "And we are now?"

He met my eyes, the corner of his lip pulling into an uncertain smile. "Maybe."

"What convinced you?"

"The cat."

So it was a test. Since I had taken the kitten to Doug, I'd wondered why Archer hadn't taken it straight to him and why he'd felt it necessary to involve me at all.

There was so much unsaid between us. So much I wanted to tell him, so much I wanted to hear. Our classmates shrieked in excitement all around us, yet all I could hear was the silence growing between me and the boy who had taught me how to love again, and to take the risk of getting hurt and learning that the risks were totally worth it.

"I miss you."

Epilogue

It was a weird sight, the room that would be my home for the next year. Half in chaos, half still and naked. The walls were a boring beige, the carpet threadbare and scratchy. Two desks on opposite walls and two beds with bedside cabinet and two dressers and two wardrobes crammed into the room. I dumped my bags on the empty bed and sighed.

The contrast between my half and my roommate's half of the room freaked me out, so I figured messing my half was the only thing for it.

A blonde force of nature stormed into the room a half hour later, grinning from ear to ear. "Hey! You must be Lori!"

"That's me. Cheryl, right?"

"Right!"

I stuck out my hand for her to shake but she knocked it aside, hugging me so tightly I feared for my ribs.

"This is exciting, right? That summer was loooong!" Cheryl dropped down onto my bed, crushing half my clothes in the process. "Want a hand unpacking? I'm already finished. Ooh, who's the hunky dunk?"

I turned around and saw Cheryl clutching a photo frame she had plucked from an open box. "My brother, Derek. He died."

She glanced at me, maybe wondering why I was over-sharing. I figured best just to get it out there. I took the photo from her and set it on the bedside cabinet.

"Ooh, can I have this one?" she gushed, grabbing another frame.

I laughed. "That one I'd fight you for."

She groaned. "Some girls get all the luck. He's cute.

What's his name?"

"Archer. Jack. Jack Archer — I call him Archer."

She giggled. "Can I get a copy of this?"

"No." I grinned and set Archer's picture beside the one of Derek and me. "He's coming to visit next weekend. You can see him in the flesh then."

Cheryl grinned. "Awesome. Where does he go to school?"

"Nowhere right now. He's enrolled to start here in January."

Her grin widened. "I bet you're counting down the days, huh?"

"Like you wouldn't believe." My cell buzzed on the table and a smile teased my lips when I saw the caller ID. "Hi," I answered.

"Hey, superstar. All settled?"

"Not yet."

"Slacker."

"I miss you."

"I know."

"I'll see you soon?"

"I'll see you soon."

"I love you."

"I love you."

More books from Finch Books

Volatile and unstable, Amy stands at the precipice. Will she fall into the chaos and despair of insanity or ascend into brilliance and redemption?

Every teen has dreams, but only Joe Knightley can make his dreams reality. Even the nightmares…

Deep in the mountains of Perry County, Kentucky, a troubled young woman enters a new life of magic and danger.

Taking care of a pet is one thing, but when orphaned teenager Karen Fox is kidnapped to service an interstellar zoo, she gets more than she bargained for.

About the Author

Lillie Todd

I have been a storyteller for as long as I have been a reader. There is no greater pleasure in life than diving headfirst into a new world, meeting new characters and falling in love over and over again. There is a certain kind of magic in books, and I hope to weave a spell over my readers.

I grew up in the countryside of Southwest Scotland and it was amongst the rugged and sprawling landscape that my imagination was set loose. When I'm not spending time with my favourite characters of my own creation, I can be found running around like a headless chicken trying to catch up on everything I have ignored since disappearing in my head.

Lillie Todd loves to hear from readers. You can find contact information, website details and an author profile page at https://www.finch-books.com/